REVEALED TO HIM

OTHER BOOKS BY JEN FREDERICK

REVEALED
TO HIM

JEN FREDERICK

Text copyright © 2015 Jen Frederick
All rights reserved.

Published by Montlake Romance, Seattle

www.apub.com

Amazon, the Amazon logo, and Montlake Romance are trademarks of Amazon.com, Inc., or its affiliates.

ISBN-13: 9781503947559
ISBN-10: 1503947556

Cover design by Marc J. Cohen

Printed in the United States of America

To my sister, whom I once lost and found again.

CHAPTER ONE

NATALIE

Every long journey begins with one step.

I read that on an online forum a while back. It was one of those photoshopped inspirational quotes done in a curly typeface on top of a beautiful sunset. To this day, I remember the image vividly not because it featured a blonde beauty clad in a sports bra and tight shorts with a golden retriever by her side, but because my best-friend and editor Daphne Marshall pointed out that the cliff formation in the background looked like a penis. Once someone points out a penis in a picture, it can't be unseen.

"Do you remember the Mount Dick photo?" I ask Daphne. She and I are standing at the kitchen island as I stare at the door of my apartment.

"The one with the chick running on the beach with her dog? How could I forget?" She arches an eyebrow. Daphne is tall, slender, and every inch the fashionable New York working woman. She could be on the cover of *Women's Wear Daily* with her slick black outfits and perfectly shod feet. In contrast, I'm wearing pink flannel pajama pants decorated with penguins and a faded NY Cobras T-shirt that I'd stolen from my cousin Oliver a few years ago. I did brush my hair and teeth, though. That's a plus. "Did we decide that she was running toward Mount Dick or away from it?"

"Away. There was genuine terror in that dog's eyes. Like whatever lurked behind that penis would haunt him forever."

"Maybe that's just you projecting."

"Ouch." I slap a hand over my chest, but I can't deny her charge. I am haunted by a lot of things in my past, but I'm trying to move past them, which is why Daphne's with me today. Today I'm going to push the elevator button, and she's going to make sure that if something bad happens, I'll get back to my home safely.

It's a huge step forward for me, metaphorically speaking. The elevator is only twenty steps away from my door. And there are only fifteen steps between me and the door of my apartment. I know precisely because I've documented them in the journal I started keeping three years ago. The journal doesn't contain my thoughts and dreams—it's a collection of numbers and tally marks recording how many times it took to open the door, then step into the hall, then push the elevator button, then wait in the hallway before puking, crying, and losing consciousness because my throat closes up from fear. Not fear of anything in particular. Nope, my fear is of fear itself.

The worst kind.

The stupidest kind.

The seemingly incurable kind.

Two weeks ago I was able to leave my apartment and go down to the subway stop three blocks away. It was a huge victory for me, seeing as I'd not been able to leave even my building three years ago, let alone be within sniffing distance of a subway tunnel. One anonymous note that was barely threatening sent me scurrying back inside—years of therapy shot to shit.

It's safe to say that sometimes I can't stand myself.

But not today. Today I'm going to open my apartment door. I'm going to walk the twenty steps to the elevator, and I'm going to push that damn elevator button. I won't try to get on. My little brain can't handle that kind of exposure today. Maybe tomorrow or the day after. But I won't get outside again unless I take that first step.

"What if you gave me a push?" I suggest.

Daphne makes a frustrated noise. "Why are you doing this to yourself? I feel like I'm watching you volunteer for torture. Your face is shiny and your skin is clammy." She pats my cheek with the back of her hand. "Shit, you're already going into shock."

"I'm not." I take two deep breaths and start counting. Counting helps to slow my breathing from freaked out back to semi-panicked. So does focusing on the picture of the Eiffel Tower that I have hanging near the entry. Also pressing the large middle vein on my wrist repeatedly.

I do all of those things so that I can unstick my feet and move toward the door. Just to the elevator, I tell myself. Heart pounding so hard, I'm sure Daphne can hear it, I take my first step and then another. I keep going until I'm at the doorway. Daphne's slim body is a welcome presence behind me.

"I'm glad you're here," I say between heaving breaths. I raise a shaky hand to wipe away the cold sweat that's formed on my forehead.

"Of course. If you were to pass out, I wouldn't get the next chapter in your book that is due in, oh, thirty days."

"You'd get it," I protest, ignoring the doorknob in front of me. "It might not be for a few days, but you'd get it."

"So you say." She leans around me and places her hand on the door. "Want me to open it for you?"

I hesitate, but then nod reluctantly. If she doesn't open it, it might take me another fifteen minutes to muster up the strength to even place my hand on the knob. With her taking the initiative, I only have to concentrate on putting one foot in front of the other.

When her hand reaches for the doorknob, I avert my gaze and focus on the Eiffel Tower. I should have put the picture of Mount Dick up there instead.

One step.

A long journey.

Hell, I'd take a short journey. The click of the latch releasing ratchets up my panic. My heart starts racing again. I rub my slick palms together and try to start breathing from my belly instead of my chest.

In through the nose.

Out through the mouth.

My heart is strong. It beats so powerfully because it is strong and I am alive.

In through the nose.

"Maybe you should come back inside?" Daphne says quietly.

"No. I can make it." I want to turn and hug her for enduring this with me. It must be hard. When my cousin Oliver, who plays quarterback for the NY Cobras, gets hit on the field, my heart stops until he gets up. She's an amazing friend.

I press my hand against my stomach and take one step. Only thirteen to go.

Out through the mouth.

After each step, I stop and breathe. I reassure myself I am doing fine. Daphne waits patiently behind me.

I don't know exactly how much time passes, but after thirteen steps and thirteen deep breaths, I find myself at the elevator bank. I choke out a laughing sob. "I made it."

"Good job," she says.

Licking my lips, I raise my hand and press the DOWN button. The walls of the hall seem to shake as the elevator rises from the lobby. The lights above the elevator shift as the elevator passes each floor.

"I should go back," I say, but apparently I'm not loud enough, because Daphne doesn't respond. She's staring at the elevator doors, waiting for them to part.

What if there's someone inside the elevator? What if it's the note writer? What if it's someone from my past? My stomach starts churning and I can feel the acid rising. "I should go," I say again, but no one hears me. I must be so quiet.

I clear my throat, but all I taste is bile. I choke it back.

The note. That goddamned note.

Five words on a throwaway piece of paper shouldn't get to me. The threat is stupid and vague and clichéd. Although if it is from who I think it is—one of those cowardly, dickless wonders whose unwashed sweatpants are filled with Cheetos dust and whose only form of social activity is hurling insults on the Internet—then it should come as no surprise that the threat sounds like it was cut and pasted from the cheesiest pulp novel ever.

And I hate that it gets to me. I hate that I've been driven inside, a prisoner of my home. I hate that I'm gasping for breath standing in front of this goddamn elevator. I hate that the first fucking breath of fresh air that I sucked in took two years to achieve. I hate all of it, but my hate isn't stronger than my fear.

That's probably what I hate the most.

"Daphne." I reach out for her.

She's lost in her own thoughts. I'm drowning in mine.

Why should that note affect me so greatly? There has never been a robbery or assault in this building. There are famous people, like my cousin Oliver, who live here. All signs point to being safe.

I'm safe and I'm at the elevator.

I'm at the ELEVATOR!

Black dots start to swim in front of my eyes as my stupid brain starts telling every part of my body that we're in danger. My heart is pounding so hard and fast I fear it might leap out of my chest. My breath is stuck in my lungs and can't get out because my throat has completely closed up. I've got no strength in my legs and I'm shaking so hard my vision has blurred. When the bell dings and the elevator slides open, I collapse.

And then there's nothing.

CHAPTER TWO

JAKE

"Does that disguise work for you?" I run my eyes over one of the most famous figures in New York City. Despite the battered cap over his hair and mirrored aviators covering his eyes, I can still tell it's Oliver Graham, quarterback of the recent Super Bowl–winning NY Cobras. With the new season right around the corner, everyone in the city is ready to start another run for the ring. His face is plastered on buses and subway cars and billboards. There's hardly anyone more recognizable.

He tugs off his cap and runs agitated fingers through his hair. "Worked all the way from Tribeca."

It's seven and I meant to close two hours ago, but I've had a steady stream of new clients and investigators this afternoon. Given that Tanner Security is a young company, I don't have the luxury of turning anyone away, particularly not a client of Graham's stature.

"I fear for the city then. Jake Tanner." I offer my right hand.

"Oliver Graham."

I resist the urge to say "I know" and Graham avoids any mention of the fact that my left hand is a prosthetic. We shake and I gesture for him to follow me down the hall to my office. Graham's got a good game face.

I lost my left foot and hand to an IED explosion in Afghanistan five years ago. For some people, the prosthetics bring out pity. For others, it's a turn-on. Athletes like Graham are often in the first category. They are afraid my loss of limbs is contagious.

Early on, I might have felt that way too, but the long war had consequences and veteran amputees were one of them. I came to terms with my loss and decided I was just glad to be alive.

I take a seat behind my desk and wait for Graham to settle into one of the leather club chairs that set me back a cool grand. My sisters and mother decorated my office and I'd sat in the damn things for a month before the credit card bill showed up or I might have sent them back to the store.

"What can I do for you? Crazed fan or scorned woman?" I ask. A man like Graham, who lives much of his life in the media spotlight, probably has more than a few security concerns. Or it could be that he wants to run a background check on a potential employee, or hell, even a new girlfriend.

When I began Tanner Security four and a half years ago after getting out of the army, I didn't realize that my bread and butter would be made off of people who wanted to know other people's secrets. Eight years in the army failed to ferret out every atom of idealism, but security work did it in half the time.

"I'd like to say it was either or both, but I'm here because of my cousin." He hooks his sunglasses on the collar of his dark gray T-shirt and pulls a large envelope wrapped in plastic from his messenger bag.

I try not to look surprised, but plastic wrap suggests evidence and fingerprints.

"Hold on." I leave and grab a box of latex gloves in the bottom shelf of the storage cabinet down the hall. Back in my office, I snap a glove over my good hand and strip the plastic film from the envelope.

"Sorry," he apologizes as I peel off a second layer of wrap. "We didn't have any plastic bags."

"This is better than nothing." The side of the envelope had been ripped open. I tap on it and two ordinary sheets of cheap copy paper slid out. "I know who you are." As I read the words aloud, Graham's brows tighten in anger.

The second page is a printout of a screenshot of someone's Twitter feed dated three years ago. The tweets are innocuous. The avatar is of a cat wearing sunglasses in front of a planet. The tweets range from horror over a *Bladerunner* remake to a posting of a cat wearing glasses. There are *a lot* of cat-related tweets.

"'I'm surmising that there is something more to this story than a cat tweeting pictures of other cats." I look inside the envelope, but there's nothing else there.

"Some sick motherfucker sent this to my cousin Natalie a week ago." He jabs a long finger on the desk. "I want you to find out who it is."

"Why not go to the police?" I turn the papers over as I process Graham's statement. I didn't know he had a cousin. He's kept that well hidden. There aren't any identifying marks that I can see. Devon Zachs, my computer expert, would probably be able to tell me which printer was used just by smelling the ink.

"Because we've tried them before and they were completely ineffective. We don't trust them."

"You and Natalie?"

"My whole family."

I'd never heard of the Grahams having any problems that necessitated police intervention. As far as I recalled, Graham's family was from the Midwest—some state starting with a vowel—but I don't follow the gossip papers. My baby sister, Sabrina, might know something. I make a mental note to check with her tonight.

"Is your cousin hiding somewhere? She in witness protection?"

"No." He looks confused, but I am too. "I know who you are" is a threat directed at people who are hiding their identities.

I try a different angle. "How was it delivered?"

"It was delivered with the rest of her mail. She has a different last name. Beck."

The envelope was unstamped and had no address. Only the words N. Beck were written in block letters.

"How'd it get in there?"

"I don't know. I asked the building manager and she said that it was probably left with the doorman or at the concierge's desk and shuffled into the mail at the end of the day. I haven't asked any more questions, because Natalie was against raising a stink about it."

"She hopes it goes away."

He nods abruptly. Clearly he doesn't agree with this Natalie's decisions. "All right. Tell me the background."

"Are you familiar with the game Saturnalia?" he asks.

I pull out a recorder. "Mind if I record this?" When he hesitates, I assure him, "It's all confidential. This is so I can refer back to it as I investigate." At his nod, I press record. "I'm not a big gamer, particularly of first-person shooter games. I've lived it, so it's not my idea of relaxation." Some guys who were in the service loved those games, but I always thought that was a good way of triggering PTSD. Besides, as a thirty-five-year-old male living in New York City, there is plenty of live entertainment, particularly of the female persuasion.

"It's not a shooting game. It's a role-playing, civilization-building game. You start out in a pod in space containing biogeneration units, having jettisoned yourself from dying Earth. There's a planet ahead of you and you have two different entry choices. You can crash land or take extra time to circle the planet. At every juncture you have choices and the decisions you make throughout the game yield different results. Your objective is to re-create human civilization. The game allows you to do it a million different ways, but each choice that you make delivers different rewards. Make enough of the right choices, and as the game progresses, you meet a potential mate, have children, find more people. If you make too many of the wrong choices, your options are bad. Like your mate dies before you can have children or your potential mate will have a fundamental belief difference and won't accept your advances and your civilization will eventually die."

"Sounds interesting." And it did. Re-creating civilizations—or effectively playing God—appealed to a lot of people.

"Lots of people thought so too. Natalie wrote the game—not the code. She's not a coder. She's a writer. She was at college, majoring in English. She thought she'd be an English professor—" He waves his hand. "That's not important. She wrote the storyline, the dialogue, all of the choices the gamer can make. It was *her* writing that made that fucking game. It was praised for its 'lifelike and emotionally engaging storyline.'" He makes air quotes as if he is parroting an actual review. "It was hailed as one of the best stories in a game that year. The game developers convinced her that she should not be credited as Natalie Beck, because the gaming community is largely male and is resistant to female developers. But somewhere along the line, it became known that Natalie was female, and this set off a firestorm of controversy."

"People reacted badly?"

He snorts, a rough and unhappy sound. "She couldn't turn on her computer or pick up her phone without being inundated with the worst kind of messages—ones suggesting she kill herself and some from people who said that they were going to take the game and rape her with it."

"You reported these threats to the police?" I ask, but I know what the answer will be before Graham opens his mouth. He wouldn't be here if the police were able to help them.

"We didn't at first. I'm not a stranger to online criticism. There are a lot of assholes who hide behind a monitor. But a sports fan is different from a computer gamer who can write programs that populate a hundred accounts a day—sending you anonymous emails and messages and tweets. Vomiting out a dozen messages of hate every second."

"How did Natalie take this?"

"It was tough at first. Her feelings were hurt, but we all thought it would blow over. She's worked with men all of her life—first living with me and having to deal with all my jackass friends and then in the gaming world. But it didn't stop. She started having panic attacks, wondering if the guy in front of her at Starbucks was the one who wrote she should be train-raped by a pack of rabid dogs, or the one wearing the Star Wars T-shirt at the market was the one who emailed her a picture of a beheading."

I wince.

"They posted her personal information online, including her address. For shits and giggles, they sent stuff to her house, like dozens of pizzas that she'd have to pay for. One asswipe called 911 on her, saying that they heard gunshots and a baby crying. It was fucking terrifying for her. They made a game out of tormenting her. Finally"—he chokes up and his head falls forward hiding what I presume to be a fuck ton of emotion—"she was attacked in the subway. He was never caught, but someone pushed her and"—he pauses and shudders—"and if it weren't for a couple of college girls who caught her and dragged her back, she would have fallen onto the tracks and been crushed." Graham raises his head, and by the haunted look in his eyes, the memory of his cousin's near-death experience is still fresh. I have two sisters—it's easier to accept danger to yourself than it is to someone you care about.

"Three years ago she was attacked and the person was never caught," I sum up. "You think this is the same person?" I gesture toward the letter.

"I don't know who it is," he says with a lot of frustration. Graham is a big guy and has big hands, which are currently fisted and look ready to drive a hole through my desk. "The subway attack triggered a big problem for Natalie. She became housebound, because stepping outside her apartment brought on disabling panic attacks. It took her another year before she could leave her apartment and walk outside. She still can't ride the subway, but at least she could walk around the building, go to the park across the street. Get coffee at a coffee shop. This letter," he practically spits, "set her back. She tried to leave her apartment two days ago and got as far as the elevator before puking on herself and passing out. Thank Christ her best friend was with her or who knows how long Natalie would've lain like that."

I've watched Graham play football in New York, both in person and on television, for going on six years now. I've seen him pissed off and jubilant, but this is the first time I've seen him defeated. Not even during the 24–21 loss to the Green Bay Packers in the NFC Championship game when he threw two pick-sixes did he appear this upset.

"What happens when I find this guy?"

"You think you can find him?" His head jerks up.

"Why did you come to me if you didn't think I could find him?"

"These fuckers are ghosts. They create a thousand fake accounts and come after you at the same time. You can't ever pin them down." He leans forward, his big Super Bowl–winning hands clutched together. "Natalie went through hell three years ago. She's not the same person she was. Getting her out of her building was an enormous victory. This fucker has ruined it and I want him caught. Yesterday."

"I'll look into it. I'll have one of my men—"

"No." He holds up a hand. "This is Tanner Security and you're Jake Tanner. I want you."

His tone allowed no room for disagreement. Mentally I review my current assignments. I'm busy, but making time to hunt down someone who is harassing an innocent woman isn't hard for me to do. I give him a nod of agreement.

"Then I need to meet Natalie."

He heaves a big sigh. "Yeah, that might be a problem."

CHAPTER THREE

JAKE

That might be a problem?

I know plenty of men and women with PTSD. They don't like crowded spaces. They don't like loud noises. Many of them don't like to be surrounded by a lot of people, but from what Graham is describing, this is a level of anxiety I haven't encountered before.

"How so? Is meeting new people a trigger?"

"What's not a trigger?" He sighs with resignation, seeming defeated and guilty, as if he's frustrated by his cousin's mental state and angry with himself for being frustrated. "That's not entirely fair. She's fine with people she trusts, in a controlled environment. She's fine in my apartment, but getting there is a problem because it requires her to enter the hallway and ride the elevator—both are tasks that are very difficult for her. She's okay with familiar people—like the doormen, although she likes the night guy better than the day guy. They can bring stuff to her door and ring the doorbell, but a food delivery person would freak her out."

"Not being able to get into her apartment will make it difficult for me to implement security measures."

"I'll talk to her about it," Graham promises.

I flip my legal pad around and shove a pen toward Graham. "Write down her email address. I'll send her a note and see how she feels about a visit."

Graham scrawls out her email and then pushes the pad back toward me. "I'll text her to let her know to expect a message from you. Good luck," he says, and his tone implies I'm going to need it.

As soon as he leaves, I make a new file for Natalie Beck and then wait about ten minutes before shooting her an email. Most of my clients are businesses who hire us to protect a high-ranking executive overseas, or to ferret out embezzlement, or to track down the selling of trade secrets. A personal request like Graham's is rare because of the high price tag associated with Tanner Security services. But the idea of meting out some justice to a punk who's terrorizing a traumatized woman awakens the same sort of righteous anger that had me throwing away a banking career to join the army after 9/11.

Me: Jake Tanner here. Your cousin Oliver Graham has asked me to look into the note. Mind if I come over and take a look around?

Her response is nearly immediate:

Her: Like inside my apartment? If you have spoken to Oliver, then you know I'm not comfortable with that. How do I know that you're not the person who sent the note in the first place?

Me: Didn't your cousin text you? If not, here's my website.

I send her a link to the site.

Her: There aren't any pictures on your site. I feel like there should be pictures.

Me: We're into guarding people's privacy and protecting them from danger. The fewer pictures, the safer everyone is.

Her: I don't know whether to be creeped out or impressed by your ready answer for every complaint I have.

I'm a professional. Very quiet. You wouldn't even know I'm there, I write back.

Her: I'm already hyperventilating just emailing with you. Actually having you here would make me pass out in fear. Aren't there special things you can do from afar with spy cameras and listening devices? I watch a lot of movies on Netflix—those things definitely exist somewhere in either Hollywood or Washington DC.

I smile reluctantly. Her emails are funny enough to make me wonder what she's like in person. It's a damn shame that she's got some asshole on her tail. Graham never did answer my question about what he is planning to do when I find the perp, but if some guy did that to my sisters, I'd find him and break his fingers.

Me: Think about it.

Her: Can I have a day or two to prepare?

Me: Absolutely. Text me if you need to. I'm more responsive to my texts than emails.

I send her my phone number. I'm a one-handed texter, but my typing isn't much better. One of my employees has dyslexia and she prefers to send texts using emoji and pictures. I haven't quite succumbed to that.

I work for a few more hours, tackling paperwork that I had been avoiding for the past couple of days. Both my phone and my inbox stay unnervingly quiet. The mini fridge behind me yields a day-old ham sandwich, which I wash down with two cans of Coke. Reviewing reports, calculating payroll, and reading résumés of potential new hires fall under things I don't enjoy doing but can't seem to delegate to others. Around midnight, I'm close to wrapping it up when the text message alert on my phone goes off. The phone number is unfamiliar to me, but the message reveals it's Natalie. A tenseness in my gut I hadn't realized was there eases.

Her: Oliver told me you were in the army. Can I ask an intrusive question?

Me: Sure.

I wonder if it's about my prosthetics. Graham may not have paid attention to them, but he noticed the hand. It's hard not to.

Her: Were you afraid? Ever?

Her question isn't one that I expected, but maybe I should have. PTSD sufferers fear their response to current events and have anxiety over future ones. I suspect Natalie's disorders aren't much different. Fear is a big issue for her.

Me: Yes. Frequently.

Her: Thought army guys ate fear for breakfast. Also lunch, dinner, and for snacks in between.

Me: Nah. We ate shitty meals from a bag heated up by a chemical triggered by water. Snacks were candy. Fear lived with us.

Her: Shouldn't you be sleeping? I thought you'd read this in the morning.

Me: I'm still working. Reports. Very boring.

Her: If I was alone in an office, I would be afraid. I'm afraid all of the time. During breakfast, lunch, and dinner. Also during snack.

Me: Fear is a healthy thing. When you stop being afraid, you aren't as careful and alert.

Her: But at some point fear becomes the only thing. Then what?

I stare at the messages, wondering what I could say. I don't want to feed her platitudes. When I was recovering from my injuries, I felt suffocated by the pain. It took me a while to come to the place where I am now. Five years ago, I wondered why the IED hadn't just killed me instead of taking my hand and foot. Five years ago, I was a frickin' mess. She's not going to get judgment from me.

Me: Then you try to go to sleep and wake up to face the next
day. And the next, until fear is the thing that keeps you sharp
instead of the thing that makes you bleed.
Her: God. I like that. I like that a lot. I'm going to bed now to
prepare for tomorrow.

Tomorrow will be a good day. I pause, my finger hovering over the
screen. Text me when you wake up.

She sends me a thumbs-up and I leave the office with a smile on
my face. The long day makes my stump throb inside its vacuum-sealed
socket, and since no one is around, I let my left leg drag a little as I
climb the stairs to the part of the townhouse that serves as my living
quarters. But I avoid the elevator that I used frequently when I first
moved in because pain, like fear, is something I've become accustomed
to. It reminds me I'm alive and that's a good thing.

Someday Natalie's fear will be a good thing too.

In my bathroom, I pull down my jeans and push the button to release
the pin holding the prosthetic in place. Once I tug off the limb, the instant
relief is followed by a pins-and-needles sensation. I give the stump a good
massage until all that remains is a low-grade ache. The arm comes off
next and instantly I feel better. With my one hand balancing me against
the wall, I hobble into the bathroom for a quick shower. After drying off
and making my way to the bed, I drop my cell phone on the nightstand,
face up. Just in case someone needs to text me in the middle of the night.

The number of people I'd stay awake for is small, but with wry
amusement, I realize I've added Natalie to the list.

I wake up a few hours later, my body having long since rejected
sleeping in. A quick glance at the phone tells me that no one else is
awake, or at least not needing my attention. From the closet, I grab
the blade for running, strap it on over the gel liner, and quickly dress. I
don't need the arm to run, and leave that off. It's a lot more comfortable.

The one big benefit for an amputee with money is that I don't have to rely on the government or insurance for my prosthetics. I get what I want and as many as I want. Whenever I visit another vet, I'm keenly aware of that particular privilege.

Ordinarily when I run, I like to zone out, but this morning I think of Natalie, stuck inside her apartment with all her great progress shot to shit. What kind of wart on humanity intentionally messes with a woman like that? Makes me want to punch something . . . hard.

The house is empty when I get home, which makes me wonder if I'm avoiding Sabrina or she's avoiding me. Either way, I haven't seen her in a couple of days. Upstairs, I shower again—a cold shower because heat makes my stump swell and then the prosthetic doesn't fit as well. That was a hard lesson I learned early on.

When I get out, I see a message alert. Is my heart pumping a little faster because it's from Natalie? Nah, it's because I just got done running, I tell myself.

Her: I'm feeling anxious now that Oliver's contacted you. I want to feel safe in my own home.

Me: Who doesn't? I have a shit ton of security in my home. Biometric sensors. Cameras. Pressure pads.

Her: Pressure pads?

Me: Those are weight-sensitive sensors. Anything over a certain weight triggers an alarm. We could put those on your balcony. Or radio-frequency sensors that determine the size of objects based on the interference of radio waves.

Her: Have you already made the trip to LA? Because all of that sounds very Hollywood.

Me: Where do you think Hollywood gets its ideas? ;)

I stare at my phone. Fuck. A *winky face*, asshole?

To regain my manhood after sending that message, I go downstairs and yell at a few employees.

CHAPTER FOUR

NATALIE

"Oliver's security guy sent me a text." I show Daphne the message and grin.

"Is that a winky face?" She arches an elegant eyebrow and scoffs, "Only a hipster on Molly would send that. One who wears flannel ironically because he's never seen the woods and would never be caught dead in a cabin unless it's in Vail and has a full-service butler on call. He probably thinks John Cusack is the epitome of manhood and aspires to have as many vinyl records as possible." She wipes the sauce from her mouth.

She's here for lunch and lunch only, she told me when she arrived with bags of food from 'wichcraft. I try not to pout because I like having Daphne here all day whenever I can. It's almost like going out. Almost.

"I think John Cusack *is* the epitome of manhood. Like, if that was in Jake's Tinder profile, I'd totally swipe right." I push my food aside because all I want to do is talk about this Jake Tanner guy. And privately I disagree with her. Only a guy with a lot of confidence sends a winky face.

"That's all you need to swipe right?" Daphne says in amazement. "I'd need at least one pic of his face, none of this 'nose and lower' shit."

"I'm not picky." I shrug and pick up the phone to reread the messages. His replies are instantaneous, as if he just can't wait to interact with me. When's the last time that has happened? Even before I was housebound, I never had that kind of interest from males. The last guy I'd dated was more of a convenience. I'm not even sure you could call it dating, because we were working seventeen-hour days getting ready for the game launch. And then after? We had sex because he was a boy and I was a girl and we had been in close proximity with each other for two years. There wasn't even a flame to burn out when it was over. "I'd swipe right if the guy was the Son of Sam at this point."

"That's not saying much about either your taste or his appeal."

"True." I stop at the message *Then you try to go to sleep and wake up to face the next day." And the next, "until fear is the thing that keeps you sharp instead of the thing that makes you bleed."*

He's been where I am now because that is the only way he can write sentences like those, full of understanding and compassion. I want to keep texting him, sending nonstop messages all day to see what he'll send me next. I don't, though, because even someone as socially awkward as I am knows that kind of behavior would drive anyone off, even the sensitive hipster types. Plus, I need to work on my book, not write to Jake, because I'm perilously late. So late I'm concerned Daphne might develop her own anxiety disorder.

But maybe I can sneak in a few messages before I lock myself in my office. I guess it *is* best that Daphne leaves after lunch.

"I'm done," I announce. "I just had an idea for the next chapter." Jumping off the counter stool, I gather up the lunch items and stuff them in the trash. Daphne gives me a strange look, but doesn't object, because no one wants this book finished more than she does. Not even me.

She wipes her mouth once more and crumples her half-eaten sandwich up in the wrapper. I throw it away and then wipe down the counter as she's gathering her purse. "Maybe I'll see some pages later tonight?"

"Sure," I promise. I actually have a few I've been working on that I can send to her even if I get distracted by something . . . or someone. "I'll send you something tonight or early in the morning."

"I take that to mean you'll be staying inside and not trying to take field trips down the hall?"

"Scout's honor. I will be in my office until I produce something printable." I hold up two fingers in what may be a Scout's salute. I wouldn't know, having never been a Scout.

Once she's gone, I do go to my office and I do settle in front of my computer and I do open my manuscript. But I also text Jake.

Me: You were right. Today's a better day.

Him: I'm always right.

Me: Really? You're going with that?

My image of Jake as a flannel-shirted, skinny-jeans-attired male with a trendy beard is reshuffled. A sensitive hipster does not say he's always right. My first instinct, that he was confident and maybe even arrogant, appears to be correct.

Him: What's the better response? Because I've got "I know" and "Yes" saved in my autotext.

I lift a hand to stifle a giggle even though no one is around to hear me.

Me: Are you now or have you ever worn flannel?

Him: Whoa. Whoa. Are we already at the What-are-you-wearing stage? Because if so, you need to go first. And if you're fully clothed, please feel free to lie and say, "Nothing."

My eyebrows shoot so far up my forehead, I fear they are going to be lost. I reread his message. And then read it again. I might lack a lot of experience with the opposite sex, and I have been a shut-in for nearly three years, but I'm pretty sure that Jake Tanner, former army person, according to Oliver, and owner of a high-profile, very expensive security firm, is flirting with me—Natalie Beck.

And while I'm contemplating this, I get another message.

Him: There should be a message retrieval. Some kind of feature that allows someone to take back a stupidly written text before the recipient reads it. (1/2)
(2/2) That was very inappropriate. Please accept my apologies. Not sure what came over me. Probably blood loss. Or just being a man. Men are dumb. Always right but dumb.

This time I didn't even cover my mouth when I laughed out loud. I look down at my penguin pajama bottoms and my pink tank and lie like a politician.

Me: I'm not fully clothed, but I'm not naked either. Your turn.

There's a pause, and for a moment I worry. Maybe he did mean for me to forget it. I never had much game before eliminating contact with the outside world. Even before the sight of a full inbox gave me sweaty palms, before doorbells made my heart stop, before the thought of stepping outside the safety of my apartment caused dread, I was a nerdy, socially awkward girl. An alpha male like Jake, full of testosterone, wouldn't have paid even the slightest attention to me before, so why do I think he's flirting? But then the phone dings and my eyes devour the words he sends back.

Him: I don't remember wearing flannel. Since I've already revealed that I'm an asshole, what with the winky face and the blatant and inappropriate request, I should probably admit that I don't even buy my own clothes. My mom and sisters still shop for me.
Me: Don't feel bad. Oliver is the same. The only clothing interest he has is workout gear.
Him: I have a friend, Ian, who has a personal shopper. Is that more manly?
Me: So he has to pay someone to do what your mom and sisters do? I don't think that's more manly. More expensive, but not more manly. Is that important?

Him: Being manly? Yes. I grunt in the morning and five times at
night to inject the right amount of testosterone into my system.
Me: Grunting is the key to manliness?
Him: It's one of the keys. Also belching, scratching of the balls,
being able to spit—not spray—actually spit.
Me: I don't think I like manliness. Can we revisit the flannel?
Maybe you should look into it. I bet you'd look good in flannel.
Him: I shave. Daily. I think you have to have a beard to look
good in flannel. Also, you are required to be holding an axe. I
prefer guns. Besides, all my manliness is done in private.

If I were braver, I'd take that innuendo-laden statement and launch
into something sexy and provocative such as: "Not an exhibitionist?"
Or, "What else do you like to do in private?" But I'm not. Plus, I want
him to keep texting me. I want him to text me forever. I want—oh,
what am I even thinking?

I can't even open the door. The idea of Jake Tanner in my apartment
terrifies me. It's one thing to joke and flirt via innocent message bubbles,
but normal people want face-to-face contact, skin-to-skin contact.

Him: Did my keys to manhood scare you off? Manliness also
requires you to recognize a good Scotch, know how to kiss, and
know that you drive a woman home after an evening out. No
matter how late or early it is. Is that better?

He's so sweet. He probably does wear flannel and because of that,
I text him the truth.

Me: I want you to come over. But I'm afraid I won't be able to
open the door.
Him: There are things I can do without coming inside.
Me: But not as effective for you.
Him: It helps to have eyes on the inside to see exactly what
we're dealing with.
Me: What if I can't open the door?

Him: Then you don't open the door and I deal.

A wave of emotion swamps me—part gratitude and part yearning. This man, with whom I've only exchanged written messages, is killing me with his humor, his understanding, and most of all, his kindness.

Me: Why are you so kind?

Him: As opposed to what? Making you feel bad? Seems to me that you have a lot on your plate without me adding guilt to your fight against anxiety.

I decide right then and there I don't care if Jake wears flannel, if he's mean to small children, if he forgets Mother's Day, and if he uses the horn too much when he drives. He's perfect and I'm half in love with him already. Of course it will never go anywhere. Because I live inside, and every other normal person is outside.

I wish I was okay with my current status—that I didn't long for human interaction. It would make life so much easier. Then I could look in the mirror without disgust. I could take my fear and wrap it around me like a warm comfortable blanket. I could stop wanting what I probably can never have—a real relationship with someone like Jake.

But the part of me that hates my fear? It wants out and now it wants Jake. That part drives me to type: Come over tomorrow.

CHAPTER FIVE

JAKE

The next day, I drive down to Tribeca early enough that there's still street parking available. The seven-story brick condo complex the Grahams live in isn't much to look at from the outside, but given that Graham just signed a five-year, $145 million deal this summer, I'm guessing the inside is much more interesting. Security consists of one doorman and no visible exterior cameras, which doesn't surprise me. Cameras require someone to actually look at the tape, and a complex like this is too small to have on-site management. The company that owns and manages this property is probably down in the Financial District.

"I'm here to see Oliver Graham," I lie to the doorman. He's young, 20 to 25 years old, with enough gel in his hair to style an entire boy band. It's easy to peg him as an aspiring actor or model. I want to see how simple it is to get inside.

"You need to sign in," he says, swinging a ledger book toward me.

"Did I see you in *The Lion King*? You look familiar." I push the ledger to the side.

He takes up the invitation immediately. Excited that someone, anyone, has recognized him, he leans forward and his elbow pushes the ledger farther down the marble-topped reception desk.

"No, but I have been in a couple off-Broadway shows." He rattles off the names of them. I haven't even heard of the theaters he names let alone the plays. My youngest sister would. She's pretty artsy.

"Why don't you give me a flyer?" I invite and close the ledger. He doesn't notice because he's too busy digging under the desk for a piece of promotional material.

"Here you go. We're doing a reinvention of *Waiting for Godot*, only the characters have been transformed into animals. So it's like a cross between J. K. Rowling's *Fantastic Beasts* and *Death of a Salesman*."

I nod like I would ever want to see something like that. "Sounds good, man."

"So you a friend of Mr. Graham's?" From his skeptical expression, I must not look like Graham visitor material. He takes in my boots, jeans, and T-shirt. I have a nylon jacket despite the early spring heat because I'm carrying. I'm *always* carrying.

"Business." Graham's visitors are probably leggier, shorter, and sporting much longer hair. Mine is still military-short. Some parts of the army can't ever be carved out of me. I can grow a beard and leave my bed a rumpled mess, but the minute my hair touches my collar, I start to get itchy.

Business must make sense to the doorman because he nods twice and jerks his head toward the elevators. I wave the flyer at him in thanks. The elevator doors slide open when I reach them and the top floor—the seventh floor—is already lit up. Over at the desk I can see him on the phone, likely calling Graham, who I know for certain is not home right now.

I watched him leave two hours ago and he hasn't returned, something the doorman missed when he darted out to get a coffee. I wonder if Graham knows how shoddy the security is here.

When the elevator stops on the top floor, I take one quick look around and then jog down to the third floor—the one Natalie lives on. There were two doors on the top floor, but six on this one. Sounds come from only two of them. I pause to make a calculated guess as to which one is hers. I asked Graham not to tell me because I wanted to see how easy it was to find her.

The middle units had the fewest number of windows whereas the front and back units had at least six windows each. Natalie's fear of the outside world could mean she'd want as little access to it as possible or she may enjoy what little access she had through greater exposure. I take a chance and knock on 3A, a corner unit with eight windows.

Behind the door there's a slight scuffling noise, which stops and then starts and then stops again. Someone is walking toward the door, but can't get close enough to open it. Bingo.

Because I'm not here to scare the shit out of her, I announce myself. "Natalie. It's Jake Tanner."

"How do I know you're who you say you are?" a distant female voice calls back. "Your website didn't have any pictures, remember?"

The low, husky tone sends a chill up my spine. Graham failed to mention that Natalie's voice is the sultry kind that hits a man in the solar plexus. Silently I cough into my hand to chase the vague tingle of interest away. Completely unprofessional. That said, nothing about our contact so far has been professional. I try to regret that, but I can't seem to summon up any outrage. I spent the night thinking about her.

"I'm sliding a card under the door."

"Anyone can print up a card."

Her voice is closer, unfortunately for me. I slide the cream card with the bold black print under the door and give it a shove. Graham said she wrote the damn game, but I'm wondering if she did voiceovers for it. A game with that voice crooning into a headset would sell millions of copies. She could convince half the male population to open their wallets and buy dirt with that voice.

"Think you're up for opening the door?" I lean against the wall to the right of the door and watch the doorknob, but it doesn't move.

"I don't know." She sounds nervous and I don't want that, but . . . I also want to meet her. Shake her hand. Or, if I'm completely honest, I want to put a face to the ill-advised fantasies I'm starting to have.

"You don't sound like you're hyperventilating. Besides, I thought I'd give it a try."

"I'm big on trying," she says. She's close enough to the door that I can hear her sigh, an extended exhale full of longing. This is a woman who doesn't want to be locked in her apartment. I respect that. "But not so much on doing."

"All you need to do is open the door. Let me take a look around."

"Jake, I'd love to be able to open the door," she responds with a touch of asperity and I can't help smiling. Housebound she may be, but she's got bite. "I might not be gasping for breath, but right now it's taking everything I have to just stand in the entryway talking to you."

Graham had said she'd been making progress getting out when the note arrived, which made it all the shittier. My fingers curl into a fist and I have to force myself to straighten them. People who prey on the vulnerable are bottom-dwellers. I might have to be there when Graham doles out the punishment.

I shouldn't care. She's a client. Feelings interfere with a rational review of the facts and evidence. I've terminated more than one security employee because he couldn't keep his pants zipped, yet I'm breaking all the rules for her. "Go into your bedroom and call me. You already have my number, and it's the same one on the card."

As the footsteps fade away, I pull a simple lock pick set from my wallet. The phone rings and her name shows up on the screen.

"Why should I go into the bedroom?" she asks.

"Because it's the room farthest from the front door. Once you're in your bedroom, I'll come in and take a look around." The phone line doesn't reduce the effect of her voice. I try to shut it out and concentrate on the task at hand. Her lock is a standard pin tumbler. It will take me all of a minute to pick.

"How do you know where my bedroom is?"

"The floor plans are on the Internet from when this building was being leased." Sticking the tension wrench into the keyhole, I press until the plug begins to rotate. Time for the rake. Three passes of the rake later, the pins bounce into place and the lock disengages.

"Ugh," she replies, but she doesn't hang up.

She'd probably never leave her bedroom if she knew how easy it was to gain entry into her home.

Natalie's apartment is good-sized by Manhattan standards. She has a fairly large living room with floor-to-ceiling windows that run along the far wall. Two of the windows are actually doors that open onto a small balcony overlooking Howard Street. To the immediate left is the kitchen. My card lies on the granite island counter. To the right a door rests slightly ajar.

"You and Graham could live in a place with more security." I poke the door and it falls open. Inside is an office. There's a treadmill with a platform attached to it at elbow height. A laptop sits on top of the platform. She must . . . type while she walks? I hadn't seen one of those before. There's a whiteboard filled with text, arrows, Post-it Notes. The room is ringed with bookshelves. I venture further in.

The shelves are filled with nonfiction and fiction alike. Romances, science fiction, mystery. She has eclectic taste.

"This is a small condo and we don't get a lot of attention here, which Oliver really likes. Plus, we have a doorman."

"He's pretty useless."

"You are the bearer of not very good news. Are you like that with everyone or am I getting special treatment?"

If she'd texted that, I might have thought it was a come-on, but she sounded weary rather than flirtatious.

"I give out facts. How my clients choose to interpret those is up to them." At the very top row of the bookshelves are multiple copies of the same book by the same author—a very famous author. "M. Kannan?" I murmur.

"Are you inside my apartment?" she shouts.

I pull the phone away from my ear.

"Yup."

"Oh my God, you picked my lock. You're in my apartment!" Her too-quick breaths fill my ear.

"Natalie, go sit on the bed. Imagine a square. Breathe in for four seconds and then walk to the other side of the square and exhale. Breathe in for four seconds and then out for four seconds," I command in my best drill sergeant voice. I wasn't a DS in the army, but I got yelled at by one enough that I can replicate his commanding voice with ease. I can almost taste her panic over the phone. "Start counting. One, two, three, four." She doesn't obey, and I hear her breathing coming in short pants. "Now," I bark.

There's a shuffling and then I hear the numbers. The first one is quavery and it takes her about five seconds to get the second one out. "Louder. I want them loud and crisp."

She starts over at one. By the fourth set she's breathing more easily. Yeah, the guy who did this is going to have a real pleasant visit from both Graham and me. "Good girl, Natalie. You're doing fine. I'm almost done here. Keep counting."

"Fuck you," she gurgles out between numbers three and four.

The insult makes me grin, but my smile fades as I spin around. This place isn't *that* big. And if it's the only place she feels safe, then her life is pretty miserable.

In the soft blue living room are three large framed posters of the covers of a bestselling science fiction series—a series that is being made into a movie. The light bulb turns on over my head. Natalie Beck is M. Kannan. That must be how she affords this Tribeca condo. And it makes sense. She wrote the storyline for one of the most famous games of recent memory, and now she's writing bestselling science fiction. And it's a series I fucking love.

"I've read you." I don't get starstruck. I've worked with too many celebrities to be awed by them, but I am standing about twenty feet away from the person the *New York Times* has called "a revolutionary new eye into the future." "I thought M. Kannan was a man" is my first thought.

I know who you are.

The threat takes on a different dimension.

She snorts, interrupting her counting. "Male readers don't read female authors. It's more lucrative to be gender neutral, especially when you're writing science fiction."

The words rush out, as if she's saying them all in one breath, but at least she's talking and thinking and not passing out. The panic attack is tapering off.

Mentally I run through my bookcases and realize I have embarrassingly few female authors on my shelf. "Like I said before, men are dumb."

"Yes, yes they are." When she half laughs, I exhale and realize I'd been holding my breath, waiting to run into the bedroom. Phobias are a bitch to fight off. Too many of my brothers-in-arms suffer from them and mental illnesses are viewed differently than physical illnesses. If a friend is sick with the flu, or God forbid, something worse like cancer, everyone is sympathetic. But depression? Fear of being in your own head? Folks just want you to get over it and if you can't, you're a weak-ass sadsack.

I don't know why I don't have PTSD. It's not because I'm better or stronger than my squad mates—more likely that I'm just a cold bastard. That's what my youngest sister claims.

"I'm going to need you to sign my books." She has a big-screen television, one of those curved ones, and three different game consoles underneath. Whatever happened in her past, it hadn't killed her love for the medium. I finish my inspection of the interior and walk to the kitchen.

"Just bring them over. You know how to get in." Her sultry voice is about an octave lower than earlier, and scratchy, as if she's spent a long time screaming. A quick vision of sheets, bedposts, and an arched back flash through my mind.

All right, Jake. Get a hold of yourself. It's only been a few weeks since I last got laid so I'm not sure why I'm having such a visceral reaction to this woman whose face I haven't seen.

"I'm almost done here."

The last room is her bedroom and while I need to see inside of it, I know she's not ready. Not today. Resolutely I turn away. "I'm leaving now."

At the kitchen counter, I pull out a small jar of powder and a brush. "A pre-Hollywood invention. Fingerprint dusting powder so you know where I was in your apartment," I write on a notepad I find on the counter.

I hope my token apology for interfering with her life, causing a slight panic attack, is offset by this. As I climb the stairs to the top floor, so it looks like I was with Graham the whole time, and then travel down the elevator to the lobby, something about the whole sweep of the apartment nags at me. Was it that I didn't get to see her bedroom and complete my assessment of her security needs? Was it that I didn't get to take Natalie's measure by looking her in the eye?

It isn't until my feet hit the sidewalk that I realize that I want Natalie to like me, not to be afraid of me. I look down at my arm, the one that is missing a hand, and then the leg, the one that is missing the calf and foot. Turning around, I stare up at the window in the far right corner. There's a movement there, a twitch of the curtain. I hold up my good hand and shove the bad one in my pocket.

No, let's be honest. I want Natalie to be attracted to me.

CHAPTER SIX

JAKE

Her call comes just seconds after the window curtain twitches.

"You left me a present."

"It's a thank-you for letting me in. I figured it would give you some peace of mind to know where I was and what I touched."

"I didn't let you in. You picked the lock!"

Her indignation makes me smile. I give her another wave and walk toward Hudson. We're both on the West Side so I decide to walk back to my office rather than catch a cab. I need to clear my head and the exercise would do my leg good. "You let me in. Or at least you gave me permission by going to the bedroom."

"So now you know all my secrets." She sounds nervous, as if I'm going to start blabbing to reporters about what I saw in her apartment.

"They're still your secrets. I'm hired to protect you, not to bring you more harm by revealing your secrets. That's why we have a nondisclosure agreement." As the sun warms my skin, I wonder what it's like to be locked inside the four walls of an apartment. Does she open her balcony windows? How often does she feel the sun on her face or the wind in her hair? "Is the author thing a big deal?"

"Meaning will it hurt my sales if it is revealed that I'm not male? Who knows? I already don't do book signings," she sighs. "I didn't want to use a male pseudonym because of where it got me before. I had to fight for the ambiguous first initial, but I knew if I used my real name it would be tainted by everything that had gone on in the past. I wanted the books to succeed or fail on their own. Not because people felt sorry for me or because they hated me for something other than my writing."

"That makes sense. How many people know you're M. Kannan?" That could narrow my suspect list considerably.

"Oliver. His parents. My therapist. My editor." She ticks them off one by one. "There might be a few other people in the publishing house, but we also have a nondisclosure agreement and they'd pay hefty damages if they broke it."

"But the resulting publicity could be good for them," I suggest.

A foul stench hits me as I reach Hudson. Being indoors isn't all that bad. Natalie's apartment smelled like cinnamon and lemons.

"I don't want to sound like an asshole, but we're doing pretty well on the publicity part."

A metro bus speeds by wrapped in an advertisement for the upcoming movie. "Good point. Do you think the note is from someone in your past or your current life?"

"Past," she replies firmly. "It has to be. My life . . . it's so small now and everyone in it is a friend. I can't imagine someone I know and love doing this to me."

Just because you don't want something to be true doesn't mean it isn't. But I suspect she knows this. "If it's someone from three or four years ago, then he has a real hard-on for you to be coming back after all this time. Can you make a list of the most determined guys who threatened you?"

"It wasn't just guys. A few of the worst were women."

That surprised me. "They threatened physical harm?"

"No, but they sent me other stuff. Women know how to hurt other women so well." She pauses. "Will it be very difficult if I don't want to delve into the past? I mean . . . yes, God, I did not like getting the note, and yes, it set me off, but digging through all that shit is only going to make me more stressed out."

"Why don't you have someone forward it to me?" My leg is starting to ache. I probably shouldn't have planned to walk this far with this prosthetic. I'd traded out the blade for my normal device with the vacuum-sealed socket and the carbon foot. It's not made for strenuous activity, such as walking forty blocks. And while I'm fairly comfortable with the fact that I'm walking around with a fake limb on my leg and arm, I don't enjoy the looks of pity when I have to turn on my vacuum pump to adjust the fit of my socket. It's noisy as fuck and it makes it harder to convince people that they really don't have to feel sorry for me when I'm grimacing in pain because the damn device isn't fitting well as my stump swells or shrinks.

I face the street to hail a cab.

"Can we talk about something else?"

"Like what?"

She takes a deep breath. "How about a picture of what you're wearing?"

I look down at my jeans, Windbreaker, and T-shirt. "It's not flannel. I promise."

"No picture?" She's disappointed. Maybe she wants to see my prosthetics. Did Oliver tell her? She never said a word before. When I meet women, it's the first thing they check out. I don't hide it, because if they're turned off by the fact that my left hand and foot are made of steel, plastic, and synthetics, I'd rather know that up front than later when I'm taking my clothes off. But for some reason I don't want to acknowledge, I don't want the focus on those things just yet.

"I'm six feet three. Weigh about two sixty."

She's silent. Am I too tall for her? Too short? A cab stops as I'm scratching the side of my shorn head. Why do I care?

"So not a runner's body?"

"I'm not sure what a runner's body is." That's not the comment I expected. "Because I do run."

"How long?"

"Depends, but usually about six miles a day."

"Six miles?" she yelps. "That's like half a marathon."

I cover the phone and give my address to the cabbie who stops. Returning to Natalie, I correct her. "It's a quarter of a marathon."

"It's a marathon compared to what I run."

As if the distance is what's offensive. Of all the things about me I figured she wouldn't like, the fact I work out isn't one of them. Most women like my body, if they can get over the stumps. They coo over my muscles and wonder how I can even have any on my left side. I've had more than one run her tongue over the ridges of my abdomen. The last woman I slept with—a financial reporter, whom I stopped seeing because she was a little too snoopy for my taste—told me that my physique and big cock made up for a lot of deficits. Come to think of it, I probably dumped her for more than a few reasons.

"You have a treadmill so how much do you run?" I ask.

"Three miles with no resistance either. I run flat with no incline."

"Three miles is a lot."

"I could never keep up with you."

"Did you plan on racing me?"

"No, but it'd be nice to run outside."

I've never run with a woman, never wanted to. But I could picture Natalie running beside me along the Hudson River, telling me I'm going too fast or too slow in her sultry voice. My jeans start to get a little tight and I shake my head. Getting turned on by just a voice is a first for me.

"If you go early enough, the route along the Hudson is pretty empty." I rub my chin. Am I asking her to run with me? Maybe the cell phone radiation is scrambling my brains. This is probably the longest conversation I've had with a woman not in my family.

The cabbie stops at my townhouse and I hand him two twenties and climb out. "Keep the change," I mouth.

"Yeah, man, thanks," he says and his voice is an intrusion on whatever weird intimacy that Natalie and I had developed over the phone.

She senses it too, because she clears her throat awkwardly. "Gosh, look at the time. I can't believe I kept you on the phone this long. I'm so sorry. You must think I'm totally friendless and weird. Anyway, um, send me a bill for this and whatever else."

"Natalie," I say gently. "I enjoyed talking to you."

"Um, right. Just, ah, send me the bill."

Then she hangs up.

With a sigh, I tuck the phone into my pocket. We have a connection, a different sort of one, but I think we're both caught off guard. I did enjoy talking to her, and generally speaking, I'm not a phone person. I text, I email, but spending thirty minutes on the phone isn't something I've done in a long time. The lights to Tanner Security, which is housed on the ground floor and garden level of the townhouse that I bought with the inheritance I received when I was twenty-one, are off. I glance upward to see if my sister is home.

All the rooms are dark with the exception of the front bedroom on the fourth floor. She's home, then, but doesn't want to have anything to do with me.

My sister and I were close once. When I was shipped home after my unfortunate run-in with an IED in Afghanistan, she was still in high school. I hadn't wanted to live at home and I hadn't wanted to have a live-in nurse, so Sabrina volunteered to come and stay with me. It worked out great. By the time she began attending Columbia, I'd become self-sufficient again, learning how to redo simple things I'd once taken for granted—such as buttoning my shirts. I solved that by wearing pullovers. She'd since moved out, but still spent a lot of time with me.

Yet somewhere along the line, possibly the moment she met Tadashubu Kaga, she stopped appreciating having me as a big brother and started accusing me of interfering with her life.

While I admire Kaga and view him as a friend, I don't want him anywhere near my innocent baby sister. He's a powerful and wealthy man with very specific taste in women.

I finger the phone in my pocket, wondering what Natalie would say about this. She and Graham seem pretty close. I have the phone out and in my hand before I realize what I'm doing. I just met this woman. Hell, I hadn't even *met* her. I talked to her on the phone for nearly thirty minutes and I've been inside her apartment, but we aren't even friends and I'm thinking of calling an agoraphobe for fucking advice?

I need to go inside and take a long cold shower.

When the phone rings, my heart thumps like a fucking twelve-year-old's until I see my mom's face on the screen.

"Hey, Mom."

"Are you still working? I can hear the noise on the street. You should be inside having dinner. It's nearly eight o'clock at night." She sighs, an exhale of frustration.

My mother has been nagging me about working too much and this moment of insanity is proof she's right.

"I'm going in right now and eating a cow," I reassure her.

"Save some for your sister," she replies. "She's looking tense and hungry these days."

The last thing I want to think about is what might be causing Sabrina's unhappiness. I shuffle that thought toward the back of my head and lean back against the stone railing of my stoop and enjoy the brisk night air as Mom catches me up on the news of her friends. She murmurs something about my ex looking me up but that's another thing I don't care to pay any attention to. After I promise to feed Sabrina, Mom lets me go.

I put the phone away and jog up the stairs. The front door has a lock and key, but it's for show. Access to my townhouse is gained through a biometric hand scanner and voice recognition. I press my hand against the pane of glass in the door that serves as the scanner and give an audible command. The three locks disengage and a chirp of the alarm acknowledges my entrance.

I wonder if Natalie would feel more secure with a system like this—

Stop, I order myself.

This is not me. I don't obsess over women. What I need to do is sit down, evaluate what I know, suggest a security system, and start viewing her as a client, not a potential bedmate.

In the kitchen, I find that Sabrina hasn't totally written me off. There's a plate of pasta covered in plastic wrap with a note that says "reheat, two minutes."

"Bless you, my child," I murmur as I stick the plate into the microwave. I can boil water, operate a microwave, and cook a steak. That's about the extent of my cooking skills.

"You're welcome."

I hide my surprise and turn nonchalantly to lean against the counter. Sabrina stands at the entry of the kitchen, her arms crossed and her mouth pressed into a hard line. Despite her angry stance, I see confusion in her eyes. She loves and hates me at this moment.

"Mom called to make sure you were eating."

"I ate earlier. Tiny came up an hour ago and said you were out on a call."

"New client," I answer. Tiny's an investigator for Tanner Security, but she's also married to Ian, whose best friend is Kaga, so I know where this is headed—nowhere good. The only mystery is how long it will take for us to get to the subject of him.

"Is it Kaga? Is he in trouble in any way?" she blurts out.

Not long, apparently. I pinch my nose because just the thought of her wanting to know about him gives me a headache. "Bri, honey," I begin, but before I can finish my thought, she interrupts me.

"What? I can't even ask about him?"

"What purpose does it serve for you even to imagine yourself in a relationship with him?"

"We're friends." She's stubborn.

"If you were friends, then you wouldn't need to ask how he's doing." Immediately I regret my words as she turns ashen and the skin around her lips whitens as her lips thin. "Aw, fuck me, honey. I'm sorry. I love you and I just want to make sure that you're happy in life." Pushing away from the counter, I move toward her, but she backs away.

"Really? You could have fooled me. Every action you take is designed to keep me away from people I love!"

She loves Kaga? She doesn't even know him. I reach a hand toward her. "Sorry you feel that way."

"If you were truly sorry, you wouldn't do this. You're only sorry that I'm mad at you." She whirls on one foot and runs out of the kitchen and up the stairs. My leg aches too much to run after her and frankly, she's right.

I'm sorry she's mad, but I'm not wrong about her and Kaga. Their differences are too vast.

The microwave dings and my stomach growls in response.

For a moment, I let my forehead rest on the heel of my hand. Maybe I'm thinking about Natalie because she's the one woman in my life that I haven't disappointed . . . yet.

CHAPTER SEVEN

NATALIE

"In my next book, I'm killing off the protagonist on the first page."

"Because you're tired of success and you want to shit all over your readers?" Daphne doesn't even look up from the magazine she's paging through as she predicts the demise of my career.

"How can I write about anything even remotely brave and heroic when I can't even put my hand on the doorknob without puking and fainting?"

"It's fiction. You can't do martial arts either, but your famous protagonist, Soren Blake, is a master at it. You haven't flown in outer space and fucked three alien dudes, or if you have, you are completely holding out on me."

"Why are we friends again?" I stare out onto Howard Street, wanting the six-feet-three, 260-pound Jake Tanner to reappear. I hadn't gotten a good look at him the other day and my image of him is fuzzy. I've crafted him with a Seth Rogen physique, which is comforting for me. The guys with the real hard bodies are usually the biggest jerks. In my fantasy, Jake Tanner is a sweetheart who helps old ladies across the street and talks to virtual strangers on the phone for thirty minutes or so. The fact that it isn't entirely a fantasy makes it all the more amazing. This guy texted me, talked to me, and flirted with me, all without meeting in person. He knows I'm fucked up in the head, but still made time to chat.

How could I not tumble head over heels in lust with him? I don't even want to stop the fall. It's harmless to have a crush—harmless and a little exciting. The rush of blood to my fingertips, the tingle up my spine? That's not due to fear, but excitement. I welcome those feelings. I *want* them.

"We aren't merely friends. I'm your editor, and a kick-ass one at that."

"I wish you could edit my life." Put me in a story with a hot security guy. He falls madly in love with me despite the fact that I don't like leaving my apartment and that the prospect of meeting new people sends me to my bed for several days.

Daphne sighs and throws the magazine aside. "Isn't that what Terrance is for? What does your therapist have to say about all of this?"

Dr. Joshua Terrance is probably the only one who knows the full extent of my crazy. "Too much. I preferred it when I had minimal contact with him." Minimal for me was once a month. Since I got the note, I've been talking to him nearly every day . . . except for yesterday, when I spent thirty minutes on the phone with Jake.

"Good thing you earn so much money selling books, or you wouldn't be able to afford him."

"I know." Daphne's sympathetic look borders on pity, so I gaze outside again, away from it and toward the direction of uptown where Tanner Security is. In different circumstances, I could leave my apartment and take the subway uptown. From there I could walk a few blocks and end up outside Tanner Securities. I'd march in wearing some saucy dress and high heels and tell the receptionist to hold all of Tanner's calls because he was going to be too busy servicing me to help anyone else.

A tingle of excitement causes me to clench my legs tightly together. I had a few naughty dreams about Jake last night. Ones that I shove into my mental closet so I don't get flushed and aroused while I'm sitting with Daphne.

"It's been so long. I think I've forgotten what sex is like."

"It's good, just FYI."

"I keep thinking about him." I run the back of my fingers along my collarbone wondering what it would be like if they were Jake's and not mine.

"The asshole who sent you the note?"

"No, Jake. The security guy."

"I have no idea who he is."

"He's tall and has a potbelly."

"You let him in?" She sounds shocked, and that annoys me even if it would be a giant surprise that I let someone other than Oliver and Daphne inside.

"No. He told me."

"He told you he was tall and had a potbelly? How did you have this conversation?"

"I asked him what he looked like."

"And did you ask him what he was wearing at the time? Are you sure this is an actual security person and not some rent-a-cop?" She looks at me as if my conversation is entirely fiction, like my books.

"Oliver hired him. And I looked him up on the Internet. He's got a real website, but no pictures. Isn't that weird? Like, does a person exist if there isn't a picture of him on the Internet? It's like the Internet version of 'if a tree falls in the forest.'"

"Not everyone is on the Internet twenty-four/seven like you."

"True."

"Why do you think he has a potbelly?"

I shrug. "I don't know. He said he weighed 260 pounds, and based on the background in his bio, he might have muscular arms and stuff, but he's probably soft around the middle. Right? I mean, that's like a hundred pounds more than me."

"Oliver weighs a hundred pounds more than you and there's not an ounce of fat on him anywhere."

"He's a football player. They work out every day. This guy eats donuts in his office."

"You have made some weird assumptions."

He needs to be average. Really average, because the only way some guy would ever be interested in me was if he had no other options. My fantasies have always been weirdly realistic. Like I never fantasized about running into Ryan Gosling at the airport and having him rub his fine form against mine, but I was guilty of inserting a few random guys from around the city into my sexier thoughts. That was back in the day when I actually got outside and could see random people on a regular basis.

And these days all I have are fantasies. I don't, of course, imagine being in a crowded rave, but I do dream of a day when I can walk outside, go to a bookstore, see a movie.

There are a whole host of things I could be doing, like visiting the set of my book's movie, to which I've been invited more than once.

But I can't and so my life has shrunk to the four walls of my apartment, three people, and the things I can conjure in my own head.

Today and yesterday, Jake is playing a big starring role in those imaginary happenings.

It's completely harmless—for both him and me.

Outside there is only the regular traffic. I see all these people and I know—*I know*—that not one of them down there would hurt me, but the minute I try to go outside, my heart seizes. I can't breathe. I start sweating like it's 110 degrees and I'm running wind sprints. Even getting near the front door can cause me to hyperventilate. All that Jake will ever be is a fantasy. "It's so fucking stupid, the power our minds have over us."

"It's also what makes you a great writer. Your imagination is big and powerful and sometimes it's too powerful for even you." She sets down the magazine.

"Thanks for trying to make me feel better."

The chair squeaks as Daphne pushes out of it to join me at the window. "Think of it this way. Two weeks ago you were telling me you couldn't write another word. Since the note came, you've been writing like you were possessed."

"Because I *am* a madwoman. I have the actual crazy person diagnosis." I don't tell her that last night I got out of bed and wrote the steamiest scene I'd ever put on the page. My readers would probably be shocked, and in the end, I probably won't include it, but damn, had it been hot.

"You are not mad. I know Dr. Terrance doesn't like you to use that word. Hell, I don't like you to use that word."

I don't like it either, but sometimes when I take a good hard look at myself, I can't shake that I am not right in the head. The glass feels blessedly cool against my skin. I'm somewhere along the scale between normal and not, otherwise I could step outside my apartment without wanting to puke. I need to force myself. "Daphne, would you—?"

"No!" she nearly shouts. Hurrying, she tries to explain, but there's no explanation necessary. I know what she's going to say and I don't blame her. "We are not going to the elevator again. I'm sorry, Natalie, but I just can't. That was terrible. I know you want to recover, but what's the rush?"

"It'd just be nice to go to Barneys. Try on shoes. Maybe go eat a Shake Shack burger." *See Jake Tanner in person. Put on a sexy dress and seduce him. Have some intimate contact with a real human being for the first time in forever!*

"All those things can be delivered here. Stay here. Write. Get better. Before you know it, we'll be having lunch at David Burke's in Bloomingdale's."

"I know. Isn't New York great?" I say without enthusiasm.

After Daphne leaves, I heave the biggest sigh known to womankind and then slump down in front of the French doors that lead out onto the balcony. The room-darkening curtains are pushed to the side. The sun's rays burning through the glass are about the only sunshine and outdoors I get. Two weeks ago, I was able to go up to Oliver's penthouse apartment. We had dinner with his parents, who were visiting from Ohio.

Two weeks ago, I was standing outside the subway stop. Sure, I hadn't been able to make myself go down the stairs and into the tunnel. That was my next goal, though. I would've made it—no. I'm *going* to make it.

It's happening. In the future. All my progress isn't relegated to the past.

What I need is for the good doctor to write me a prescription for elevator visits, because frankly with both Oliver and Daphne telling me that I need to stay inside, I'm beginning to wonder if I am pushing too hard.

Picking up my phone, I press the second contact on my Favorites screen. Favorites is a misnomer. If I never had to see or talk to Dr. Terrance again, I would be so happy. He's not a bad guy but he's a visible reminder of my psychosis. If I could, I'd make a list called "Un-favorites I have to stay in contact with." I wouldn't have gotten to the point of being able to stand outside without his aid. Even so, every visit and phone call is just a reminder of my weakness, my mental illness.

While another person might have fired him and found a new doctor, Daphne recommended Dr. Terrance, and I'll admit that up until two weeks ago his methods have worked.

"Hello, Natalie, how are you today?"

"Not bad, Dr. Terrance. I was wondering about getting out of the apartment."

He *tut-tuts*, the clicks of his tongue against the roof of his mouth as clear through the phone line as if he is standing next to me. It's just as annoying in person.

"And what happened the last time that you ventured out?" he asks. Psychiatrists ask questions—at least that's what I've learned. If I wrote a book featuring a psychiatrist, I'd wear out my question mark key. *Were you sad when your parents died? When Oliver went away to college, were you upset? Why did you move to New York? When the person called you a whore and threatened to send dogs to rape you, were you scared?*

Yes, yes, because Oliver came here, yes. He always knew the answers, but wanted me to say them, as if saying the answer, acknowledging my pain, somehow lessened the sting. It hasn't yet, but I keep going back to him because I *did* get better. I was improving and I'm not going to let some note from some faceless neckbeard keep me from going outside again.

"I made it to the elevator." I project as much gaiety as possible.

"And then you felt faint, vomited, and lost consciousness. You frightened your cousin, who called me in a panic and, had you not been revived, he would have taken you to the hospital where you would likely have been admitted—at least overnight—for observation."

Hot-cheeked, I remain silent because his recitation is terribly accurate and nothing scares me more than being admitted. The feeling of suffocation inside the white walls of the psych ward with the antiseptic smells and the constant interruptions by the nurses and aides is a million times worse than the fear that overtakes me when I try to leave my apartment.

"Natalie?" he prompts.

Natalie with a question mark. I answer with my own query. "When do you think I'll be able to leave my apartment?"

"It all depends. I've written you a scrip for Tofranil and you should take four 25 mg tablets a day. With food," he adds as an afterthought. "Stay away from triggers like visitors and leaving your apartment. Once you've been on the dose for seven days and your anxiety is down to manageable levels, you may call me and we'll try the elevator together, which is how we should have done it in the first place, isn't that right?"

I ignore that question, which probably doesn't require a response anyway. Dr. Terrance likes to be with me for every big "breakthrough."

"Are you saying that I shouldn't see Oliver or Daphne?"

"You can talk to them on the phone, but no in-person contact."

"How am I supposed to eat?"

"Order in and have the food deposited outside your door as you usually do. You are still comfortable with the doormen delivering your goods, correct?"

I drop my head into my hands. Seven days of forced solitude? Well, Daphne would say to look at the bright side and think of all the writing I'll get done. "Yeah, I'm okay with the doormen. Does it have to be Tofranil? I feel like a zombie on that."

"You and Prozac have never gotten along, Natalie, or have you forgotten?"

"No." Prozac makes me violently ill.

"Good. Take the Tofranil and let's get ready to face the elevator together, hmm?"

Suitably chastened, I reply, "Right."

"Oh, and Natalie, think about my proposition again, will you? I think it would be a wonderful service for the community."

"Sure."

Never happening in a million years, Dr. Terrance, I silently vow.

Hanging up, I stretch out on the floor and press one hand against the glass. Dr. Terrance wants to write a book about my experience. He says when I recover it will be a triumphant story of recovery and provide hope to other sufferers of extreme anxiety.

I don't believe him, but partly because I don't want it to be true. If it is true then repeatedly turning down his offer is super selfish of me because I should want to help other people, but it would mean laying my entire life bare; I had enough of the fishbowl three years ago when someone leaked that I was Natalie Beck. The unhappy trolls, who'd discovered that their favorite game had been written by a woman and not a man, made it their mission to uncover every piece of dirt in my past—who I'd slept with and how many times was of greatest interest. They read my innocuous tweets about cats and movies. Looked me up on message boards. They discovered my Facebook page and proceeded to comb over every status update as if they were the Watergate reporters.

Thankfully my connection to Oliver was never revealed. It was apparent early on in Oliver's high school career that he was someone special. To prevent me from suffering abuse from nosy people on the Internet as he became more famous, we hid our connection. It was easier to do that now when we lived in the same building. Most of the people here were very private for one reason or another, and Oliver's visits to my apartment or mine to his have never been remarked on publicly.

After my identity was revealed, he wanted to blast everyone who hurt me, go on talk shows and the like, but I begged him not to. I knew it would only make it worse. He'd been coming off a terrible season and his social media accounts were filled with hostility too. It would have been gasoline on a fire.

No, there won't ever be a book written about me—at least not without my permission.

I roll to my side and stare out the bottom of the glass door. It's all academic anyway. There's no triumphant recovery. Not yet.

And after the note?

Maybe not ever.

CHAPTER EIGHT

JAKE

"Glad you could make it," Ian says with sourness as I slip into my courtside seat.

"Work," I answer. I'd spent the afternoon running down possible leads in Natalie's case. Oliver provided me a list of her former coworkers, people they thought could have been behind the subway attack, and her ex-boyfriends—only one actually lives in New York City; the other two were from her hometown in Indiana. I put an investigator on the one who lives in Brooklyn. "How long has he been like this?" I ask Kaga, who is seated next to Ian. Their long legs are stretched perilously close to the out-of-bounds line. Anyone who thinks Asians are short hasn't met Kaga, who tops me by an inch.

"Since the opening tip-off," Kaga replies with a roll of his coal-black eyes.

We both turn to look at Ian, who apparently came from the office since he's still wearing his suit. His collar is unbuttoned and his undoubtedly very expensive silk tie is hanging halfway out of his pocket.

He invited us out tonight to witness the shellacking of the Knicks by the Atlanta Hawks. He flips us off but doesn't take his eyes off the court.

The Knicks haven't been good since Willis Reed, and I suppose it's a measure of Ian's steadfastness that he still pays good money for this type of torture. And if there's anyone who has money to burn, it'd be him.

Ian Kerr is a billionaire. When he plays poker, there are only a few people in the world who can afford to sit with him. I'm not one of them. I only have a few million to my name, and unlike Ian, who transformed himself from a street rat who ran small cons on the Atlantic City boardwalk, my paltry millions are inherited from my grandfather. The Tanners have a long history of modest wealth based on the founding branch having manufactured and sold gunpowder during the Civil War—a decent work ethic interrupted by a few spendthrifts means our money has lasted but hasn't grown.

Besides, a seven-figure net worth in the city is nearly a dime a dozen. One in twenty New Yorkers can lay claim to that.

"Watching the home team lose makes me thirsty," I declare and hold up my arm to signal the beer hostess.

Kaga's lip curls. "How can you drink that piss water?"

"Don't have much choice here."

Kaga's one of those men whose fortune rivals Ian's. His large Japanese conglomerate distributes everything from domestic beverages to some of the best brandy known to man. Kaga's making inroads in the international real estate community as well. Soon half of New York will be owned by Kerr and the other half by Kaga. Since both pay me a lot of money to do investigative and security work for them, I'm completely fine with their impending takeover. Could be worse.

It was Ian's and my mutual interest in cars that led to our first meeting at a Long Island body shop that worked on foreign sports cars. I was getting my tires rotated on my Audi A8, one of my few extravagances, and he was eying a custom remake of a 1970s McLaren F1, which cost about as much as an apartment on the Upper East Side.

When he found out what I did for a living, he had me investigate a couple of principals in a company he'd wanted to take over. It worked out well, and after that the acquaintance grew into a sort of friendship. Through him I met Kaga, who'd done a few deals with Ian, and I'd connected with these men, despite our varied backgrounds.

Kaga and I had watched with bemusement as Ian fell hard for Tiny, just a year earlier. He'd seen her on the sidewalk and told me she was the one.

The one to what? I'd asked.

She's going to either remake me or break me, he'd answered.

I'd been remade and broken and I wasn't interested in going through that again, but I won't deny that seeing Ian and Tiny together has made me feel . . . restless. Maybe that's why my thoughts have been lingering on Natalie. She'd been bent by a rough hand but was fighting back. That's intriguing to me in a way that the popular supermodel who has been gazing longingly in our direction isn't.

"You should take her up on her offer," Kaga says, dipping his head toward the model.

"I think you're the one she's trying to consume with her eyes."

"No, I don't think she's that discriminating. Any one of us would do." He nudges me as the beer arrives.

"Not interested." I take my beer with my prosthetic and give the server a twenty. "Keep the change."

Her eyes widen in surprise that I can hold the plastic cup, but holding things isn't an issue. Gross motor tasks are fairly easy for me. It's the fine motor skills that are problematic.

"I thought you had finished with your journalist friend." Kaga makes a shooing gesture toward the waitress and she scurries away.

"I did. What about the girl over there don't you like?" It'd be nice if he started seeing someone. That way Sabrina could move on.

Kaga weighs his response carefully, his tension visible. Finally, in deference to our friendship, he says, "I am not interested either."

He wants to say that he has interest in only one woman and, to give him credit, I haven't seen him with anyone in recent memory. Granted, he is not in New York for great swaths of time, so he could be fucking a dozen different women in different cities, but Kaga's too decent for that. It's his honor that keeps him from Sabrina as long as I disapprove. But it's also his honor that has gotten him into his current predicament.

I take a long draft of the flavored water that the Garden serves as beer. A shift reveals Ian's interest has been drawn away from the game. Both of them look at me expectantly.

"You have to clean house first," I say in answer to the unstated question as to when I'll give my blessing.

"Maybe I will," he responds quietly. Ian nods in satisfaction and turns back to the game.

I hide my surprise by lifting the beer again. It looks like I'm not the only one unsettled by Ian and Tiny's pairing.

"Sir, would you like to come out at halftime and be honored for your service?" A dark-suited young man with a lanyard around his neck proclaiming his position as Entertainment Staff appears at my side.

Kaga covers his face to hide a smirk, while I try to summon a smile to soften my emphatic response.

"No. I never served. I lost my hand in an unfortunate meatpacking incident," I lie.

The young man colors and his gaze flicks behind him. "I must have been mistaken then. So sorry to have bothered you."

As he leaves I scan the crowd behind him, only to see my old therapist, Dr. Crist, in the mix.

I give him a one-fingered salute with my prosthetic, which he acknowledges with a wave and a laugh.

"You know him?" Kaga asks.

"Isaiah Crist served in the army during the first Gulf War, and suffered a hip disarticulation." At Kaga's raised eyebrows, I elaborate. "His amputation is at the hip instead of below the knee like mine." I tap my lower left prosthetic. "After he was medically discharged, he went back and got his head-shrinking degree. He's expensive as fuck and has a clientele list that would make your head spin, but I met him when he was doing pro bono work down at Bethesda."

"What was that all about then? I know you do not enjoy being on display."

"He's just fucking with me. It's an army thing."

Kaga looks unimpressed. "Did the nosy journalist turn you off women?"

"The game must really bore you if we're delving back into my personal life."

"Yes," he says with a grin and an expectant look. I'm not ready to talk about my surprising attraction toward Natalie. I can't explain it to myself yet, but I'm honest enough to admit it exists.

I like her taste in books, her plucky attitude, and her unwillingness to be cowed by her fear. She's interesting in a way that the other women I've been with since I was discharged haven't been. That may be a bigger reflection on me than the women of New York, though.

"When I have something to share, I'll be sure to call you up right away," I reply.

"I'd share my own personal female woes, but I suspect it would make you uncomfortable."

"You'd be right." The last thing I want to hear is what he wants from my sister. But I like Kaga, so I add, "Sorry."

Kaga shakes his head slightly. "Your devotion to your family is one of the things I admire most about you, so there is no apology necessary. But you realize it is in my best interest to see you helplessly in love like our friend Ian."

Ian gives a nod of acknowledgment, though he doesn't turn away from the game. "He's right. You need to pair up so that Tiny has someone to do shit with when we go out to dinner. She's tired of your single asses. If you aren't going to give Kaga and Bri your blessing, then you need to step up."

"Oh well, then I'll get right on that for your wife. Hey, single lady, want to hook up for an unspecified period of time? My buddy's wife is tired of talking to penises when we go out."

"I'd phrase it slightly differently," Kaga offers unhelpfully.

"What if I had an agoraphobic girlfriend who couldn't leave her apartment?"

Ian scoffs. "That's your excuse now? How'd you meet this agoraphobic person if she doesn't go out?"

"I'm extraordinary," I say, in hopes that the ridiculousness of my reply deters further inquiry.

But Kaga looks at me thoughtfully. "This is happening in large numbers to young people in Japan. It is called *hikikomori* and means a withdrawing or pulling inward. They do not socialize with anyone but their own families and retreat to their bedrooms. It can last for a few months or even years."

Surprised, I gesture for him to continue.

"I don't know much more about it," Kaga admits. "I have only heard small pieces. Supposedly it affects at least one percent of our young male population. It is a concern. As time passes, the withdrawal feeds upon itself. Social abilities atrophy and even the desire to escape is eaten away."

"She's not like that," I find myself saying. Kaga merely nods—his perceptiveness is eerie at times.

"I thought you were joking," Ian says. He's abandoned the game, probably because the massacre is too painful.

Sighing, I give in.

"I'm looking into something for someone." I hold up my hand to forestall further questions from Ian. He shuts his mouth and slides back in his chair. "I met a woman who has severe anxiety, but she's not withdrawn. She's actively trying to get better—she's suffered a setback and I'm investigating some circumstances that might have adversely affected her recovery."

"She's a fighter, then," Kaga muses.

"That's right."

"Of course," he says. "You, as a soldier, must not only admire that, but respond to it as well."

Ian makes a gun with his fingers and points them at me. Is he saying I'm dead or down? I'm neither, but I might be falling and it doesn't seem to be painful at all.

CHAPTER NINE
NATALIE

I allow myself to have a brief pity party that my wonderful progress has been halted and then peel myself off the metaphorical floor. Daphne is correct when she says my best writing comes from torment. But as I stand and type out an entire chapter, I find myself inserting a tall, pot-bellied space ranger. He's got a wry smile and good hands that capably manage his phaser.

I work for hours until I forget the outside world exists and my fingers are cramped and my own shoulders ache. When the sun becomes just a thought on the horizon, I put my computer to sleep and fall into the darkened bedroom, asleep before my head hits the pillows.

Somewhere around noon the phone wakes me up. I try to ignore it because I'm having a very nice dream involving Jake. He's under the covers with me, nuzzling my neck. My hands cling to his broad shoulders as the coarse hair of his legs rub against mine. His hands move down my sides and I start aching in places that I didn't know could ache.

His head follows the direction of his hands, pausing to lick on my tightened nipples and then lower still. The first touch of his tongue is so tender, I almost weep. He draws his tongue in slow, long movements until I tilt my hips forward in an unspoken plea for more. He palms my butt and rocks me toward his mouth. I'm shaking with pleasure and desire, desperate for more. I beg him to stop tormenting me. He rises to his knees and drags me down with hungry hands until my wet heat presses against his hard erection. He leans forward, all two hundred and sixty pounds of fierce need, sinking on top of me, but the stupid phone will not stop ringing. I shut my eyes tighter, but the heavy pressure of his body dissipates and I'm left clutching my sheets.

It's probably Oliver. Unhappily, I stick my hand out and fumble on the nightstand without emerging from the covers. If I don't lift up the sheets, maybe the dream will come back.

"Hullo?" I mumble.

"Did I wake you?"

It's Jake and he sounds amused. My heart gives a silly pulse as I scramble to answer him. I feel off-balance, as if he somehow knows I was having a naughty dream about him. "I went to bed at four in the morning. It's still early for me."

I run a hand over my hair, smoothing the wild strands down, and then laugh silently at myself. Jake can't see me. If he could, he'd hang up and never call me again because I know from experience my bed head is frightening. My ex used to say that for someone with thin hair, I was able to create an alarming Medusa-like cloud after only a few hours of sleep. Although seeing my hair is the least of the reasons he should run away. The first and foremost is that I'm using him as fodder for my sexual fantasies.

"Were you having trouble sleeping?"

"No, I was working. The words kept falling out and I didn't want to stop."

"I'm sorry I woke you up."

"I'm not," I answer with frank eagerness. I don't want him to hang up. Talking to him feels good, like spring in my heart after a long dark winter.

"Then I'm not sorry either. I called about some security ideas."

Oh, I like that he called me and not Oliver—that he thinks I'm capable of making decisions like this. "Thank you," I murmur, huddling deeper into the covers. I wish he was here with me. We could discuss this over coffee, still in bed, our limbs tangled together. I barely remember the last time I slept with a man. Daphne's stayed over a few times, but she sleeps in my pull-out in the living room, and as much as I love her, she's no substitute for a warm male body.

"For what?"

"For treating me like an adult."

"You look like an adult."

Is that . . . an innuendo? I want to tell him that I'm very adult. That I just had a grown-up sex dream he starred in, and would he like to come over and act it out in person. Of course, I don't because rational people don't go around telling strangers that they are spank bank material, and even if he is okay with that, what if he showed up and I couldn't bring myself to turn the doorknob. That would be a humiliating experience.

Abruptly I sit up, tossing the covers aside and banishing my foolish thoughts. Jake is not flirting with me; he's being kind and I need to start acting like the adult we both are pretending I am.

"What are your ideas for improving the safety of my home?" I ask with brusqueness.

He picks up my cue and responds in kind. "I'd like to place proximity sensors around your doors—the front and the balcony. The alarms are outward-facing and wouldn't be triggered by opening the door from the inside or even walking onto the balcony."

"You can do that?"

"Technology is pretty great."

I guess it is amazing. It'd be great if we could implant a device in my brain that would turn off my fear, but then I'd probably walk into traffic and get myself killed. "That sounds good. You wouldn't have a proximity sensor for an individual, would you?"

"What do you mean?"

"Like, let's say I fell. Could you have a proximity sensor that could detect the motion of falling and then a period of, say, thirty seconds of no movement?"

"I don't have anything like that, but it's possible it could be rigged up. A proximity sensor can detect certain motion, like the deceleration of mass, but it's not a system I stock and could bring over today. Why?"

I blow out a stream of air and then decide what the hell. He already knows I have *issues*. "I've been trying to force myself to go outside, leave my apartment."

"Is that safe?"

"It's how I won before. After—" I don't even like to bring up the attack, but I force it out. "After the attack, I got scared of everything and everyone, but after like six months of solitude, I started going a little stir-crazy, so I tried to leave. I got as far as the stairs—I lived on the second floor—and had to turn around and go back. But I kept going back and I'd mark down in a little journal how long I stood there. After a couple of weeks, I looked at my log and saw I had stood five minutes outside my door. That was . . ." I try to find the right word to describe my triumph that day. "I felt like I'd won the Pennant and the Super Bowl all at the same time." *Please don't find this pathetic*, I cringe.

"I understand," he says. "When I took my first step with the prosthetic, it felt as good as when I'd passed Ranger School."

Okay, he did get it. Wait, did he say prosthetic? "You have a prosthetic?"

"Yes, left hand, left leg, below the knee."

"Wow." I didn't know anyone who had a prosthetic. A couple of my characters in the Dark Worlds series had biomechanical limbs, but I'm a science fiction writer, so I can write any kind of thing I please, within the rules of the world I'd built. While I'd done some research, I had no idea what it meant to have a prosthetic.

"Is that a problem for you?"

There's a hint of defensiveness behind his strong voice. If he only knew how exponentially more attractive he just made himself, he'd be frightened. He'd suffered a terrible blow to his body and probably his self-image, yet he had started his own business and is clearly very successful or Oliver would have never hired him. He is someone who's overcome. Basically the person I want to be someday.

"No, not at all. I was just thinking how amazing you must be."

"How do you figure?" He snorts.

I shrug, but he can't see me. "Because you're a bad-ass at protecting other people. Not to mention you can go outside whenever you want."

"Are you saying you would give your left arm to be able to walk in Central Park?" It's a joke. At least I think it's a joke, but I'm not sure, so I don't respond right away. He clears his throat. "Bad gimp joke. Anyway, let me know when I can come over and install the system."

I chew on my lip. I'd like him to come over right now. I'd like to look at him, his tall frame, his prosthetics, what I presume to be a sweet and decent face. But then if I puked, passed out, or did anything embarrassing, I could kiss all my dreams good-bye. Actually, no, that's all I'd have left of him—those dreams. "This will require you to come inside, right?"

"It would."

"I . . . I just don't know."

"Can I help you in any way, honey?"

It is the endearment that does me in. Whatever defenses I had against him, and I didn't think I had many, tumble down. I want to impress him, but more than that, I want to know him.

"I don't get you."

He doesn't answer right away and I like that. Maybe I read more into it than I should but his hesitation makes it seem like his response is important enough to him that he's not going to throw out a glib answer. "I like the sound of your voice."

"Really?" I'm skeptical and thrilled all at the same time.

"Really." Sometimes his responses are so dry I think he must be making a joke. "Why don't I bring some food over?"

"Why?" I ask like a fool.

"So we can share a meal. Get to know one another."

"What if—what if I can't open the door?"

"Then I sit on one side and you sit on the other."

"You'd do that for me?" My heart pounds frantically at the thought—half in panic and half in excitement.

Another of his long thoughtful pauses follows before he answers. "You'd be surprised what I'd be willing to do for you."

♦ ♦ ♦

For the next few hours, I write and then take breaks to practice opening the door. I visualize my portly fellow with the receding hairline—I added that detail because it fit with my safe image of him—outside, wearing khaki cargo pants, tennis shoes, and a white polo. No flannel. I shake my head and remove the receding hairline and replace the white polo with a dark blue polo, otherwise he looks too much like the cable repair guys on television. By the tenth time, I'm able to make it to the doorway and twist the knob. I don't open it yet. While my palms are sweaty and my knees are weak, I don't feel bile at the back of my throat and I'm still standing up.

Success. I can do this. I can let him in. I shut out the little voice in my head that chirps *Dr. Terrance would not approve.*

Excitedly, I call Daphne and tell her about my impending date. "Can you fall in love with someone you've never seen?" I ask as I straighten my hair. The wispy brown locks usually have a slight curl in them, but I want to look older and sophisticated.

"Sure. Isn't that how Internet relationships are? You email someone or chat with them and then just confirm your lust in person. Why? Is this about the winky face person? The lumbosexual?"

"The lumbowhat?"

"That's the type of guy who is spending thousands of dollars to look like he's in a back-country camping ad, but he doesn't camp. He just looks like he does, and he'll cry if you show him a picture of a cute puppy. Hence the flannel and the inappropriate use of emoji."

"No. He is definitely not a lumbosexual." Jake didn't seem like the crying type.

"Should you even be talking to this Jake guy? Have you cleared it with Dr. Terrance?"

"I don't have to have permission from Dr. Terrance to make a new friend!" I exclaim, affronted.

"I'm just saying that so soon after your meltdown at the elevator, it doesn't seem wise to invite some stranger into your apartment."

"He's going to sit on my balcony. He's not even coming inside to act on my lust," I point out.

"He's bringing food and wants to get to know you better. That's what guys do when they want to get in a girl's pants."

She's right, but I'm okay with that because if all he wants is sex and I can actually follow through, that would be it's own small miracle. "True, but what if I'm not pretty enough for him? Because for a guy to take on a basket case like me, he must either have no other options or he thinks I'm supermodel pretty."

"You are very pretty," come the words of a best friend.

"I'm not a dog, but I'm no model." And model types are everywhere in New York. A guy like Jake who owns his own business and his own home would be attractive to them. Hell, he'd be attractive to 99.9 percent of the single heterosexual ladies in the city and half of the married ones too.

According to the little information that the Internet reveals, Jake owns an Upper West Side townhouse worth at least five million according to some real estate site. His mother was a lawyer and his father was a banker. Both are retired. He holds a degree in business management from Columbia, plus there's the added benefit of a touch of danger. He was a soldier and wore a uniform. I found a picture of his platoon—or what I think might be his platoon—on Google but I didn't know which of the dirty-faced, camo-wearing guys with guns was him. There isn't much else that Google coughed up about him. "It's all academic. I've not made a new friend or acquaintance since, you know, before."

"There's a first time for everything. By the way, the pages you sent me today were brilliant.

Whatever you are doing, keep doing it and keep sending me pages. You'll make your deadline if you keep at it. If flirting with Paul Bunyan makes you write like this, then I approve."

"So I should keep my door shut and my feelings repressed and regurgitate all the emotional mess on the page."

"If that's what is keeping your creative engine motoring . . ." She lets the unfinished statement dangle there.

"Maybe there will be lots of romance in this book."

"Everyone likes romance," she agrees. The phone beeps and it's Dr. Terrance.

"Dr. T is on the line," I say.

"Go," she orders. "I've got work to do. Keep writing!"

"Yes ma'am." I snap off a salute she can't see and switch over to Terrance.

"Hello, Natalie, did you get the delivery today?"

Guiltily, I cringe. "Um, I haven't called down for it." I've been too busy flirting with the sweet security guy my cousin has hired to worry about taking drugs. Besides, now that I've got a date with Jake, the last thing I want to do is take some antianxiety medication that will dull all my feelings and turn me into a walking, talking, monotone zombie. That will really impress him.

"If you don't take your proper medication, then we can't move forward."

"But Dr. T, I felt really good today and I was thinking—"

"Natalie, when is the last time you were able to leave your building?"

My fingers curl in anger so I take a second before I respond. "A while."

"Two weeks and three days, if my calculations are accurate."

You know they are, I say silently. Out loud, I try to convince Terrance I can do this without the medication. "I think we should just try, maybe once, without the medication."

"How did it feel the last time you tried?"

"Not good," I admit. "But I met this guy—"

"A new person, Natalie? Why haven't you told me about him?"

"I meant to, but it was just the other day."

"And who is he?"

"Oliver hired him to look into my situation, to give me some additional security."

"Oh dear, Natalie, I'm going to talk with Oliver. I don't think introducing a new person into your life at this time is good for your fragile state of mind. Now I want you to take the medication, and then I'll call you tomorrow after I've spoken to your cousin."

"But—" I start to object, but the dial tone tells me he's already hung up. I'm about to call him back when I get a buzz on my phone from the doorman downstairs.

"Hi, Jason," I say. "What's up?"

"You have a visitor. Should I send him up?" He sounds confused—I never have new visitors.

"Is he six foot three and two-sixty?" I ask wanting to be sure it's Jake.

"Um, I'm a doorman, not a doctor."

He's earlier than I expected, but maybe he's just as excited as I am. I resist the urge to clap. "Sorry, send him right up. And thank you, Jason."

"No problem. Let me know how you enjoy it!"

I raise my eyebrows at this. Jason and I have a friendly relationship over the phone wherein I call and ask for packages and he leaves them outside my door after ringing the doorbell, but we certainly aren't at the stage where I'd tell him dirty details from any intimate encounter I had.

The door rings and my heart starts pounding. I flex my fingers wide and take deep, calming breaths. I move slowly toward the door, pushing hard through the anxiety that is threatening to drag me under. "I'm coming," I call, in case he's worried that I'm not home. Ha, I'm always home. He murmurs something that I can't quite hear.

The doorknob looms large and my wet palms have a hard time turning it, but I do, slowly. "It's Jake," I tell myself. "He's sweet. Kind. He will not hurt you. He will not hurt you." I repeat it over and over as I turn the knob, as I take each breath, as I open the door.

And when it's wide enough for me to see outside, I scream. I scream and scream and scream. My breath seizes and oxygen becomes a memory. Stumbling forward, I hit my head on the door and then black out.

CHAPTER TEN

JAKE

I hear the scream from the elevator and I know it's Natalie. The metal box doesn't move fast enough for me and I pull at the doors the minute they crack open, dropping the bags full of Chinese onto the floor. The screams stop abruptly, propelling me forward at an even faster pace. My Beretta is in my right hand, and I'm down the hall in two strides with the barrel shoved against the intruder's white greasepainted face. His fake red smile and nose look macabre against the black metal of my gun.

He shrieks and raises his hands. "Don't shoot, man. I'm just a messenger," he blubbers. The gun slides against the greasy paint. I start to question him, but the smell of urine fills the air and he starts crying. Nothing worse than a crying clown. I shove his face against the wall, stepping wide to avoid the pool of piss. With my left hand pressed into the middle of his back, I pull a zip tie out of my back pocket and whip it around his wrists, pushing up his gaudy purple sleeves to gain access.

Quickly, I secure him and then let him go. He slides to the floor, leaving a track of white greasepaint and red lipstick streaking down the wall. Just inside the apartment's entry, I hear whimpering and I steel myself against what I might see. There's no blood, but Natalie is curled into a ball. Her knees are tucked against her body and her hands are clenched to her head.

"Shit," I mutter softly. Kneeling down, I pat her slowly, feeling for any broken bones. She shudders under my touch. Her skin is clammy from shock. Concerned she doesn't want to be touched but not wanting to leave her on the floor in the entryway, I opt for the lesser of two evils and pick her up. She feels slight, not substantial enough to fight this by herself. I hold her tightly against me, trying to send her whatever strength she can draw from me. I carry her into the one room new to me—her bedroom.

I'm nearly struck blind by the assault of pinkness. Thank Christ the walls at least are white. There are the hot pink chairs with no arms that flank a window with pale pink floor-to-ceiling curtains drawn shut. They manage to block out all of the afternoon sun. It's dim and cool in here.

I sweep the pink floral comforter back and tuck her under the pile of down and blankets. Despite the warmth, she continues to shake. The good thing is that she's conscious and I don't feel any wounds on her skull. Probably fear shut her down for a moment, but she's awake now, just very afraid.

"Natalie, honey." I kneel down with *shh* noises, but she can't hear me—or doesn't want to. She needs to warm up. I could strip down and climb in bed with her, but I've got the dipshit in the hallway to deal with. Plus, I doubt that a woman who suffers from severe agoraphobia would be okay with waking up to find a stranger in bed with her.

Leaning over, I brush aside the light brown hair and press a soft kiss against her temple. She stills and her hand reaches out to wrap around my wrist. The touch of her palm against my skin sends an electric shock through me, and for about five seconds, my heart beats double-time.

"You came," she whispers, her words a stutter on her shortened breath.

Shit indeed.

"Yeah." I squeeze her hand. "I got you."

She snuffles and tucks her head under the covers, as if for refuge. With another squeeze to reassure her I'm still here, I look around for her phone. I wish I had someone to come and sit with her while I go interrogate the piece of trash outside.

"Natalie, sweetheart, I'm going out to talk to the clown. You stay here."

There's a slight movement under the covers, which I take to be agreement. I bend down and press another kiss to the crown of her head, the only part of her that is still visible. Then I draw the comforter up and over so that she's completely engulfed. If that's what makes her feel better, then so be it.

Out on the counter, I spot her phone. In the Favorites, there are five choices.

Editing goddess

Dr T

Big daddy

Papa

Mom

I make an educated guess that Oliver is big daddy. I tap the contact and the phone rings. Oliver picks it up on the second ring. "Natalie?" He sounds slightly breathless, as if I've interrupted a sex session or a workout, but I don't really give a shit which one.

"This is Jake Tanner. Someone sent a clown to your cousin's place. She must have opened the door thinking it was me and got this joker instead."

"A clown? Like a real live clown or an asshole from the Internet?"

"He could be both, but yeah, he's got the white face, a stupid wig, and a fake red smile."

He curses. "She's fucking terrified of clowns. I'll be down in a second. Don't move."

Ignoring him, I walk out to the hall and pull out the Beretta I'd tucked into the back of my jeans. With my prosthetic, I grab the back of his purple coat and haul him upright so he can see the barrel of my gun. "Sit up."

"Don't shoot," he cries again and tries to raise his arms. He forgets they are bound behind his back and the motion tips him over. I don't even bother to set him right again. He whimpers as he lands in the puddle of his urine.

The doorway at the end of the hall bangs open. Oliver obviously took the stairs. He's on us before I can begin questioning.

"Who's this piece of shit?" He nudges the clown with his sneakered toe. He's clad in workout shorts and a side-vented T-shirt. I mentally cross off sex session.

"Don't know. I was bringing Natalie dinner and heard her scream. Ran down here and found this piece of shit standing outside her door."

"Why does it smell like piss?" One nostril curls in disgust.

I point to the wet stain on the clown's pants.

"Fuck. That's foul." Oliver takes a big step back. For a football player, he seems remarkably fastidious. Maybe I've spent too much time in the trenches. A little urine is nothing when you're on a mission.

I tuck the gun into my harness. I'm not going to need it for the incontinent clown.

"You always wear that?" He gestures at my holster.

"Always." Turning to the clown, I give him a little tap on the face to get his attention. "Why don't you start talking?"

"I'm just doing my job," he whimpers. "I was told to deliver a message. That's all. The chick took five days to answer the door and when she saw me, she freaked out. *She's* fucked up, man!"

Oliver sucks in a breath at the insult toward Natalie and I move between them. I don't need Oliver hitting the clown before he babbles out his answers. The elevator dings and a small man with a shiny suit and even shinier black hair steps out. He moves purposefully toward us and stops behind Oliver. Oliver looks over his shoulder and gives a tiny head nod of recognition. I peg him as an accountant or financial advisor. Maybe agent.

Interrogating people in front of an audience isn't my preferred method of operation, but I want to eke out what I can here and now. I don't want to have to chase him down, plus later he'd have an opportunity to change his story. I want it fresh.

"What's the message?"

The span between me shoving my gun in his face and him catching his breath has given him a false sense of security. He lashes out. "What's your badge number? I'm reporting you for police brutality!"

"I'm not the police, dumb shit. Now tell me what the message is."

"I think you should leave, Oliver," the small man suggests quietly and tugs on Oliver's T-shirt.

The clown's eyes shift away from me as if noticing all over for the first time we aren't alone. "Wait, holy shit. Are you Oliver Graham? Jesus fucking Christ. My brother is going to shit his pants when he hears this." His eyes dart to the open foyer door and then back again, narrowing in an opportunistic gleam. "Aren't you dating Fannie Carter? Is this your side piece? I can be quiet, you know. You got any signed jerseys?"

My gut tightens at the reference to Natalie belonging to another man. A reaction that I try to ignore. Meanwhile, Oliver sizes up the clown, probably debating how to respond. Given that Natalie and Oliver's connection has been secret for years, he's going to deflect, and for some reason I just don't want to hear it. I think it would hurt Natalie, and the last thing I want is for her to be caused any more pain.

It's damn irrational, I know, so I push that aside with all the other little things that I don't want to examine at this point.

"Listen up. Who's your employer?"

"I'm an indie." He lifts his chin proudly.

"How do you take jobs?"

"People fill out a form online and pay via PayPal."

"Great. Pull it up."

"Pull what up?"

"Your PayPal account."

He shakes his head. "I'm not pulling up my PayPal account for you!"

I move before he has time to react. I reach inside his coat pocket, pull out his phone, and then spin him around so his cheek is kissing the wall again.

"You can't do that. It's an invasion of my privacy. Oliver, are you watching this?"

Oliver backs away. "I don't know who you are or what you're doing. I heard someone scream and came down to help."

"I'll testify to that." The suited man raises his hand. "I'm his agent and we do not know anyone here."

"Wait," the clown calls out to Oliver's retreating back. "What about the signed jersey?"

He barely notices that I've pressed the phone against his finger to bypass the screen lock. I pull up the mail app and find the PayPal receipt. I pull out my phone and take a picture. I scroll through his contacts, swiftly snapping his favorites and his last ten emails. I look as his photo roll. Big mistake. He's got a bunch of porn saved. I cut the zip ties and jerk him to me.

"Don't come back here," I warn and then give him a hard push down the hall. He steps in his urine, slips, and falls. From the elevator bank, I can see Oliver smirking at the insta-karma. I enter Natalie's apartment and close the door firmly.

The phone rings before I can get two steps inside the apartment.

"Call Terrance," Oliver barks as greeting.

"That her therapist?"

Oliver grunts. "Yeah. They have a love/hate relationship, but he's the professional. She'll need to be medicated."

I don't know Natalie as well as I'd like, but I'm not calling some guy she loathes. "Let's have her sleep it off. When she wakes up, she'll remember what happened and it won't be an issue. We don't need to make it an issue," I clarify.

"Did I miss your PhD certificate in your office? Call fucking Terrance."

I decide to hang up on Oliver.

Natalie has her issues. She's scared of new people. She's scared of going outside. Guys with extreme PTSD lock themselves up because they're worried that they'll fall apart in public. She's scared of being scared. I get it. I've had my own mild case of it and so I don't stay, knowing when she wakes up, she needs things to be comfortable and familiar. I'm neither of those things . . . yet.

If anyone is calling her therapist, it won't be me.

I invade her office and grab a piece of paper out of the printer.

"You still owe me dinner. Call me."

CHAPTER ELEVEN

JAKE

"Are you going out?" Sabrina asks. "Because you're kind of in a shitty mood for going out."

I haven't heard from Natalie, which is why I'm in this shitty mood, but I try to summon a smile for my sister. She's back to talking to me . . . barely.

When she follows me into my bedroom, I put her to good use. "Yes. I'm meeting Ian and Victoria at Club 69. Pick out something suitably clubbish."

I wait for her to beg to come with me. Club 69 is one of Kaga's newest ventures. It seems like he is opening a new club every other month.

She avoids the subject and instead points to my closet. "What look are you going for? Trendy? Urban? Bridge and Tunnel?"

"What's Bridge and Tunnel?" I ask, rubbing my chin. I've got quite the scruff going, but I'm too lazy to shave. In a couple more weeks, I'll be headed into full hipster beard mode. I told Natalie that I preferred to shave and now I wonder what she likes. Clean shaven? A little scruff? A full beard?

Her skin felt petal-soft as I carried her into her bedroom. I tried not to stare at her legs or how the big shirt she wore clung to the curves of her ample chest and hugged her waist. Perving on a woman who had passed out from fear is probably one of the lower points in my life.

"Bridge and Tunnel is in from New Jersey to pick up chicks who don't know better. Axe body spray or Drakkar, open collar, lots of chest hair showing." Her head is stuck inside my closet, making the words sound like they are coming down some tunnel—although maybe not all the way from Jersey.

"I'll pass on that. Isn't there anything that looks like 'I'm here because my friends think I'm a stick-in-the-mud'?"

"Only everything in your wardrobe." She makes a face as she holds up a pair of camo pants from my army days. "Seriously, why do you still have these?"

"They're clean. Sturdy."

"Ugh." She throws them back into the closet. Sabrina doesn't like to remember the time I was in the army. Says it gives her nightmares. She pulls out a black suit and a plain gray shirt. "These things. No tie. Do you want to change your hand?"

I look down at the metal-and-plastic prosthetic on the left side, and flex. The design isn't much to look at, but it is more functional than the other ones I have, like the more realistic flesh-looking one. That one is really nothing more than a mannequin piece. I choose function over form any day. "What? You don't think the Terminator look is in? When your robot overlords are arrive, you're going to be glad your brother is half man, half metal."

She makes a face. "I just don't want a bunch of stupid bitches at the club to say stupid shit to you."

"Not everyone is like the old lady at Barneys."

Sabrina is still hurting from the incident a month ago when we went shopping and an old socialite at Barneys nearly fainted when I reached down to tie my shoelace. My metal prosthetic, which looks more like a silver/black titanium glove, brushed the back of her tiny dog. She thought I was going to crush it. Most people ignore my hand or stare covertly, but she was elderly and had no problem shrieking and then apologizing all over, exclaiming how pitiful it was that a man like me had to have a prosthetic.

The pity gets to me more than the fear, but I don't know if Sabrina understood that. I step into the bathroom to begin the semi-elaborate task of changing clothes. I usually keep my day-to-day limb in my boot. It's easier to dress in the morning. My routine consists of pulling on my gel liner followed by the suction suspension sleeve. After that I stick my prosthetic in the bottom of whatever pants I'm wearing, pull the pants over my good leg, and then drop trou until my artificial limb is attached. That process takes less than a minute.

Getting undressed and into another set of clothes is a different story. I have to remove the prosthetic because the pants are a bitch to get over the artificial foot, and then while I have that off, I might as well change the liner and sleeve so I can last a few more hours without significant pain, which is why if I go out, I prefer to wear jeans. But Club 69 is not a place for jeans, and Ian and Kaga are good enough friends for me to make the extra effort.

"You never said why you broke it off with Deena?" she asks, rummaging in my sock drawer as I exit the bathroom having changed pants, reattached my limb, and shrugged on the button-down shirt.

"Why is it me doing the breaking? Maybe it was Deena who had a change of heart."

Sabrina turns toward me with a give-me-a-break look on her face. "Has anyone broken up with you?"

"Sure."

"Who? Name one girl."

"Anna Madden." I sit on the edge of the bed and motion for her to throw me the socks.

"Who's she?" A belt lands beside me and I dodge a pair of black leather shoes, which land neatly, sole-down on the bedspread. I pull on the socks, one over my right foot and the other over my prosthetic foot. I don't need a sock on my fake foot, of course, but it looks better.

"Nice throw. Anna Madden was my soulmate. She crushed me when she told me she wanted to see other people," I say cheerfully.

Sabrina's eyes narrow.

"Was this in like sixth grade or something?"

"Second. She was the cutest thing in elementary school. She wore pigtails and her brown hair curled around her face when she sweated. I liked to chase her around the playground until the hair started forming little ringlets."

"That's weird. And perverse. What's Anna doing today?"

I shrug and stand. Sabrina comes over and buttons my shirt. Small buttons are a struggle for me. I swallow my resentment at needing help to dress. Reaching for the belt, I loop it through the pants. She makes a motion to ask if I need help with my buckle. I shake my head. The buckle I can do with my right hand. There's never a moment that goes by that I'm not grateful I lost my left instead of my dominant right. "Hopefully breaking more hearts. Then I'm not the only sap she rejected."

"The fact that no woman has broken up with you since second grade pretty much proves my point."

I'm not sure where Sabrina is going with this, so I tell her what I told Deena. "We wanted different things in our lives at that point."

She'd understood. She was—is—ambitious and wants to make a name for herself. While I want Tanner Securities to be successful, I didn't need it to be big. I didn't need to own half of Manhattan to feel good about myself. Deena wondered why I wasn't expanding, hiring new people. Why I kept turning away business. She blamed it on my trust fund.

I'm not sure how she knew about that, because I'm pretty tight-lipped about my money, about everything in fact. That was another thing she didn't like. In retrospect, the only thing Deena and I had going for us was our compatibility in bed. She liked to be fucked hard and often and I was happy to oblige.

After a while, though, having only sex in common became boring.

"Mom wants you to get married."

Sabrina follows me out of the bedroom and down the two flights of stairs to the main level.

"She wants a lot of things, but she's been a mother for over thirty-five years. She knows life is full of disappointment."

"Maybe if you had a girlfriend, you wouldn't worry about my love life so much."

And there it is. Sabrina has decided to switch tactics from yelling at me to trying to divert attention away from her feelings toward Kaga. It's working, although she doesn't know it. My mind has been preoccupied with Natalie since I left her.

I glance at my watch. I could sneak down into my office to check my messages. I have yet to hear from her. Was she mad that I was in her bedroom? Would she have wanted me to stay? *Call me* wasn't an invitation. It was a command. Maybe she didn't understand that. I hadn't abandoned her, but I didn't want to freak her out more by staying.

If I'd stayed, I would have wanted to climb into the bed with her, that pink-and-white monstrosity of a thing. She had more pillows than the bedding department at Macy's. Hell, it could have been the bedding department at Macy's.

I'd left with an uncomfortable ache in my pants and another pang slightly higher and to the left. The feeling hadn't gone away either. I'd had to take myself in hand in the shower both last night and this morning; something I hadn't done for a long time, because I either had someone else around to take care of that or I went without.

But last night when I got home, I couldn't stop thinking about Natalie. She felt right in my arms. She fit—in a way that Deena and all my past women had never done. I wouldn't have gotten any sleep that night if I hadn't taken care of my hard-on, so in the shower I'd fantasized about pulling down the sheets, licking my way from her calves to her core.

By the time I had my tongue deep into her pussy, I was coming. After a quick cold-water rubdown, I'd been able to fall asleep, only to wake up with her on my mind. So I took the same course of action again. I was left just as hungry and nearly as hard as when I'd started.

She has until tomorrow to call me back before I take matters into my own hands.

"What are your plans?" I ask Sabrina.

"Going to a bar with some friends."

"Have fun tonight, squirt." I lean down to give her a quick kiss on her forehead. "Be safe. Call me if you need a ride."

"Tell Kaga I said hi," she says softly into my shirt.

I stiffen at her words, but wanting to avoid another fight, I give her a half smile. "Will do."

◆ ◆ ◆

Priya, Kaga's drop-dead gorgeous assistant, meets me at the side door. "You're late," she says in greeting. Priya lives and dies by her schedule, and his. I've suspected more than once that she suffers from at least a mild case of OCD. I once accidentally moved the stapler on her desk and she about melted down until it was repositioned.

But her attention to detail was why she was the perfect match for Kaga, a guy who ran two empires—one in the US and one in Japan. I often wondered if they had a thing. Priya is almost too beautiful not to make at least one play for, but I never got anything but a boss/secretary vibe. Probably Kaga would say that it was dishonorable to take advantage of an employee.

"Only by fifteen minutes. That's early by New York standards."

Priya frowns, but says nothing. She silently leads me up the stairs to the owner's suite. In every bar Kaga owns, he has a private suite that overlooks most of the club. It's equipped with televisions if you are bored with the floor show, a private bar, catered food, and several flat, soft surfaces for when you want to take your dancing from vertical to horizontal. I've done my own share of fucking in his private suites. There is just something about clubs that makes women want to take their clothes off. The one-way privacy mirror feeds their exhibitionist fantasies without exposing them in any way.

I wonder what fantasies Natalie has.

"You look fierce. Kaga's not even here," Ian says as Priya opens the door. "Japan. A family issue," he adds before I can ask where and why.

Kaga's comment about cleaning house followed by his quick departure gives me pause. I'm glad when a knock at the door interrupts us. A dark-eyed beauty walks in with a sultry smile and a tray holding two glasses of amber liquid. God love Priya's efficiency.

She bends near Ian first, her body brushing his. He draws back and makes a show of reaching for the glass with his left hand so that the platinum of his wedding band flashes in the light. She's smart enough to recognize the rebuff and turns her attention to me.

My left hand is noticeable too, but in a different way. Either Priya gave her a heads-up or she's got good self-control, because she doesn't react at all. She treats me with the same seductive attention. A cynical part of me knows that of course she's going to treat me the same. A guy with a prosthetic—who is a personal guest of Kaga—likely has a big enough bank account to make up for all kinds of deficits, including the lack of a limb. Or two.

"Anything else I can provide?"

Ian raises his eyebrows to indicate that the invitation and response are mine alone. Another time, maybe I would've taken her up on it. Ian would have excused himself and this young lady would discover that the rest of my body still worked just fine.

Instead, I shake my head. "We're good."

Her regret seems genuine as she nods and leaves.

"Not feeling it tonight?" Ian asks. "Too easy?"

He likes the chase—a waitress offering herself along with Kaga's aged whiskey wouldn't have enticed him before his marriage. I don't mind easy offerings. "Not interested."

"Why not? She was gorgeous. All legs and boobs."

"There are dolls for you if all you are interested in are legs and boobs."

He nods and without another question turns back to the large windows overlooking the show.

In the cages and on the stages at Club 69, couples simulate sex acts—there's something for everyone. Gays, lesbians, heteros. In the center a rotating stage rises and lowers on a hydraulic lift—something that gave Kaga a dozen headaches pre-opening.

From this room, we can see the various acts and the clubgoers writhing on the dance floor. Ordinarily one of the acts would've stirred me, but tonight all I can think of is Natalie.

"How can you even see her down there?" I ask, referring to Ian's wife and my employee, Victoria. Ian calls her Tiny, which I freely admit I don't get. She's average sized.

"I just know. I could pick her out from a thousand look-alikes. She's on the dance floor, northeast corner."

I squint and make out a pretty light brown head next to a curly-topped head and one security guard, standing as a buffer between the crowd and the two girls.

"That doesn't look like one of mine," I comment, pointing to the guard.

"Kaga's security," Ian admits. "Steve wouldn't come. He's too busy chasing that waitress."

"Still? I don't know what to be more impressed by. His persistence or her ongoing refusal." It seemed like months since we'd discovered that Cecilia Howe, a wealthy socialite, was blackmailing a number of people in order to maintain their silence about her husband's infidelities—among other things. One of Howe's victims was a waitress trying to keep her younger brother from going back to prison.

"His persistence," Ian says. "Because who'd want to wake up to his crabby ass every morning?"

Steve is Ian's bodyguard, driver, and good friend, but surly is his default setting.

"Why are you up here with me? Shouldn't you be down there marking your territory? I think I saw a male hand come within six feet of Victoria."

He scowls at me. "I'm up here learning to be an evolved man, not the Neanderthal she keeps calling me."

"How's that working?" I note his hands are curled around the arms of the leather club chair.

"I'm here, aren't I? Instead of down there, pissing a circle around her," he responds drolly.

I could needle him more by talking about how hot she looks in her sparkly dress, which is so short I swear I can see her underwear, but she works for me and that feels vaguely wrong.

"I'm surprised you even let Victoria out of the house after dark."

"It was either ease up on the chain or face divorce. We compromised with the guard after she was kidnapped off the street." He nods toward the solidly built man keeping the crowd away from the dancing pair.

"Good call."

"Thanks. Tiny doesn't seem to appreciate how much of a sacrifice I made for her."

I can't tell if he's serious or not.

"If we're mentioning surprises," he continues, "I'm surprised there's nothing here that interests you. You weren't interested at the game, and you aren't tonight. I think your reporter girlfriend is down there." He gestures toward the main bar. I don't even bother to look.

"We parted ways a few weeks ago."

"Too clingy?"

"Too nosey."

"She is a journalist."

"So I noticed."

"Tiny's got a friend," Ian starts.

"No." I raise my left hand. "I get that enough from my mother. I don't need it from my friends."

"Okay, but don't say I never warned you. Tiny's worried about your long hours and thinks that her friend Sarah would be perfect for you."

Great. I could see I was going to have to avoid Victoria for the next few weeks.

Our conversation changes to the Mets and Yankees and which team is going to disappoint the city the most this year. I stay for one more drink and then use my aching left leg as an excuse to leave.

But I don't go home. When I get in the car, I head south instead of north, and I find myself in Tribeca, sitting outside a seven-story apartment building watching the third floor for signs of life. I thump myself a few times with my prosthetic because it's heavier than the skin and bones on my right hand, but it doesn't have the right effect. No sense is knocked into me. I'm not suddenly free of my growing Natalie obsession. In fact, I don't leave for a long time, not until after the cop car circles the block a second time.

The lights in Natalie's apartment never turn on—at least not from my vantage point.

Tomorrow.

She has until tomorrow to call me, because I'm not going to sleep well until I know she's all right.

CHAPTER TWELVE

NATALIE

I read the note for the umpteenth time. *Call me.*

Is he even serious? I feel like there's some hidden message in the seven words on the page. Maybe it's an anagram for "You're the craziest loon I've ever met. Stay away."

My mind is sluggish today. Oliver called Dr. Terrance, who ordered me a whole new cocktail of drugs and put off any attempts of mine to go outside for another couple of weeks. After Dr. Terrance chewed me out for opening the door to a stranger, someone he hadn't met and approved of, Oliver showed up with the new prescriptions and wouldn't leave until I'd taken my recommended dosage. Poor Oliver. He tries his best to cope with me, not calling Dr. Terrance until the last minute. Even Oliver grapples with Dr. Terrance's need to vet everyone in my life and every action I take, as evidenced by Oliver hiring Jake without preapproval.

I'm not even sure what my biggest fear is anymore. Is it really breaking down in the middle of the subway or is it never being able to leave my apartment again?

I haven't written in two days, just sat on the couch or laid on the floor near the French doors, looking outside without the lights on. Last night a dark car slid into a parking space and sat there for a long time. I stared at it, wondering who was inside, wishing it was Jake. But eventually it drove away. Probably a tourist—few people in the city own cars.

I probably should have been freaked out by it, but I was mostly sad it left. I'd felt like there was at least one person in the city still awake other than me.

Daphne has sent me a dozen unhappy emails about my lack of progress on the manuscript. I don't need her to remind me of my looming, already-missed-once deadline, but my creativity is stifled when I take the drugs.

I can't write emotion if I don't feel it.

Call me.

The note is the only thing that interests me and really, what do I have to lose by calling him? He's already seen me at my dismal worst. If he acts embarrassed and unhappy, I'll hang up and that will be one more thing I've sacrificed at the altar of my anxiety. It's eaten everything else that is decent and good. Why not Jake?

The phone rings so many times I nearly hang up.

"Tanner here."

The sharp bite of his tone throws me, but I've called and he answered so I might as well plunge ahead.

"Beck here," I mimic.

"Natalie." His voice drops into a low, rumbly tenor. Comforting and sexy. I want to wrap myself up in that voice. "How are you doing?"

"Hungry," I joke. Although it's not entirely a joke. Now that I think about it, I haven't eaten anything in a while. I lower the phone from my ear to check the time. Holy crap. I haven't eaten anything in seven hours. I've just sat on my ass staring at the blank wall across from my sofa. "I'm sorry I missed our dinner date. I could be eating Chinese leftovers right now."

"Maybe I would've taken the rest home with me," he laughingly suggests. "I like leftovers too."

"I don't believe you would have. If you bring it to my house, you have to leave it here."

"Is that a Natalie Beck rule?"

"I think Emily Post says it. If you are visiting, bring lots of food and leave it."

"I'm taking notes."

I love talking to him. Love it so much. I could talk to him forever. I stretch out on the sofa and pull a throw over myself. Snuggling down, I pretend he's in the room and we're having that date—just two normal people hanging out after dinner. Would he allow me to put my feet in his lap? Some guys are adamantly against feet. My last boyfriend, if I could really call him that, had an anti-foot fetish. He didn't even like to see toes and was freaked out whenever I'd run my feet along his calf. Suffice it to say, we never played footsie. Not that *that* was what turned me on, but his aversion to my bare piggies kind of hurt my feelings.

And like I'd turn Jake down if he was anti-foot. I've already concluded that he must have some terrible personality trait that has not yet revealed itself to me. Like maybe he has bad personal hygiene and he smells terrible. Maybe he clips his toenails in bed.

Whatever it is, I am down with it. Because he wanted me to call him even after I freaked out about the clown. And it wasn't just a courtesy gesture, because he could have made an excuse to hang up by now, but instead he's talking to me, joking about our missed date.

He can have bad breath, leave the toilet seat up, and I'll buy lots of paper towels to place under his feet. Hell, I'll give *him* pedicures.

"I was worried when I didn't hear from you," he says softly.

"I'm drugged up," I admit. "Oliver called Dr. Terrance. He was cursing because he told you to do it and you refused."

"He said you had a love/hate relationship with your therapist. I wasn't going to call someone to your place you didn't fully want there."

"What else did you look at while you were here?" I ask. He'd seen it all except for my overly froufrou bedroom. I wait for him to remark about the girliness. It's emasculating, Oliver told me once.

"Your bedroom is very pink," he admits.

"Would that turn you off? Affect your performance negatively?" I tease.

He chuckles, though, apparently not offended or turned off by my question. "My manhood can withstand a little pink. I grunted a lot this morning."

"That's nice to know." My cheeks are pink to match the decor, part in embarrassment over the other night and part delight. I burrow under the covers, where I can pretend that we're talking in person. His next sentence surprises me.

"We need to reschedule our dinner."

It's a joke. It's so clearly a joke so I respond in kind. "Yeah, tomorrow night." I force a light laugh.

"I can do tomorrow."

"It's too bad you can't come. Wait, what?" *Did he just say tomorrow?*

"How about tomorrow night?" he repeats.

"I, uh, I don't know." I can't process his question right now because the thought of opening the door again, not knowing what is on the other side, is terrifying so I avoid it, but I can't have him hang up on me. I change the topic hastily. "What's your office like?"

He accepts my avoidance, just like he accepts every weird thing about me. "It's very boring. White walls, gray carpet. It's on the bottom of my townhouse, the garden level and the main level. I live in the top three with one of my sisters, Sabrina, who will be graduating from Columbia this year."

"What's your other sister's name?" I want to know everything about him.

"Megan. She's thirty-two. My parents had Megan and me a couple years apart. Sabrina was a late-in-life surprise for them. You?"

He's thirty-four or thirty-five then. Nearly a decade older than me.

"Oliver's like a brother to me. My parents died in a twenty-car pileup when I was five. The roads were icy and a truck on the interstate did a three-sixty, took a bunch of cars out, and caused a huge accident. They were coming home from a lecture at the university. My dad's sister took me and raised Oliver and me together. He's only two years older than me."

"So you're twenty-six?"

"You know how old Oliver is?" I guess he's as good at math as I am.

"Since he won the Super Bowl, I think that everyone in the city not only knows how old he is, but how much he weighs, how tall he is, and what he bench-presses."

"Good point. Are you a fan?" Maybe that's it. Maybe he's a huge Oliver Graham fan and he's going to try to get to Oliver through me. He'd be disappointed to know that the most I can offer is a signed jersey, and I tell him so. "I don't get free tickets to the game. Oliver's given up on me attending so he gives them to other people. I could get you a signed jersey, though."

I try hard to keep the disappointment out of my voice.

He's quiet for a heartbeat, maybe two. "This may sound like I'm bragging, but I have a good friend who has a box at Cobras Stadium and I've got a freestanding invitation, and while I'm a fan, I think I'm a little old for a signed jersey. Besides, your cousin offered me one when we first met and I turned it down."

"Oh." There is a subtle rebuke in there, as if I should know better.

"Honey, are you trying to find something wrong with me?"

"No, I'm . . . oh Lord, this sounds pathetic and I know it's going to sound worse when I say the words out loud, but I don't understand why you're even talking to me."

"Tell me what flaws you've given me." His voice warms me like a hot chocolate on a snowy day.

"No." I'm not saying even one of them.

"I'm not going to be offended." He's having trouble hiding the amusement in his voice, I can tell.

"But I'll be embarrassed. Or more embarrassed. If you could see me now, I'm rivaling a tomato in color."

His voice drops at least a pitch. "I'd like to see how red you get. Do you blush all the way to your toes?"

If I wasn't before, I am now. I'm hot, and not from shame, but from his suggestive tone and words.

"I, ah, I'm very red." God, I suck at this phone-flirting thing but he . . . seems pretty adept at it. "Have you done this before? This, um, phone thing? You're better at it than I am."

He chuckles. "You're doing just fine. But, yes, to answer your question, when I was deployed, I used Skype and emails to stay in contact with an old girlfriend."

"How old?" I ask, instantaneously jealous over this nameless, faceless woman.

"In age or time since our separation? We broke up a few years into my deployment. I haven't dated seriously since. How about you?"

"Not since Adam Masterson. He was a senior programmer for Saturnalia. I worked with him every day and after a couple of years, he seemed better than being celibate. We didn't even date. We just kind of . . . fell into bed with each other. Neither of us were heartbroken when it ended."

"My heart wasn't broken either," he says softly, as if to reassure me that he isn't holding out for a rekindling of any lost love.

"Did you like it? The phone stuff? The Skyping?" I truly want to know. Can anyone be fulfilled by this? I suppose they must to some extent, or cam girls and 1-900 numbers wouldn't exist. But with someone like Jake, I'd think he'd have a dozen better offers than sitting at home having a virtual relationship with a shut-in.

"It was better than nothing."

I'm one step up from nothing at least, I reassure myself. Curious, I ask a question that has sat in the back of my mind since the first time we exchanged messages. "Why do you want to know what the girl is wearing?"

"It grounds you. Gives you a visual. Men are very visual."

"But the person on the phone could be lying."

His text message—which I've read repeatedly—comes back to me. *And if you're fully clothed, please feel free to lie and say nothing.*

"Doesn't matter. If you tell me you have your hand down your panties and your shirt pulled up to show off your spectacular breasts, that's what I'm seeing regardless of what you're really doing or wearing."

I lift the blanket and look at my breasts. They've flattened out a bit now that I'm on my back, but my nipples are hard. I wouldn't categorize them as spectacular, but I haven't had complaints. They're just . . . breasts. Maybe if he was holding them they would *feel* spectacular. I tingle at the idea.

"I'm too honest. Like right now I'm wearing jogging pants and an old T-shirt."

"And nothing else?"

"Well, underwear."

"Hmmm." His hum enters my ear from the cell phone and shoots straight between my legs. I squeeze my thighs together once as if to catch his touch and hold it there.

"You?"

"Jeans, T-shirt. Gray socks. Boots."

I want to know more about this phone sex thing, yet what he's wearing doesn't interest me. I guess I want to know what he's *doing* or rather what he would do with me.

"So you just say sexy things to each other and then hang up?"

"I had more involvement than that."

"Like what? You had the phone-sex pillow? I saw that on the Internet once. You programmed it to shake or something when you wanted to alert your long-distance partner to some activity back home. I'm not entirely certain how a vibrating pillow does anything for anyone."

"No." He sounds a bit as if he's strangling on a laugh he doesn't want to release. He clears his throat and answers frankly, "I'd jack off."

"Oh."

The image of him sitting with his legs spread and his big hand around his big dick appears immediately. He'd handle himself with sure strokes and his chest would heave as he took big gulps of air. But his eyes would be pinned to mine as if we were magnetically pulled together.

"You still there, Natalie?"

"Yes." I lick my dry lips. "Just, um, visualizing it. It's been a long time."

His voice gets lower, quieter. "Tell me what you've been missing."

He must read the yearning in my voice, but he doesn't ask if I'm lonely, because he knows I am. So instead he asks what I want.

"Everything. I miss just the cuddling, but I guess a lot of guys aren't into that. Just lying around for hours, wrapped up in each other."

"What else do you want?"

You.

"Touch. The warmth of a palm on my knee." I breathe in, once and then another time, trying to regain some control. I'm breathless and anxious but not panicked. The need for reassurance is strong. I hate that I'm so vulnerable, but I need to accept my weaknesses. That's one thing Dr. Terrance has impressed upon me and truthfully it works. Other, more experienced women might be able to play coy but I can't. Uncertainty generates panic for me, and I'd rather ask a dumb question and be shot down than not know what is going on. Bluntly I ask, "What's happening between us?"

"We're getting to know each other better."

"I wasn't expecting this," I admit. I rub my neck, imagining that it is his palm on my chest and his weight against my body, his flesh pushing into mine.

"True for me as well," he says. "But not all surprises are bad. I'm a big believer in the whole concept of things happening for a reason."

"What about your loss? What was the reason behind that?" I hope it doesn't come across as snotty. I am genuinely curious.

"I saved a friend," he answers immediately. "And just so you don't think I'm bragging, I'll tell you it was pure accident. If he'd have jumped out of the Humvee before me, he'd have been hit, and he didn't have the resources like I did. I'm pretty fortunate that I'm alive. I have a great family and a healthy bank account that allowed me access to things other folks don't have."

I can't respond right away because my throat is thick with emotion. Of course he views himself as blessed by his circumstances, but what he won't ever acknowledge is how he's embraced his losses and healed both in body and spirit. In reality, his good life is due to his hard work at achieving that spiritual equilibrium that has eluded me for so long. But his courage inspires me.

"I'm scared of many things," I whisper into the phone. "But not of you."

"Good. I'll never give you a reason to be afraid of me. I understand where you are coming from, Natalie. If your only contact with me is over the phone for a while, we'll get creative." His throaty words thrill me. "I suspect writers are really good at being inventive."

It seems impossible, but this man appears to be telling me that he's willing to *date* me over the phone for as long as it takes for me to open the door. With someone who fainted at the sight of a clown. How is this even possible?

"So tomorrow night? I'll bring the Chinese food with me and leave you the extra food. How do things get delivered?"

Trying to stop myself from smiling, trying to stop my heart from fluttering, I answer as evenly as possible. "The doorman calls me, tells me he's going to bring them up. He sets it by my door. He rings my bell and I wait to hear the elevator ding as he leaves, and then I open it. A lot of stuff Oliver brings up."

"Okay, then, tomorrow that's what we'll do."

"What if I can't open the door?"

"Then you don't open it." His response is matter-of-fact, as if he doesn't care that our date might be aborted because I can't even twist a doorknob.

"How can that be okay for you?"

"Why don't you let me worry about what's okay for me, and you worry about you?"

"Okay," I say, and the last syllable is swallowed by a hiccup. Tears are forming. They aren't unhappy tears, but tears at this man's amazing generosity. "Excuse me. There're onions everywhere in my apartment."

"Take your time."

"I'm really having a hard time keeping it together. Because of, you know, the onions."

His reply is full of understanding. "I'll call you tomorrow, sweet-heart. Have sweet dreams."

"Thanks." I manage to hold it together until he hangs up, and then I roll over and cry the happiest tears I've felt in a long time.

CHAPTER THIRTEEN

JAKE

"What kind of progress are we making on the note and the clown messenger?" I ask my tech guy, Devon Zachs.

Zachs's inky black hair is stuck up in fifty different directions, and from the number of crumpled potato chip bags littering his desk, I'm wondering when he last left the cellar office.

He claimed this space when I first opened, jokingly saying he planned to drink all the wine from my nonexistent collection. The space was originally designed to house hundreds of bottles of wine and liquor. We tore down the shelves and put in storage units and a bunker that held all our electronic equipment as well as a storage locker full of enough ammunition to arm a small militia. Too many years in the army.

He taps his pen against the far left monitor in his bank of five large screens. "The note is a nonstarter. It's plain white paper used in millions of offices around the world. It's printed with an inkjet printer, which probably points to home use. I don't know what type of ink. We can get that analyzed, but it's probably just standard ink.

"The clown messenger information is more interesting. The email address that was used to pay him comes from an unverified PayPal account. We can try to hack into it, but hacking individual accounts is a lot harder than a system-wide hack, if you can believe that. We'd need to use a bit of social engineering, and we don't have enough on the account other than the username dd1995dd. 1995 is an interesting choice, because it's kind of a bland year. Could be his birthday. I tried a few passwords based on a 1995 date of birth, but came up empty. We don't really have the computer processing power for hacking, though it's not like we couldn't get it. We've just never done it in the past. But as we both know, that would be illegal. And given that it's a financial institution, the penalties could be quite heavy."

Zachs looks unperturbed and almost a little excited about the idea of hacking into a bank. "What are our other options?" I ask.

"I set a tracer on the email. Maybe he's left a review about bad service in the city or something. We'll see. People leave unintentional tracks all over the place."

"You think it's a he?"

He furrows his brow. "I guess so. What's he get out of it anyway?"

I tend to agree with him. "He likes the power, the feeling that he can make her afraid at any time, which is why I want you to look into Joshua James Terrance. He's a psychiatrist. His offices are on Madison and East 59th Street."

"So you think he's the asshole?"

"I don't know. But it's someone who knows her very well, and currently her circle of people is small."

"What about the ex-boyfriend?"

"Our tail on him doesn't think he's the guy. We can't find any connection between him and the clown."

"If it's the doc, man, that's so wrong. You make her sick so you can keep treating her? That's fucked up."

"I'll have the boyfriend tail take a look at his other patients. See if we can't identify them and then see if they've made any harassment reports. Maybe we can nail him on pattern and practice."

"On it, boss."

I leave Zachs to his work, silently berating myself for not asking more questions instead of flirting with her. This is why you don't get involved with clients. But backing away now isn't going to happen. I spent the night hard thinking of her in the ratty clothes she described with all that smooth golden skin underneath. I can tell she wasn't ready, not ready to open the door and not ready to have dirty sex with me over the phone. But I am. Fuck, I am.

I can't stop thinking about her. I've never talked to anyone on the phone so long. Not my mother, not my sisters, not Laura Severson, the girl I dated for four years before I signed up to join the army. We'd made it two years into my deployment before I broke it off. The man she thought she'd fallen in love with didn't exist anymore. I'd changed from a snot-nosed kid with an Ivy League degree to someone who felt more comfortable sleeping in a ditch than at home in his parents' multimillion-dollar townhouse.

We'd done those things I'd told Natalie about—the Skype sex, the phone sex. It'd been good. Shit, after days and nights of seeing nothing but the grimy faces of my fellow soldiers and acres of dust, any slight reveal of a boob or ass would've gotten me hard back then. She only had to smile or toss her $600 salon-colored, wheat-blonde hair over her shoulder to get me ready. Until it didn't work anymore. Until I began to dread those phone calls, those Skype sessions, the visits with her back home.

She'd wonder aloud when I was getting out, suggesting various investment firms that would love to have me.

We'd have sex on those visits and I'd wonder how soon I could leave. And the answer was *not soon enough*. She felt like she couldn't break up with a patriot, so I did it for her. I was the asshole who left her and she could move on without guilt. I was glad to hear she had gotten married.

At the bottom of the stairs, Victoria greets me. "Jake, do you have a minute?"

I open my mouth to say yes, and then I recall Ian's warning from last night. The tentative smile on her face signals that business is probably not what she intends to talk to me about. Suddenly I remember I have an appointment.

"Not right now. Just leave me a message." Victoria has dyslexia and her hastily scribbled notes are a conglomeration of letters and little pictures that only Ian understands. Her partner writes the reports and Victoria leaves me voice messages. In my office, I grab my jacket, phone, and keys.

"It will only take a minute," she says.

A highly uncomfortable minute, I think.

"Sorry, leave a message." I brush by her, but she's dogged and follows me out to the car.

"You can't escape me this easily. I work with you. I know where you live." She points upstairs.

"But I have a car so I can escape."

"You're going to have a bitch of a time parking."

"Maybe so." I move her to the side and unlock the black four-door Audi A8 that she eyes with undisguised interest. Ian had been teaching her how to drive and she's developed a new interest in cars—a good replacement after she'd traded her cycling shoes in for a private investigator's license.

I didn't lie to Victoria, though, because I did have an appointment to see Dr. Crist. It occurred to me after the game that he might have some insight on Natalie. I worry that her doctor is doing her more harm than good. There are good therapists and then there are assholes. I served with assholes and I served with good people. No organization or group of people is devoid of the dreck of humanity, the ones who like to kill for shits and giggles or the ones who are so irresponsible, they'll shoot themselves in the face by accident. Problem is that sometimes you have difficulty discerning who's the good guy and who's the fuckstick.

The tree-lined street where Isaiah's office is located is already full of cars. Victoria was right. I probably should've taken a cab or a car service, but I prefer to drive. I don't like to be dependent on anyone for anything, including my own transportation. I maneuver the car into a parking spot two blocks away, but halfway to Isaiah's office, my leg begins to ache—part of the drawback of getting up early and staying out late with a prosthesis.

I climb the steps of the brownstone and press the buzzer, announcing myself.

His secretary releases the lock. Sylvia has been with Isaiah for as long as I've known him, and she never looks like she's aged a day.

"Dr. Crist is running late. May I get you something to drink?"

"No, thank you, ma'am," I answer. I take a seat to stretch out my leg and give my thigh and knee a quick rubdown. I'm still squeezing it when Dr. Crist comes out.

"Looks like you're not taking care of yourself," he says in his deep baritone. Crist is slightly under six feet, but his wide shoulders create an imposing presence.

I rise and give my leg a little shake. "Just spending a little too much time on my leg. Thanks for throwing me under the bus the other night."

He grins. "I thought you'd enjoy that. Come on in. How's business?"

"Good. I've got more clients than I have employees." I decide against sitting. Sometimes the burning or ache goes away if I walk it off, other times I just have to live with it. It's the price an amputee pays for being mobile. I don't know of one person who is pain-free with their prosthetic. At some point during the day, it starts to ache, but if you embrace the pain, it can be a sweet reminder of what you survived. "I'm guessing it's the same for you. Sylvia sighed a lot before she told me I could see you at ten."

"Unfortunately," he admits, "there is no end of customers. The demand for your type of services may always be high."

Isaiah's office takes up almost half of the floor, and one side is lined with books. There are fiction, nonfiction, academic texts, and popular self-help books that rest side by side on the shelves. Toward the end, by the French doors leading to a garden terrace where Isaiah sometimes holds his sessions, I even find a set of Natalie's books. I pull the first one out. *Don't Sleep* by M. Kannan.

I'd have to ask her some time how she came up with her pseudonym. I hold out the book. "You plan to see the movie?"

Isaiah settles behind his desk and puts his feet up as I wander. "Opening night with my wife, I hope. You?"

"Yeah. Opening night," I echo.

I wonder if Natalie would go or if that was one more thing that she would miss due to her illness. On the other side of the room are pictures. Some are of Isaiah when he was in the army, some when he was in college, but many are pictures of his family—old, deceased, and new. Isaiah lives the life dreamed by every soldier. His wife is literally a supermodel. She doesn't model anymore but hosts her own reality-TV show. They have three beautiful children. In their wedding picture, the one that he has chosen to showcase in the middle of the wall, his tux pants are rolled up and you can see the titanium leg and blade that served as his foot that day. His wife is holding his hand tightly, her dress pulled up to reveal her perfect ankles and toned calves.

Isaiah is the perfect doctor to talk to if you're a soldier who thinks his life is over. He will tell you it has just begun.

"I have a friend." I put the book back in its place and turn around to lean against the shelves. "She suffers from severe anxiety. To the extent that she is housebound. She has difficulty even opening her door at times for fear of what unknown may be on the other side."

"Anxiety disorders can be seriously debilitating, as you already know."

I nod slowly, trying to explain the situation as best I can without breaking a confidence. "It's been going on for at least three years. Recently she had gotten the courage to leave her apartment and go to places close by. A couple weeks ago she was able to make it to the subway entrance but not down in the tunnel. A subway attack was the trigger to her current situation."

"Then something happened to impair that?"

"She received a threatening note. It disturbed her to the extent that a lot of the advancements that she had made were eradicated."

He rocks in his big leather chair, the ancient brass ball bearings squeaking with each rotation. "And you want to know what? How to help her? I'll certainly see her, if that's what you're asking. Although my schedule is full, I would make the exception for you."

"She already sees someone her family trusts, but I don't have a good vibe about him."

Isaiah sighs and sits up. He folds his hands on his desk and peers at me over his glasses. "A patient's relationship with their doctor is a unique one. Particularly when you're talking about psychotherapy. Many people believe the type of therapy I do for soldiers is inappropriate and that in the long term, even if I solve some of their problems, they will suffer. And I'm sure that some of them would rather go back to the front line than enter my office."

"She wants to get better and he's holding her back," I state plainly.

"How so?"

"Yesterday she told me she wanted to try some of her aversion therapy again and slowly start the process of going outside, but her doctor refuses and has told her to take a bunch of drugs that numb her out. His advice to her is to avoid new people and stay inside."

"New people like yourself?"

I make an impatient noise and push away from the bookcase to stand near Isaiah's desk. "He doesn't know I exist. But her circle of acquaintances and friends is otherwise quite small. It's two people—one she works for and one who is a family member. He's tightening the bonds around her, corralling her into a spot where she only has a few contacts vetted by him. I don't like that."

The good doctor replies with an evenhanded tone, "Being patient has always been difficult for you. You wanted to be walking before you had the prosthetic on."

"I *did* walk before I had the prosthetic."

He laughs. "I remember you hobbling around the halls with your one crutch, nearly taking out nurses and aides with your recklessness."

I felt my cheeks heat slightly. "It was one time. I almost ran into a nurse once."

"Sit down, Jake. You're looming." He gestures toward one of the big leather chairs and I drop into it. "You care for this woman, which is wonderful, but I cannot tell you whether this other therapist is doing right or wrong without knowing more about your friend, without talking to her. It may be that she won't respond well to aversion therapy at this point. My best advice to you is to listen to her. Be encouraging. Don't force the issue. Everyone has their own timetable for healing."

"That's it?"

He stares at me and I stare back. I'm far better at this than Crist. He's been out of the army too long. "Distractions are good. She can't focus on two things at one time. If you distract her, completely, then she won't be able to focus on her anxieties."

I can do distractions.

"Thanks, Isaiah." I stand and hold out my hand.

He rises, takes my hand but delivers a slow, disbelieving laugh. "I don't think you heard anything I said but the last part."

"You'd be wrong," I reply cheerfully. "I heard it all."

I just planned only to follow the last part. Once back in the car and armed with new information, I shoot off a message to Natalie.

Me: What would you like for dinner tonight? Rice or noodles?
Her: Noodles.

She answered immediately. I let out a long breath that I didn't even realize I was holding.

CHAPTER FOURTEEN

NATALIE

Good, I'll be there with the food at six.

I'm having a date? Oh crap, I'm having a date. The first one in years. Although to say that Adam, the gaming software developer I'd slept with before my subway attack, and I had dated was a stretch. We were two individuals who spent a lot of time with one another who ended up in bed and decided it felt about as good as pizza and a beer after a long day at work.

But my stomach never filled with butterflies at the thought of eating with Adam. I never thought about Adam when I wasn't with him. I never fantasized what it would feel like to run my hands over his chest or tangle my fingers in his hair.

I didn't touch myself at night wishing it were him. I spent last night with my old vibrator, which had run out of batteries. I was too embarrassed to ask the doorman to run and get me new ones because it felt tantamount to asking him for tampons. I couldn't ask Oliver because he would wonder what I needed the batteries for. I ordered a bunch off the Internet, so last night I had a dead vibrator but an active imagination.

And imaginary Jake did things to me that I'm sure are illegal in several states, and if they aren't, they should be. He licked me and sucked me and spent hours running his hand all over my body. He took me hard and then gentle and then hard again.

I went to sleep excited and woke up hungry for him.

I still wasn't convinced when I got up that yesterday wasn't a mirage, that I hadn't dreamed up the whole conversation, the flirting, the mere existence of Jake. But then he texted me and I couldn't type my reply fast enough.

The only problem remains whether I can open the door. As I stand here looking at it, I think I can. I've spent hours looking at it and psyching myself up to open it. As I walk toward the white metal rectangle, I remind myself that the hallway is empty. I haven't heard an elevator ding since this morning when everyone on my floor left for work. There's no one out there. Not a clown. Not a faceless tormenter. Not even Jake.

You can do it. I tell myself. *Just a step. Just one. Take just one!*

But I'm frozen, three feet from the door as if there's an invisible shield.

I steel myself to make a mental push, to break through that wall, when my phone dings, alerting me to another message.

I rush to read it, thankful for the reprieve.

Don't open the door, it says. Or the curtains.

Me: Why?

Him: I'm going to install sensors on your balcony and after I'm done, I'm going to sit there and have dinner.

Me: On the balcony?

Him: Affirmative.

Me: Where will I be?

Him: Inside. Eating the food I bought you.

Me: That's—

I don't know what to type after that. Ridiculous? Thoughtful? Outrageous? All of the above?

He texts again before I can reply.

Him: Don't stress over it. See you tonight.

I can't let it go, so I call him.

"Natalie," he answers.

God, I love the way he says my name. It sounds so seductive rolling off his smooth tongue.

"Is it because you think I'm not ready? Because I'm ready," I tell him. "I can open the door or if not the door, at least the curtains."

Thankfully no one is here to call me a liar.

"I know you can and I want you to open the door, sweetheart. I have plenty of ideas about the things that we could do once we are face-to-face. But there is no hurry. So no door. No curtains. No stress tonight."

My entire body tingles at Jake's words. Apparently I'm not the only one who has an active imagination. "You sound like Dr. Terrance," I grumble, but inwardly I'm so relieved.

"As reluctant as I am to push advice on you from someone that you don't like very much, I have to agree. I know you want to get out there and do stuff, but there isn't any hurry. There is no time line by which everyone should be recovered from a trauma they've experienced."

"You don't think three years is too long a time?" I say in a small voice. Dr. Terrance has said the same to me for years, but I never believed him, not really. Hearing Jake say that is balm on a wound in my soul, one that I didn't even realize was so painful and exposed until now.

"No, I don't. I think the more that you press yourself, the harder it is to push past it because then your anxiety builds on your anxiety. That's like a girl who can't come. Every guy that she's with becomes a new test for her, but because she puts so much pressure on herself, she can't relax and enjoy the moment."

His reference to other women and orgasms makes me scowl. "You sound like you have a lot of experience with women who've never had orgasms."

"I was talking about hypothetical women. As far as you know, I'm a virgin."

I nearly swallow my tongue in shock. "Wait, are you a virgin?"

He bursts out laughing. "No. I'm not. I'm sorry if I've disappointed you."

"Well, I'm not either. Is that a disappointment?"

"No. Pushing past that particular barrier has never been a fetish of mine."

"So you have fetishes?" I can't help myself.

He chokes. "Hold on a minute." I hear a rustle and then a door closing. "I'm in my office and I don't know if I should be talking to you with the door open. Someone might come in at the wrong moment. I don't know if I have fetishes. I'm pretty sex agnostic, if there is such a thing. Do you have fetishes?

"I don't know. While I'm not a virgin, I don't have a lot of experience." I shrug, but since he can't see it, I tell him, "Adam, my ex, wasn't anything to write home about."

He makes a *tsk* sound. "I don't know whether to be glad that Adam was so inept in bed or whether I should find him and punish him for being such a poor representative of the male gender. Your sex life should be fucking spectacular, sweetheart."

It occurs to me that I've never asked him about a wife or girlfriend or anything. I've just assumed he is single, but now that seems spectacularly dumb. "When's the last time you were horizontal with someone, and was it spectacular?"

"I broke it off when it stopped being spectacular."

I don't like the kind of sex talk where he admits to having great sex with some other woman.

"Is this your hypothetical woman or some piece you're currently banging?" I ask, and I can't keep the snideness out.

"And I don't love hearing about your past sex life either," he growls back immediately.

A silence so long that two moon cycles could have taken place passed before either of us says another word.

"I'm afraid," I finally admit.

"Of what, sweetheart?" He's no longer growly. Instead he sounds relieved.

"Of everything. You know that. I'm afraid to open the door. I'm afraid of being outside. I'm afraid of talking about your past sex life because I don't think I could please a man like you."

He snorts. "What kind of man do you think I am?"

"A really wonderful one," I say, getting tearful again.

This time the quiet that settles makes me feel prickly and hot.

"I want you," he says with calmness. "Think about that and forget the rest. I'll call you when I get to your place tonight."

I want you.

Those three words ping-pong around my head all afternoon. I manage to pound out a few words on a page, but they look like gibberish and I end up deleting everything.

I ignore the inbox that contains three emails from Daphne, each of them wondering where my next chapter is. I wish I knew. The medications that Dr. Terrance has prescribed sit in a precise row on the edge of my desk. I'm tempted to push them over, right into the wastebasket.

I hate not feeling. It's almost worse than being anxious. Daphne says my writing is completely toneless when I'm on the drugs, and I end up having to do major revisions on those pages that I do write.

From the middle drawer, I dig out my journal. Even though I didn't agree with Dr. Terrance's therapy direction, the small, red, leather-bound notebook has been more helpful than all of the prescriptions and breathing techniques.

It holds the history of the times I've left the apartment and how far I got. It took me 108 tries during the first year to open the door and then 74 tries to push the elevator button. That process took about a year and a half. After that, each step took fewer tries, with a lot less time in between each step. I remember the days I spent sitting in the lobby like a statue, getting up and looking out the glass doors and then returning to sit on the chairs.

The doorman at the time was Chris Murphy, a young man who was taking night classes at SUNY. He helped support his mother and his teenaged sister. Chris is now the night doorman. He takes classes during the day because of a new building scholarship. He doesn't know that the scholarship was made up by Oliver and me.

I trust Chris, but not the new daytime doorman, who always looks at me like I'm a crazy person and makes the winding gesture next to his head when he thinks I'm not looking.

Those glass doors are like mirrors! How can he miss that? But I guess he's prettier than he is smart.

With the leather journal in hand, I walk back to the door. So it took me 108 tries before. I'm going to beat that this time.

By five o'clock, I'm a sweaty mess, but I feel triumphant. I didn't get the door opened, but I had my hand on the knob, and I'm going to count that as a success. Dr. Terrance says to celebrate every victory, even the small ones.

While I'm not supposed to open the door for Jake, I still won't feel attractive or wonderful unless I shower, do my hair, and put on something sexy. Although he can't see me through the curtains he's instructed me not to open, I'm going to do everything I can to make this a real date. Because it is. It is a goddamn real date. We're just not sitting across from each other.

It's like he's deployed and we're having a Skype chat. Maybe later we'll do something naughty together. A girl can hope.

At precisely fifteen minutes to six o'clock, Jake rings. "I'm on my way."

"You are so punctual," I tease.

"I don't want to keep you waiting," he says in his warm, honeyed voice.

"So you have my noodles?"

"I've got everything you need." His tone is matter-of-fact despite the innuendo-laden words.

It breaks my heart a little to tell him I can't open the door. "I tried to open the door and I think it's going to happen soon, but maybe not tonight. How're we going to do this?"

"I'm going to sit on your balcony," he says, as if having dinner with a glass door and closed curtain between two people is an everyday occurrence.

"How?" Do I take a pill and run into the bedroom and wait for him to walk through?

"Your neighbor is letting me look at his balcony. I have to tell you that the security in this building bites."

"That's not making me feel better," I say, and then the full import of his words hits me. Is he going to leap from my neighbor's balcony onto mine? I rush over to my French doors and peer out. From inside, it's hard to judge the distance but it appears to be over six feet. I have trouble jumping over a puddle. "How do you know my neighbor?"

"It's my business to know." I hear the sound of a car door closing and then the throaty purr of an expensive engine. "The good thing is that before we eat, I'm installing proximity sensors to make your place safer."

"Won't you need a power source?" I try to figure out how all of this is going to work. I've learned that if I have control over my environment, then I feel safer—unfamiliar things can cause more anxiety. Inside this apartment, I feel safe, but now Jake is introducing new things and new fears.

He doesn't seem to mind the questions, though, and explains, "It uses a mix of solar energy and a permanent wired source. For now they will run on battery power. If the battery power is turned off by someone, there is enough energy stored from the solar panel to send a signal to our base. That alert will send someone over to check out the intruder right away."

"I like that."

"Good. It's not perfect, but it will be a start."

"What would be perfect?"

It's a throwaway question, but his response is not.

"My home is more secure than a bank."

My heart skips two beats. "I—I—" I stutter because I don't have a response to that.

"Yeah, so let's just table it for now. Call your doorman and have him let me up."

His suggestion shocks me so much I'm only able to mumble, "Okay."

I hang up and obediently call Chris in a slight daze. "Chris, I'm having a visitor at six. His name is Jake Tanner. He's six foot three and two-sixty."

"Yes ma'am."

Did Jake just invite me to move in? I know that it's for my safety as much as anything, and yet here is an opportunity, not just to get out of my home, but to be with someone who is genuinely into me.

When my phone rings, I answer it immediately. "Hi," I say slightly breathless, thinking it's Jake.

"Are you running on your treadmill? I hope you are running on your treadmill and that you've been working hard on your chapter all day."

Definitely not Jake.

I open my mouth to tell Daphne about Jake, but for some reason I stop. Which is strange, because I've always told Daphne everything. She is my closest confidante since the attack, and we've only grown closer over the years. But this thing with Jake is so new and different and strange that I don't want to jinx by talking about it with anyone.

"I'm running on my treadmill and working hard on my chapters."

In the background I hear papers shuffling. I've never seen Daphne's office, but she admits to being rather disorganized. I envision her sitting under a towering pile of manuscripts going through each with a ruthless red pen. "I'm going to pretend that you aren't completely lying to me."

"*House Hunters International* was in the Bahamas last night and I couldn't stop watching." That technically wasn't a lie, because before I pulled my vibrator out of the nightstand and settled down for a long fantasy session with imaginary Jake, I did watch television. The Bahamas looked gorgeous. I have never been, although my former coworkers and I'd joked that if Saturnalia became successful, we'd take our money and run for the border. I know that three of them bought a boat together and went on a sailing trip. I wasn't sure about the rest of them. I cut them all off after the subway attack. I don't want to lose Daphne; I can't.

She releases a long, exasperated breath. "What am I going to do with you? You know that your deadline is looming. I'm not saying this to pressure you, but I'm worried. We don't want to disappoint your fans."

"I don't want to disappoint anyone either," I say with earnestness. "And haven't I met every deadline I ever had?"

"To be fair, honey, when I signed you, you already had one book done and the second one nearly complete. The third one you knocked out before the series started to take off. You haven't written a book in a year. You need to strike while the iron is hot."

"I know. I know. I just was focused on other things." Like overcoming my anxiety. Getting outside. Doing *stuff*.

"I want you to get better as much as you do," Daphne continues, barreling over my protests. "But the truth is, you are more productive when you're not focused on going to the subway and counting how many seconds you can stand in one place. It takes so much of your mental energy to just open the door and leave your apartment, sometimes I wonder if you're not just better off staying home."

That hurts. My throat tightens for a moment. I've never heard her say that she thought I was better off being a shut-in with no life. No friends beyond her and Oliver. No dinners out. No boyfriend. No lover. No children. A long, lonely life alone in this apartment. Quietly, but fiercely, I tell her, "I would rather never write again if, in exchange, I could leave the house. I don't want this anxiety to be constantly paralyzing me and preventing me from living a full life."

She huffs as if offended by my tone or maybe my words. I don't know. "Before you had the attack in the subway, before you closeted yourself up in the apartment, you didn't live any differently. You sat in your apartment over in Brooklyn and you worked day after day, hour after hour on your computer program. You lived out your life on gaming boards, forums, Twitter, Reddit. That's how you and I met—online. That's how you met all of your friends. They were all online. You never left! I had to beg and plead to get you out of Brooklyn, because coming over the bridge was like taking a trek up Mount Everest!"

I swallow hard at this accusation. I didn't go out much before the attack due to the shyness of being a new person in a new town. But not to the extent that I could not meet new people, or go to the movies, or check out that new restaurant that just opened in Midtown. I had choices and options, and none of those choices and options exist for me now. I feel that just when the world is expanding, what with Jake coming into my life, Daphne is trying to zip me back into the bubble of supposed safety. "I'm sorry," I say for lack of anything else in my head at the moment.

"Look," she says, "I'm not trying to make you feel bad. I just want what's best for you. And what's best for you is to finish this book. You're almost done. You have maybe eight chapters left. You're over the hump."

I answer in the only way that I know is acceptable, both to her and me. "I'm going to finish on time. I will meet the deadline."

The phone beeps to inform me I have a new call. "I have to go."

"Is that Oliver?"

"Yeah, Oliver," I lie.

"Tell him I said hello." Her voice switches from business to flirtation with no hesitation. "If he's single these days, tell him I'm available."

"Someday I am going to tell him that and then he'll take you up on your offer." I know she's just joking. Other than these teasing asides, she never shows any interest in Oliver beyond that he's the quarterback for the Cobras, which is good because Oliver doesn't really have any interest in her either. "I'll have pages for you tomorrow."

After Jake and I have dinner, I'll have something to write about. I'll need to take out my sexual frustration on something, and it might as well be the book.

I switch over. "I'm sorry."

"It's no problem. Your doorman let me up. I'm in the elevator—if I get cut off, I didn't hang up on you."

"It was my editor. I'm behind on my book so I needed to take a well-deserved tongue lashing."

"Do you need to postpone our dinner?"

"No!" I nearly shout in alarm. Calming myself, I say in a more controlled tone, "No, I've got time."

I wouldn't miss this dinner for all the advances, book awards, or good reviews in the world. I've got all the time in the world to write, but only one night to have dinner with Jake Tanner.

CHAPTER FIFTEEN

JAKE

I turn my Bluetooth headset on and pocket the phone. The duffel slung crosswise over my back holds the electronic equipment. I jimmy the lock on her neighbor's door. It's so cheap and unsophisticated all it takes is a bump key. I don't even have to pull out the lock-picking set.

I wasn't kidding when I told her to move. This place is a security nightmare, with the property management offering only token protection—a doorman, a security feed in the lobby and elevators, and locks you could buy at any local hardware store.

"I'm going to need a picture," she's saying as I walk through the empty apartment. Per surveillance, this neighbor left to go to dinner about fifteen minutes ago.

It strikes me that she's never seen me in person.

What I look like clearly doesn't matter to her.

"Why do you need a picture?" I ask, not that I care. As for me, like I'd told her, I like a good visual. I'd stared a good long time at her before leaving her apartment the other day. And I am damned curious about other things I haven't seen . . . or touched.

She hurries to explain. "Not because it's important. But my phone has the little gray outline, and you are the only person in my contacts without a picture. It bothers me."

The corner of my mouth twitches up. Of course that's the reason. She likes order in her life. Her office is devoid of extra papers and paraphernalia. Her home—the two times I saw it—was clean, not a pillow out of place. Even her bedroom had no clothes on the floor or scarves draped over the chairs. Sabrina's room is bursting with *things*—clothes, shoes, handbags. There seem to be a dozen lip glosses scattered over every flat surface, but then Sabrina's not had anything traumatic happen in her life that would cause her to want to exert rigid order over everything within her reach.

"I generally don't let people take pictures of me. But I tell you what, after dinner, I'll send you one."

"It's a deal." She sounds pleased and satisfied, as if getting a picture of me was her only goal. "Where are you right now?"

"Walking through your neighbor's apartment. You have the better apartment of the two." This place is a cross between ultra-modern and man-cave chic. Lots of black lacquer, black leather sofas, and mirrors. I bet if I went into the bathroom, this guy would have five bottles of shampoo along with a cologne for every day.

"It's also a more expensive apartment."

"Yours is decorated better. This one has too much black leather, which is saying something because I'm a man and we tend to love black leather."

"Is it bad that I don't know my neighbors? Oliver once told me who lived where, thinking it would help me out, but it kind of went in one ear and out the other."

Because at the time he'd told her, she hadn't thought about leaving her safe place, is my guess. I step out onto the balcony of her neighbor's and eye the distance. I had brought a rappelling rope, just in case, but there should be no problem in jumping between the two. There's less than ten feet in distance.

"What's your place look like?" she asks.

I tighten the strap across my chest and test my left leg. I should've worn the blade for this, but I didn't want to go through the hassle of changing out the prosthetic. Plus, I'll admit to being a tiny bit vain. On the off chance she does open the door, I'd rather have her look at the straight fall of my jeans rather than the alien appendage strapped to my stump. I shake my head at my clearly wishful thinking.

Natalie isn't opening the door, let alone letting me into her bed.

"I call it breakfast decor. Lots of oatmeal-colored things along with some egg-yolk yellow and toast brown. I'm sure there are better terms for it, but those three things go together on some sort of decorator tree. My mom and sisters did it."

"You should send me pictures of that too."

"Just in case my house calls you?" I tease. I swing my arms to loosen up and be ready for the jarring impact when I grab onto her balcony railing. I don't want my real leg to crumple under the weight so it makes more sense to leap and grab for the iron railing.

"Well, you have seen my place." Then she adds quietly, "and me."

"You're beautiful," I respond. There's a small hint of vulnerability there, which shouldn't surprise me but does. With her bombshell curves and long, light brown hair contrasting with all the pale, ivory skin, she'd stop traffic if she was walking down the sidewalk. "In fact, you're probably doing the men of New York a service by staying inside."

"How's that?" she snorts.

"Fewer accidents. They'd be staring at you and not paying attention to where they were going. Bikers would crash into fire hydrants, and cars would rear end other cars."

"Ha, ha," she says, but I can tell she's smiling. I can hear the pleasure in her voice.

"Be prepared. You're going to hear a thud."

"Do you have safety equipment—like a harness or something? You know, the type of thing that window washers use."

"No." I laugh. "I don't have anything like that."

"But you might fall. It's three stories up and you could really hurt yourself." She pauses. "Or wait, do you have some super-duper type of spring action in your leg?"

She never fails to make me smile. "No, I have my regular prosthetic. My super-duper prosthetic is the one I use for running and climbing."

"I think this qualifies." She's sounding slightly indignant, which I find adorable. Can't be mad at a woman for caring about your safety. "How are you going to do this?"

"I have good balance, and your apartments are closer than you think."

"I can't believe you're jumping!"

"Believe it."

I climb onto the railing and make the leap. Surprisingly, I clear the railing and land right on Natalie's balcony. The small space, no greater than five feet by ten feet, holds a small table and one rickety chair, which I don't think has ever been sat on.

"Are you okay?" she asks.

There's almost an echo and I realize she must be standing just inside the door. Even so, I keep the headset in to hold her voice in my ear.

"Perfect."

"You're the crazy one," she sighs and I sense, rather than hear, her put her head against the curtain-covered glass of her French door. I wish I hadn't told her to keep those curtains shut, but I don't press her. Being this close is good enough for me tonight.

"I'm going to put the sensors up, which, by the way, you shouldn't mention to anybody. That's between you and me and the security firm."

"When you say anybody, are you talking about Oliver?"

"Anybody. Oliver, Dr. Terrance. Chris the doorman. You'll be safest if you are the only person that knows about your security measures.

I'm not saying Oliver's not trustworthy, but he might tell his agent or his business partner, who might let it slip to someone else, and pretty soon everyone knows and there's no use to having the security system."

She mulls that over. "That makes sense, although I'm sure Oliver has nondisclosures with his people."

"Better safe and all that. You won't share, right?" I press. I want her assurance. It's for her safety as much as it is for my peace of mind.

"I won't share," she repeats.

"Good, now let me tell you what I'm doing so you can visualize it." I draw the bag over my head and start to pull out the sensors. "I'm placing these proximity sensors at the edges of the railing where they meet the brick of your building. There will be one on each side and two above your doors. These aren't cameras, but ultrasonic sensors that detect objects based on the reflection of sound waves. They're set to emit an alarm if waves reflected back create a significant mass. It won't alert us if a feather or leaf drops in front of it, but a large rock or a body would set it off."

"I sense a disturbance in the force, Luke," she quotes.

I chuckle. "Yes, something like that. Although we have to use sensors instead of our Jedi powers."

"The technology is basically making us Jedi-lite."

I trowel on the adhesive to the back of the sensor as I respond, "I suppose, although Luke had more function in his prosthetic hand than anyone has currently."

"How so?"

I affix the first camera with industrial-grade brick cement. It will take a chisel to dislodge. If she moves, I'll come back and repair the exterior. "The signals that you can send from your brain to your prosthetic currently are only digital, not analog, meaning I can tell my hand to grip or release but not release more slowly. Think of a clock. Analog clock hands wind continuously around the face, whereas a digital clock simply flips the numbers. Those gradients can't be achieved yet, which is why it's hard to do fine motor tasks like draw, write, or even crack an egg. I can open a can of beer or unlock your car door or slip the token into the subway or apply adhesive cement to affix a sensor, but it's harder to do things that require a fine or a delicate touch."

She's quiet, real quiet and I wonder if I've shared too much . . . if the idea of my prosthetic hand is too strange for her. I've dated women who were intellectually fine with the fact I had two stumps and two fake limbs, but at times when I touched them with one of my prosthetics, they'd recoil. It might be subtle, but it was there. Hard to get excited with a woman who didn't want you to touch her a certain way.

I run a hand up my left arm, currently covered in the long sleeve of my knit shirt, and feel the industrial plastic underneath. Should I have waited to share with her? No. I walk determinedly to the other side. She either accepts me as I am or I'll move on. I quickly finish installing the three other sensors.

Her soft voice breaks into my thoughts. "Is it really gauche of me to say I find that fascinating?"

No. Fuck no. I want to reject the feeling of relief, but it's there. I like to think that I don't give a fuck how people respond to me, because there's nothing out there that I used to do in the past that I can't do now, including bringing a woman to orgasm. Repeatedly. My dick's not broken and I've got a damn strong tongue. But what Natalie thinks matters more than it should.

"Nope," I answer, trying to keep my tone even and light.

"I think my brain works in digital too. Like I have problems opening the door when I don't know who is on the other side, but when Chris or Jason, our doormen, let me know it's them, I'm not afraid. As if they've cleared out the hallway of the infestation of people and all that is left is my food or package."

"Sure. It's the unknown that scares you. If you knew exactly what would happen, every minute of the future, then there'd be nothing to fear." I finish up the install and continue explaining, "Now I'm placing the battery pack underneath your chair out here. The battery is the main power source, but if it's turned off for any reason, the sensors have small solar panels and there will be enough residual juice to emit an alarm. The battery pack should be moved inside. The best thing that you could do, if possible, is to open your door after I leave and take the battery pack inside your house. Place it just to the left or right of your door and it should work perfectly."

"I think that's amazing. I think you're amazing, and I'm trying really hard not to cry right now. I think crying is verboten on dates, right?"

"It can put a damper on things," I reply dryly.

Inside, I hear her doorbell ring. "It's Chris. He says he has a bag of something that smells awesome."

"I left your food with him. Go get it."

While she answers the door, I settle gingerly into the small chair. Thankfully, it holds my weight. From my bag, I pull out my own dinner. Three chicken breasts and plenty of veggies, courtesy of my sister. I pop off the plastic lid and dig in. It's late and I'm hungry. I guess one of the advantages of not eating face-to-face is that she can't see when I'm being rude. Even I know that starting to eat before the other person does isn't well-mannered. Mom likes to say that I use being in the army as an excuse to forget everything she's ever taught me. She's only half wrong.

A long, loud screeching noise has me rising from the table and knocking on the glass door. "You okay in there?"

"Yes," she says, slightly out of breath. "I was just pulling my coffee table over. I didn't realize how heavy glass is."

"Shit, you should have asked me, I'd have helped you move it." My voice dies off at the end. That'd only happen if she could open the door. "Never mind."

"I want to open the door. I really do." Her voice catches on the last word.

I clench my jaw. "It's nothing, sweetheart. Have a seat. Let's enjoy our dinner."

"This is bizarre."

"Only if you want it to be." I tear off a hunk of the chicken and shove it in my mouth. There are benefits to being out here. I don't have to watch my manners and I can eat with my hands.

I hear the clink of a plate on the glass-topped table she has and then silence. I imagine she's dumping her food out.

"God, this food smells great. Where did you get it?"

Bizarre or not, we're having dinner. I smile with satisfaction and swallow another piece of chicken before answering.

"There's a tiny little hole-in-the-wall near my place, with great Chinese food, reasonably priced. I think everyone in the four-block radius who knows about them keeps quiet so we can get in and out real fast."

"Well, it's delicious."

"What're you eating?" I told her, I'm a visual guy.

"My egg roll. Do you like them?"

"Don't eat a lot of fried foods," I admit.

"Everything tastes better when it's fried," she says. "I saw this one episode on television where they tested out all these different animals to see if they tasted like chicken. At first they fried all the stuff and admitted that the test wasn't very challenging because everything that's fried tastes good, even lizard. I suspect even poo would taste good fried."

I nearly spit my chicken out when she says that. Laughing, I pause and take a long drink of water before I can catch my breath enough to answer. "Let's just agree to assume, because I'm not willing to test it out."

She chuckles. "What are you eating? Same Chinese?"

"A few chicken breasts. Some broccoli."

"What? Why? Did being in the army kill your taste buds?" She sounds aghast. I hear her shift on the floor, the sound of fabric rubbing against wood as she finds a comfortable place for her ass on the big floor pillow I spotted sitting near the French doors.

"At the risk of sounding like a 'roided meathead, I'm pretty careful about what I eat. It's harder for me to build muscle in certain areas of my body, so since I was discharged, I've stuck to a diet of mostly lean meats and vegetables. I'll splurge now and then, but not tonight."

"Now I'm feeling guilty, but not so guilty I'm not enjoying the crap out of this lo mein." Her gusty sigh of appreciation is followed by a moment of silence, for eating, most likely. I polish off the rest of my chicken and lean back to enjoy the cool spring air.

While she eats, I talk.

"When I was first in, the meals were terrible. We lived on a diet of caffeine, tobacco, and stimulants. The latter are banned, but we used them anyway and the officers turned the other cheek. They weren't going to deny us Ephedra when they were asking us to carry out twenty-four-hour shifts at a time. The food we ate was basically a bunch of calories in a bag. There was mystery meat in chunks and we'd heat it up using this weird-ass chemical that would cause cold water to boil immediately. There was a ton of junk food—cake, snack foods, candy. The supply of MREs varied over the course of our time over there. Sometimes we had too many of them. Later, in the middle of the deployment, there'd be too few. All the good stuff, we'd save, and then distribute when we got low."

"What's the good stuff?" she asks, as if there couldn't be anything good, which is probably a fair assumption after what I've shared.

I wonder how long she'll let me stay out here. I should've brought a blanket and I could've bunked down, although my six-foot-plus frame would have a hard time being comfortable. "Instant coffee, cocoa powder, grape Kool-Aid. Skittles. Loved the Skittles. The Charm candies, though, we'd get rid of. They've been considered bad luck since they first appeared in World War II rations. If you're caught carrying them or eating them out on patrol, you're likely to get shot and killed, so most platoons will throw them out or give them to the Iraqi kids."

"Is it true?" she asks tentatively. "Did anyone get hurt while they had Charms in their packs?"

"People got killed all the time. Sometimes with the Charms and sometimes without. It's like the poo assumption, though, no one really wanted to test it out. Better to be superstitious and get rid of them."

"Jake." A ripple works its way down my back when she says my name. I haven't heard it often. Or maybe I just haven't heard it enough.

"Yes?"

"Can I ask a stupid question? I know it's stupid and I shouldn't ask, but I want to ask it anyway so please forgive me in advance."

Her earnestness takes away the sting of anything she could ask. "Go ahead."

"Did you lose someone you cared about?"

I look up at the sky and think of Staff Sergeant Matthew Dalton and Captain Brian McKenna. The stars wink back at me. Maybe those two are operating those stars. "You know, there were always people that you liked that you heard about dying. Guys you might have stayed with at a forward operating base or trained with out of Fort Benning, but my small unit came through the first deployment unscathed. The saddest part is that a couple of the losses happened after guys got out. That's the thing that people don't like to talk about. But so many casualties happen after the war, because you can't let it go."

"I'm not one of those people, you know," she says. "I've never thought about it."

"I didn't think you had."

"I just wanted you to know." She clears her throat. "I'm sorry you lost your friends."

"I know you are." I could hear real regret.

"How'd you get over it?" There's more to her question than how I got over the war. It's a question of how I recovered from my injuries, how I managed not to let the anxiety overtake me, how I was able to move forward. It's that question she wants answered for herself. I pick my words with care, remembering Isaiah's words.

"I didn't do anything special. I went to counseling because I had to go to counseling. That was part of my treatment to get my prosthetics.

Unlike a lot of other guys, I had the means to get other care, but I was in Bethesda for a time and when you're there, you learn quickly to be grateful for your circumstances because there are always people who have it worse than you.

"I had a very loving family and a good support network, and I knew that if I had died I would've been mad as hell if someone like me didn't get off his ass and start living. So I focused on all the things I could be grateful for. I could kiss my mom and hug my sisters. I could shake my dad's hand. None of those feelings happened overnight—I'm still a work in progress. I'm not always comfortable with my prosthetics. When I go out, a good part of me wants to shove my stump in other people's faces, and another good part just wants to be ignored. Most the time I'm just grateful to be alive, functioning. But I have my moments."

This is the most I've shared with anyone outside the confines of a hospital or therapy room, but I felt that not only did I need to share it with Natalie, she needed to hear it.

We are silent for a good long time. I don't know if she's eating or thinking or both. I'm just enjoying the company. Natalie doesn't realize it yet and I'm not ready to share it with her, but we're a match. I know it like I knew when those planes crashed into the World Trade Center that I had to go enlist. The war wasn't what I thought it was about, though I'm not sorry I served. Just like I'm not sorry I met her. I'm not sorry she's got a bad case of agoraphobia. I'm not sorry that I might have to have a hundred dinners with her on one side of the glass and me on the other.

I'm going to sit out here on her balcony until she's ready to come out. For as long as it takes—deep down, I know she's worth it.

CHAPTER SIXTEEN

NATALIE

The food he brought sticks in my throat as he talks. The things he says, the intimate, private thoughts that tumble from his lips are so moving, so real. I don't know why this man has walked into my life, but I treasure him.

And he compels me to reach deep and tell him what I don't enjoy admitting.

"I'm tired of being afraid. Tired of being tied up in knots over it and"—I take a deep breath and jump off the deep end—"I'm afraid I'm never going to get better. That this apartment will be the only thing I'll ever know."

"When you're ready, it will happen," he responds in his pragmatic way.

"How do you know?"

"Because you made it out before and you'll do it again."

He's so confident that I start to believe. I exhale, closing my eyes. I imagine what it would be like to sit next to him and stare into his eyes as he says these tender, sweet things. My heart balloons until I fear my chest might explode with all the feeling. I lay my hands over my chest, not to keep the feeling inside but to hold it close. I don't know what he feels toward me; but he's here sitting on my balcony when he could be anywhere, with any woman.

"I'm so glad you're here, Jake."

"Me too."

"Can I ask why me?"

I imagine that he shrugs, a lazy roll of his shoulders up and back, because he doesn't seem to be overly perturbed about anything. "You laugh. You listen. Perfect people are boring, Natalie. You know what you're getting with a perfect person every day, and you have to be perfect too. I know you think it's strange that I want to spend time with you. It's true that I don't spend a lot of time just talking. That's never been my style. But you're different and I'd rather spend time with you, even separated by this glass door, than prowling a club. What about you? Should I feel insecure that you're only talking to me because I'm the first male other than Oliver who will spend time with you?"

The last part is said in a teasing tone, because the last thing that Jake Tanner feels is insecure. I know it in my bones. His steps are confident; his actions decisive. His behavior is that of a man who not only knows what he wants, but gets it.

That he wants *me* is the only incredible variable in this whole scenario, but he deserves an honest and sincere answer even if he wasn't looking for one.

"No. I'd want to spend time with you, no matter what. Because to you, people really are the sum of their parts. Plus, I like the sound of your voice and the way you make decisions. There's no wavering with you. I like that. If I'd met you before, I'd have followed you home and I would've sat outside your apartment until you came and talked to me. Then I would've stalked you repeatedly until you had no choice but to let me into your life."

He smothers a laugh. "Good thing, then, things didn't play out that way or I'd be applying for conjugal visits."

My breath catches. I want him inside, next to me. No, I want him *inside me*. I want to know what it feels like to have his hand on my skin. I want to feel his lips trace a path along my neck. I want to watch in breathless anticipation as he lifts my shirt and uncovers my breasts. I want his mouth on my nipples, between my legs. I want to trace his body with my hands and with my mouth. I want him to take me and I want to take him a thousand times until we're sweaty and weary and too weak to even lift our heads off the ruined bed. "I want to open the door," I whisper shakily.

His swift intake of breath at my husky words causes me a corresponding tightening of my core.

"Why?" he demands.

"You know why."

"I want to hear you say it." His tone strains with his effort at control.

I press my lips together. It's one thing to joke about phone sex. It's one thing to write a sex scene. It's an entirely other thing to say it out loud.

"What would you do if you opened the door? Would you want me to touch you? Or would you want to initiate it? Tell me," he says with fierce insistence.

The desire we have for each other is a palpable thing. I can feel it pulsing in the air, making it harder to breathe, heating the room with its very presence.

"I'd want you to touch me and undress me." Remembering our conversation the other day, I look down at my off-the-shoulder knit blouse and tight black leggings. "I'm wearing a thin sweater. It's light blue with a black trim around the neckline. The black sets off my skin, makes it look paler, and the blue makes my eyes look more green than brown." I pause and take a sip of water. Outside I hear nothing but his heavy breaths, currently the hottest sound in the universe. The bundle of nerves between my legs are aching and on fire. I slip my hand inside my pants to ease the pain as I continue. "I have black leggings on and my toenails are painted blue to match my sweater."

"What color is your bra? Your panties?" he asks.

"I have no bra on."

He hisses in response. "How hard are your nipples? Reach up and cup your breasts. Describe them for me." Each word punctuates the silence around us.

I do as he commands, slipping my hand out of my underwear so each hand cups a sensitive breast. "It feels like they weigh more. And they're hot. It's so hot in here."

"Take off your sweater. Bare your breasts."

I whip off the offensive cloth and toss it to the side. Taking my breasts in each hand, I squeeze them. The rough touch eases the ache momentarily, but it roars back in a hurry. I pinch my nipples and rub my legs together.

"Oh, sweetheart, what are you doing to yourself? The sounds you're making, fuck—" He breaks off.

I didn't even realize I was moaning but I am. I'm moaning and whimpering. "It's not enough, Jake."

"Do you have a vibrator?"

"Yes."

"Go get it," he orders.

I rise on shaky legs and stumble to the bedroom. The batteries still haven't arrived, or they might have and they're down in the mailbox. In my preoccupation today, I forgot to check with Jason, the day doorman. Shit. Back in the living room, I slide down onto the big floor cushion in front of the French doors. Before Jake came, I drew the curtains closed as he'd instructed. Now, though, it seems too private, almost claustrophobic, but my window balcony faces the street and I'm not prepared to open the curtains so people can see in while Jake and I share this intimate moment.

"Do you have it?" he asks.

"Yes, but it's not working. I don't have any batteries," I vent in frustration. Earlier today when I used it, the relief it brought was only transient and not as powerful as the need it left behind. I don't want to be half satisfied again.

"Shhh," he soothes. I hear him shift outside. He's closer now. Before he was on the chair and now I nearly feel him, only a few feet away. If the doors were open, we could touch.

I roll to my knees and reach toward the door, but just as I place my hand on the doorknob, he speaks. "I'm going to make it all feel better."

And I'm curious. Can he, just through talking, make me come? I don't believe it's possible, but then if you'd told me a week ago I'd be having dinner with a man like I did tonight, that wouldn't have been believable either. I ease back onto my cushion.

"Are you still wearing your leggings, sweetheart?" he asks.

"Yes." And just like that, the tension is curling inside me. "Do you want me to take them off?"

"Place the vibrator on your right and then peel down your leggings, slowly. No rush." His instructions are explicit and detailed, and I wonder what he did in the army. It must have involved telling people what to do. He's very good at it—a natural leader. I heed his commands nearly without question. It's nice not to think about things, not to have to worry about my next move.

I can place myself entirely in his capable hands. I wouldn't feel this comfortable with someone else—or with anyone else.

"They're off." I kick the leggings to the side and await his next order.

"Lie on your back right along the door. Take your left hand and touch your panties. How wet are they?"

I gasp when I touch my panties.

"Dammit, how wet?" His voice is tight, hot.

"W-wet," I stammer, unused to this dialogue. I lick my lips and try to give it back to him—to give him what he wants. "I'm very wet—I want to take them off. Can I, Jake?"

He's so close I can hear his heavy, labored breaths and the way he tries to grapple for his own control. I wonder if he has himself in hand.

What would he taste like on my tongue? As these thoughts run through my head, I rub myself through the already moist cotton.

"Yes, take them off." The words have a slight shake to them, which fits my state of mind exactly.

I'm unraveling like a ball of yarn tossed across the floor. Excitement runs through me as if he's poured liquid aphrodisiac through my central nervous system and it's chasing down my veins, lighting up every neuroreceptor in my entire body.

"They're off, Jake. I don't have anything on."

He takes a breath and then another. "Pick up the vibrator and rub it on your clit. Just tip on tip."

I do as he says. As I rub, my toes curl into the floor and I draw my knees up to give me better leverage, although not for the vibrator and not for my fingers. I'm readying myself. My knees fall open and I know this will turn him on and drive him crazy so I describe it, in explicit filthy detail. "I'm rubbing myself with the vibrator and my other hand is squeezing my breast, my right one. My nipple is hard. The vibe is getting slippery. My knees are wide open. I look—" I struggle for the right word.

"—Beautiful." The compliment is bit out like a curse. "Fucking beautiful. I want to be the one touching your skin. I want my fingers to be slippery from your juice. I can see the light under the curtains. There's shadows there, hinting at what you're doing, and it's driving me crazy, sweetheart. My cock is like stone right now. I swear to fucking God, I could drill a hole in your balcony with the goddamn thing."

He's losing control, which affects me like gasoline on a fire. I'm enflamed.

"Jake," I pant, "I need . . . I need . . ." God, what do I need? More than I have here at my disposal. I need him. I want his big body pressing mine into the floor. My stomach tightens and my legs grow taut at the idea of his rough body moving in long, slow motions over mine.

"I've got you. Take the vibrator all slick with your juice and ease it inside you. Do it slow. You like your clit licked, sweetheart? When you close your eyes, what do you think about?" He doesn't give me time to answer but floods me with more sensory images. "Am I standing or kneeling between your legs? When I'm licking you, are you squirming or can you hold yourself down?"

"All of it," I cry. "All of it."

I work myself faster, thrusting the vibe repeatedly until the tight mass inside me explodes and my hand cups the vibe as if by holding it in I can draw out the pleasure. I can't hold it in, crying out, something like "Jake, my God, Jake."

When I come down off that high, I'm aching. It's too much and not enough and it's everything and nothing. Because I'm alone.

He's just outside the door.

If I make one act of courage, I could have him and this emptiness will be gone.

"Jake," I whisper.

"Yes, baby?"

"Will you come inside?"

CHAPTER SEVENTEEN

JAKE

Her words are hardly more than a whisper, but as powerful as if she'd shouted them from the balcony.

Open the door. Open the door. Open the door is the mantra that runs through my mind. But I told her I wouldn't ask. I told her we would wait. After hearing her, after listening to her sweet orgasm fill the night air, after feeling the gasp of frustration, I'm driven with the need to burst inside.

I lean my forehead against the cool glass and massage my aching erection. It was hard to stay in control when her sultry voice described her clothes, her lack of underwear, and how slick and wet she was. While I want nothing more than to open the door, pick her up, and cover her with my body before the door closes behind me, I pause to think. Is this too fast? Am I asking too much? I can provide distraction all night, but at some point, she's going to come out of her sexual haze and realize that there's a near stranger in her apartment. I'd rather wait—*No, you fucking don't want to wait,* my dick screams at me—because it might mean a greater reward later.

Risk versus reward.

I have always been a risk taker.

The sound of the lock being disengaged pierces the night like a rifle shot. I stand and turn the knob slowly, giving her every opportunity to draw back. But it opens easily and I fill the doorframe, a big hulking shape against the dark night.

I take a step over the threshold but freeze when she gasps and covers her mouth in what looks like horror. Not since my early days have I felt this prickling of discomfort at my physical appearance. I straighten, ready to march out without another word, when she knocks me off center again.

"You don't look anything like Seth Rogen."

"I—I have no response to that." I come all the way in, reach around to grab my duffel and then lock the door. Turning around, I face her, and this time I don't see horror but hungry delight. Her eyes rove over me, not stopping at my left hand but taking me all in.

"Holy crap, you're beautiful." There's a bit of dismay in her voice, and I have to bite the inside of my cheek to keep me from smiling. "I had prepared myself mentally for someone else. You look more like—I don't know—Mr. January from an NYFD calendar."

I grin at her obvious agitation. "What station? I'm curious to see what my doppelganger looks like."

She presses both hands against her reddening cheeks. She's gorgeous. I much prefer looking at her when she's upright and conscious. Her honeyed hair spills in loose curls around her oval face. Her delicate, unmarked skin is framed by the sofa throw she's draped around herself. My body tightens at the knowledge that under that blanket there is nothing but acres of her precious skin. So this is it. I can feel my bachelorhood folding its tent and packing itself away, because one night won't be enough with her.

"I wasn't prepared for you," she repeats in some frustration. "Tell me your flaws."

"Apparently I don't describe myself well. I told you how tall I was."

"I don't know what that means. I thought you were tall, but had a nice soft pooch in the middle."

Deliberately I raise my shirt. I know I look good there. It's why I eat chicken and broccoli. Her swift intake of breath at the sight of my ridged abdomen and defined obliques that form a V. "You can throw me some pillows and we can pretend, if that's important to you."

She sighs and slumps on the sofa. "You're out of my league. I can't have sex with you now. I know your type. You date the type of women Oliver dates."

"I'd think that was an insult, but I know you love your cousin, so, thank you?" I drop the duffel bag and join her on the sofa. I gather her soft body in my arms and tuck her head into my neck so she can't see my grin.

"I need you to go away and come back less perfect," she mumbles against my skin.

I shouldn't be surprised at how that almost innocent contact burns in the best possible way.

"You do remember my hand and leg, right?" I tap her with said hand.

"Are you bragging about your superhuman abilities right now? Because it's not the time," she says in an indignant huff.

I choke on my laughter. "I'm not the bionic man yet, but I bet I can make you feel better."

"You know, as Mr. January, you have to have options, right?"

I can't hold back any longer and I shake with laughter. Literally throw back my head and howl. Finally, I say, "Not as many as Mr. December. He has the whole year to collect numbers."

She grumbles but doesn't move away. She burrows into my embrace and wraps her arms around my waist. With a finger under her chin, I tip her face up. I want to kiss her, but more than that, I want to *see* her. Her hazel eyes, a golden brown, sparkle at me in rueful amusement, and behind that is banked heat ready to be stoked.

"You're not broken. Adversity has bent you, but you aren't broken. You left your apartment and went to the subway station. In another couple of months, you would have gotten on the train. You're going to do that again."

She sighs and I feel her slight body push against mine.

"Jake, I think I need you to be my therapist."

I shake my head. "I don't think so."

"Why?"

"It's unethical to sleep with your patients."

I'm done with talking. Swooping down, I take her mouth in mine. She is surprised, and then her lips fall open and she's kissing me back, just as hard and just as hungry. She moans and the vibration echoes between my ears and thunders down my spinal cord. Her tongue isn't tentative nor is her tight grip in my hair. She tastes me with the fervor and passion of a woman who hasn't been kissed in more than three years. Maybe she's never been kissed this well. Maybe she's never been wanted this badly.

I hold her jaw between the fingers of my good hand and leave my left one at my side. But she surprises me, as she always has, and releases her death grip on my head. Her hand drops down and runs lightly over my left arm until she clutches the wrist. Not once does she lift her lips from mine. Not once does her fervor let up. Not even when she lifts my wrist to place my hand around her breast.

I don't take time to examine the unfamiliar feeling in my chest. I pack it away and focus on the sensations I understand, like the ache in my cock and the desire to get inside her. I break away from her luscious mouth to run my lips along her chin and down the column of her neck. She tips her head up and to the side to give me better access.

"Oh, Jake." Her hands move to my shoulders as I travel lower, tugging the blanket down with my teeth until her nipples are exposed. I bend my head and bite.

She nearly comes off the sofa. Her hips thrust upward, seeking relief. I rip the blanket aside to expose her pale body flushed with arousal.

"Perfect. You're perfect."

Her legs fall open in clear invitation and I don't hesitate to thrust one finger inside her. I'm clutched tight and hot. My eyes roll into the back of my head at the pleasure of it.

"More," she pants. Her nails dig into my shoulders, punctuating her demands.

In answer, I thrust another finger inside her. "Is this enough or do you want more?"

"More."

Her back arches and her hips rise to meet my hand. Her tongue runs along the cords of my neck. It's my turn to gasp and writhe. Christ, I want inside her body, but I'm determined to make her come first. I want to feel what it's like as her body shudders its release.

The bright lights expose her every vein and highlight every curve. Her porcelain skin looks too delicate to be exposed to the sun or rain. The glow off the tops of her breasts beckons my mouth, and I tongue each hard peak as she grinds against me. I press the hard base of my hand against her pelvis.

"Shit, you're tight," I say before taking another rigid nipple into my mouth for a hard suck. I'm not gentle with her because she doesn't want that. She's used to her own soft hand, her own gentle touch, and now she wants a man's hand, with a man's calluses, and a man's firm pressure. I touch places inside her she can't reach, curling my fingers and dragging them along the front wall of her cunt.

She keens a low sobbing noise. "Close, so close, Jake. Please."

In the next thrust of my hand, I work in a third finger, stretching her, and it only takes two more pumps of my hand. As the orgasm overtakes her and her nerves become oversensitive, she tries to draw away.

"Too much!" she cries.

But I follow her down, rubbing relentlessly all the while whispering encouragement. "You can take more. I know you can." I bite her neck, her ear, and then capture her lips again, plunging my tongue inside her mouth in a graphic preview of how my cock will feel.

She squirms and writhes and as the sensations build again, her body tightens like a bowstring and she shrieks into my mouth. For the sake of her neighbors, I swallow it. I drink in her cries. Then I stop thrusting and slowly withdraw from her body as her tremors slow and soften.

Her clawed fingers loosen and she clasps me against her chest.

"Oh Jake, oh God, oh Jake," she repeats in some kind of prayerful litany. Her hands beat against me in jerky, random movements as if she wants to touch everything at once and doesn't know where to start.

I'm hard, harder than I have ever been, but I lie as quietly as possible under her touch, waiting for her signal for *more.*

"Is this all you got, soldier boy?"

The words cause me to spring into action. I leap off the couch and pick her up. I fling her over my shoulder, and she squeals in fake dismay as I stride into her bedroom.

"Let's see what kind of performance problems I have in here."

I toss her on the bed, thoroughly enjoying the way her breasts bounce when she lands. Her waist nips in and then flares out to nice round hips ending in long legs. This is not a girl's body, but a womanly one with abundant curves and serious dips.

She looks like a seductress, one arm braced on the bed and the other gesturing for me to come near. I unbuckle my pants and shove them down to the tops of my thighs and pull my cock out of my underwear. It will take too long to remove my pants, so I leave them there and tear at my shirt, reaching behind my back to pull it over my head.

Her eyes widen in gratifying appreciation as she takes in my broad chest and defined upper body, and I've never felt so glad I spend all that time in the gym.

"I want all of that." She makes a zigzag sign in the air as she points to me, ending with a fingertip directed toward my cock. It bobs and flexes in response.

"He wants you."

I grab her leg and pull her to the edge of the bed. From my back pocket, I pull out a small packet. I sheathe myself with one hand and with the other spread her wide. Her lower lips glisten in the low light spilling in from the living room. I'm going to need to taste her later, but the urge to get inside her before I spill in my hand like a teenager is too powerful to resist.

I take my cock and rub it along her lips, over and over until she's thrashing on the bed. Her fingers claw at the bedcovers. I resent the condom, a layer I've always used since my first time.

I clamp down on the base of my cock hard—to the point of pain— until I regain some control. Only to almost lose it again when I ease inside her. "Oh fuck," I hiss.

Despite working her earlier with my three fingers, she's still incredibly tight.

"Relax, sweetheart," I croon. I brace my left hand on the bed and use my right to soothe her in long sweeping strokes from her sternum to her navel. We share a moan as her wriggling slides me deeper inside. *Fuck. When has it ever felt this good?*

Never.

"I'm ready, really," she pants.

"Not yet you're not." I pull out and she cries out her disapproval.

"No. Don't stop!"

Ignoring her, I gesture toward the mountain of pillows at the top of the bed. "Throw me one of those."

She does and I catch it with one hand. I push her up against the headboard and shove a pillow under her ass. Crawling between her legs, I give her a wicked wink. "Now let's get you good and ready."

I dive in. I lash her clit with my tongue and rasp her inner thighs with my scruff. Her knees fall open to provide me even better access. I suck her lips between my teeth, biting down until I hear her cry above me.

Her hands dig into my head again, pressing me closer. *I'm not going anywhere, sweetheart.*

"Don't stop. Don't stop," she begs. Or maybe it's an order.

Doesn't matter, because I won't. Not until she comes all over my face.

She turns into a wild, squirming, loud being. Her words become a jumble of pleas and orders. Something about *can't, don't, please,* and then, *"I'm coming. Jake, I'm coming."*

And I feel it everywhere. Her thighs shake, her stomach grows taut, and against my tongue the vibrations of her orgasm barrel down from her head straight into my mouth. My toes and fingers are electrified. Rearing up, I drag her still trembling body to the very edge of the bed. In one quick motion, I sheathe myself in her.

The sounds of hard fucking—the slap of our skin, the draw of her sex, the sound of our breath—ratchet up my arousal.

She is so tight, her grip so hard that I almost have to fight my way out. Her hands dig into the bed covering and I use my left hand to brace myself while my right is dug into her hip, holding her body for my invasion.

"Touch yourself. Show me what you like," I say.

She obeys immediately. Her fingers start rubbing, hard—harder than I would have imagined she liked. I want to thrust forever, but I can't.

She's just too fucking hot, too fucking tight, too fucking lush, and I can't hold on for one minute longer.

"Coming, sweet," I order, my jaw clenched tight. "Come with me."

"Yes. Yessss."

At those words, I feel her clamp around me as I, hard and needy, shoot inside her in long, relentless streams of come. Her hips grip mine and I pump inside her for what seems like an endless amount of time.

Until my vision blurs. Until my mind is completely blank. Until I'm a shuddering, wracked, empty shell. She has all of me. Everything.

I collapse on the bed, barely able to roll to the side to avoid crushing her. My heart is pounding so hard I swear it is outside of my body.

"Shit" is the only word I can manage.

She laughs weakly and a small soft hand flops onto my chest, followed by her head as she snuggles into my side. "I think you wrecked me."

"No, I'm the one who's destroyed. You're able to move."

I wrap my arm around her, the one made of metal and plastic. She doesn't notice or doesn't care. She just snuggles in closer.

In the aftermath, the night air sends goose bumps over her skin. I reach across her and wrap the edge of the comforter around her. I'm too hot for blankets, plus her body provides me plenty of heat. Exhausted and sated, I hold her until her breath evens out.

After the haze of the orgasm wears off, the ache in my left arm and left leg intensifies. I need to get home and take these prosthetics off. I've worn them way too long. As quietly as possible, I ease out from underneath her. I press a kiss against her temple and wrap the comforter around her like a cocoon.

It takes me a minute to find my clothes; I locate my shirt under a dresser. Shrugging it on, I zip my pants up, but decide not to deal with the belt. I cup the end in my hand so the metal doesn't clink and wake her. Out in the living room, I gather up my duffel.

I begin to limp, slightly.

In the six years since my medical discharge and the five since I've had my prosthetics, I've never slept overnight with a woman and I have never taken a prosthetic off in her presence. It's one thing for a woman to fuck a guy standing on two legs even if one of those legs is fake. It's one thing to be held by a man with two arms, even if one of those arms is made of metal and plastic, but it's a whole different game to be touched by a stump.

I've mostly been at peace with myself over the loss of my leg and arm. I'm in better physical shape than I've ever been—even when I was deployed. I'm careful with what I eat; I run and lift assiduously. With the advancements companies have made with artificial limbs, I can even operate my prosthetics with my brain.

DARPA and others are working on making those difficult fine motor skills a reality. Already the lower-limb prosthetics are making life virtually indistinguishable from those who still have the limbs they were born with. Amy Purdy competed in a dance competition, blowing everyone's socks off. The astonishing gains we've made in science and technology are eradicating the lines between abled and disabled.

Still, for all of that, I'm reluctant, but if I want more than sex with Natalie, I'm going to have to learn to be comfortable taking my prosthesis off in front of her.

CHAPTER EIGHTEEN

JAKE

"So you're fucking my cousin?" drawls Oliver Graham as I close Natalie's door behind me.

Fatigue and a little pain makes me irritable. "You spend a lot of time lurking outside your cousin's door?"

He advances in a way I'm sure is supposed to be menacing. No doubt he's used to intimidating people, but I served in the army for eight years, four of them as a Ranger. I've seen shit and done shit that'd give him nightmares.

"How's the investigation going? You find out who sent that note yet?"

His words taunt—he knows I don't have anything to report, because if I did, he'd have already had the information. I take a moment so I don't say something I regret. This is Natalie's beloved cousin.

"We're working on it," I reply with studious calm.

He stops a foot away. "You've found time to seduce my cousin but haven't made any progress on finding the shitstain who is tormenting her."

His accusations sting, in part because they're true. We haven't made much progress on finding the guy behind the note or the clown. Neither the ex nor Dr. Terrance appear to be behind the threats either, although we keep watching both.

"We're working on it," I repeat. "I'm tired and I'm going home. I'll call you when we find out something worth reporting."

I attempt to move around him, but he's having none of it. I eye his well over six-feet-five-inch frame. He's got a couple inches on me but not much more than that. I'm confident that I'd take him in a fight, not because I'm stronger than him but because I've been trained to fight to kill. But it'd be close, real close.

"You don't want to do this," I say softly. The last thing I want to do is get in a brawl with Natalie's cousin outside her apartment at two in the fucking morning.

"Do what? Wipe the floor with your weak ass?"

I try to gather my calm. I have been accused, frequently, of being overprotective of my two sisters. Graham has every reason to be on edge given what's going on in Natalie's life.

"Fight out here and we'll wake Natalie up," I caution.

"Don't fuck with her," he says fiercely, but his voice is lowered. He doesn't want to disturb her any more than I do. "She's delicate. She doesn't need someone to sweet-talk his way into her panties and then waltz away. I don't even know how you got her to open the fucking door for you, but I'm telling you now to stay away."

"You're right and you're wrong." I gesture toward her door. "Yes, she's got some issues, but she's not all that delicate." *The sting of her nails in my back is evidence of that,* I think. "As for how I got her to open the door, she asked me to come in."

"To fuck?" he sneers in disbelief. I can see by the veins in his neck and the set of his jaw that he'd like to haul off and hit me.

I run a hand through my hair. "This is getting nowhere. Natalie's an adult. She gets to make her own decisions. She gets to decide when to call her doctor and who to have sex with. Not you. And I have no intention of fucking and running. That's not my style, unlike some people."

The snide remark hits home. Graham has a reputation for playing the field outside the stadium as well. He flinches but then rallies.

"If you aren't planning on ditching her after you've gotten your snake wet, then why the hell are you leaving in the dead of night? You know women don't like that." He throws his hand out toward the door.

"Because my leg fucking aches and I don't want to pull it off the first night I spend with her," I bite out in frustration and knock his arm down. Leaving her isn't my first choice.

He opens his mouth and then closes it. When pity leaks into his eyes, I'm done. Just done.

"Sorry, man," he says and steps back.

I fight the urge to punch him in the face. "Backing down because I'm a gimp? Thought you were better than that."

I brush by him and he offers no resistance, making me even angrier. At the elevator, I jab the DOWN button with my left hand. *See. I work my body just as well as you do.*

When he comes to stand beside me, I don't look at him. In part because I'm embarrassed by my outburst and in part because I'm angry I'm not in bed with Natalie. I should've just removed the prosthesis and climbed in bed with her. If she lay at my right side, she wouldn't even have noticed.

Now I have to explain to her why I left, and deal with her hurt feelings. I may have even damaged her trust. All because I was vain and thinking of myself instead of her. I scrub my hand over my face. With a sigh, I turn to Oliver.

"Truce?" I hold out my right hand.

"Truce." He takes it and gives it a manly squeeze.

The elevator doors open and I step on and Graham follows. I direct a raised eyebrow toward him, but he merely shrugs. We are both silent until the elevator stops on the lobby floor.

When I step onto the marble tiles, Graham's right there with me. He nods to the night doorman and exits to the street.

"I sometimes forget you even have a prosthetic," Graham says. "You manhandled the clown like a pro. I mean, it was pretty awesome seeing you zip-tie his wrists with one hand. That's a good move."

"Thanks." I accept his unstated apology and offer the explanation I wouldn't give before because I didn't like my integrity questioned. "I like your cousin a lot and I should've stayed, but the situation got the best of me and I felt like it made more sense to go home and come back in the morning."

"Which one's yours?" he asks, nodding toward the row of cars on the street.

I point to the black machine down the street.

"Nice." He whistles. "I'll walk you to it."

Because I'm too tired to argue, I allow him to follow me to my car. The lights turn on as I near, the internal sensors reading the signal the key in my pocket is emitting.

"Audi A8. Is this the five-hundred-horsepower version?"

He skims a hand over the top of the hood, respectfully not touching the actual metal but following the slope with his hand.

"Twelve cylinders, five hundred horsepower, all-wheel drive," I confirm.

"Upgraded wheels," he says, with approval. "I like the open spokes. I've been thinking about buying a car. I've never had one in the city. Parking's a beast. You have problems with that?"

"Part of the deal," I answer. "You take the good and bad, but what the hell, so you have to walk an extra block or two. Worth it." I knock my hand against the matte-black steel.

"Custom painted? I didn't see the matte black as a version on the website."

I give him a rueful grin. "A friend of mine has a matte-black Ferrari F430. It was smoking hot. Had to copy it."

"No shit." His eyes light up. "You drive it?"

"Yeah, it's a tight ride."

"Have you seen the 2010 Lotus Exige Stealth? It's matte black with a high-gloss stripe down the middle. Only thirty-five units made and none in the US."

"Haven't seen it," I admit. "But that friend I mentioned is a big car buff. He might have. Hell, he might own one."

He gives me a speculative look. "You're not just a security guy, are you?"

Graham is looking for assurance that I'm good for his cousin, and so I share a few details to make him feel better. "I'm not. I've got money in the bank. I own that townhouse where my office is located, free and clear. Bought it with the inheritance I gained control of when I was twenty-one, and I only drained a portion of it. I'm not part of the super-rich here in the city but I'm not ever going to have a problem making rent or putting food on the table."

He nods. "I know it's rude, but Natalie's got some money now—from her books and given her circumstances—" He spreads his hands out.

"You want to make sure she's not being taken advantage of," I finish.

"Right. She's gone through a lot." We both look up at her apartment. "She deserves to be happy. Anyway, I'll let you go so you can take care of business." He nods toward my leg and then turns to leave.

"Before you go, Graham, you should know that the security in your building is for shit. I wouldn't let either of my sisters live here."

He spins back. "What do you mean? It's got cameras in the lobby and a twenty-four-hour doorman. No one gets upstairs without signing in or being okayed by a resident.

"Trust me. This is my business and I do it well, which you know or you never would have hired me. There are only two sets of cameras. One in the lobby and one set in the elevators. There are none on the individual floors and none in the stairwells. The day doorman is more interested in how his hair looks than who comes and goes. The locks are so flimsy that I was able to use a bump key to get into her neighbor's apartment."

His jaw hardens and juts out in a familiar pose that I've seen on my television screen on Sundays. Narrow-eyed and determined, his look means someone's going to get an ass kicking. "I can see I'm going to have a long talk with the property management company."

"You do that, but unless they okay additional security measures, my recommendation is to sell your pricey penthouse for a profit and move into some place that has better protection. You'll need it too. If you don't have women already sneaking in at all hours trying to get a piece of Oliver Graham, most eligible bachelor, you will, and this place will make it easier for them to get you in a compromising position. It'd sell more than a few tabloids. Good luck if you're trying to have a serious relationship. Is a new girlfriend going to believe that a random woman broke into your apartment?"

He's still scowling when I drive away.

♦ ♦ ♦

At home I send a text to Natalie, hoping she's not too pissed off when she wakes up. It's a toss-up which part of my body hurts more. Reluctantly I climb into the elevator, which I rarely use but was the primary reason I bought this particular townhouse. At the top floor, I stagger out. I drop my pants and ease down on the edge of the bed.

My left thigh looks swollen. I could use a good rubdown, but it's three in the morning and the only people I could call to give me a massage at this hour would be delivering the standard happy ending. And my dick only wants one woman right now.

As I ease the rubber sleeve down and the sock, doing the same to my arm, the relief of having the artificial limbs off is tremendous. I flop back onto the bed to enjoy the air circulating around my body. I miss her already and I feel stupid for leaving. Of all people, Natalie's the last person who would judge my appearance. She seemed disappointed I was fit and attractive, I remind myself. Fatigue sets in. I should shower tonight to avoid too much swelling from the heated water in the morning. It makes it hard to get the prosthetics on. But my body has turned leaden and my eyelids drop down and then I'm out.

◆　◆　◆

The sun streams through the unblocked windows a few hours later, jolting me awake. I slept poorly. My skin is itchy from not showering and my bed feels curiously empty. I remember waking up after surgery. The pain was intense everywhere—not just around the surgical sites. The phantom pain everyone warned me about took me off guard. As time went on, that pain eased to a dull ache, until it just felt like I was missing something. Wearing my artificial limbs helped, and like Natalie, if I was distracted, it was easier to shove the pain aside.

I'm feeling that curious dull ache again. Like I'm missing something vital.

I hop into the shower and clean up. Drying off, I view the wreckage of the night before. The prosthetic is still in the jeans with the boot around it. I don't want to hassle with it, so I scoop up the mess and toss it in the corner. There are advantages to having a thick wallet and one of those is having more than one prosthetic. I pull the other carbon fiber foot and socket out of the closet and throw it onto the bed next to the arm I discarded last night.

I cover the arm with the sock and the liner and affix the stump into the arm socket. From the dresser I pull out another pair of jeans and a plain gray T-shirt. The shirt slides easily over my head. The jeans are another story. I stick the prosthetic into the jeans leg and then repeat the process I conducted for my arm. Sliding the other leg in, I'm dressed.

After four years of this, it's as habitual as brushing my teeth and just as routine, but it's a chore. One of the biggest changes post-injury was how long it took me to do even the most ordinary of tasks. The hand and arm prosthetic, no matter how great the advancements, are still tools and not real limbs. Ironically it was my injury that made me realize I have opinions about how my home is set up and what kinds of clothes I like. I prefer big furniture with plenty of places to put my feet up, and soft clothes without many fastenings. I also know who I want in my home. I want Natalie and not because I need help putting on my clothes.

The only reason I want Natalie here is because I want her with me. Not to help me dress or pick out my clothes, but because I want to watch her sleep, watch her wake up, watch her writhe on my sheets. I want to take her in the shower and put her ass up on the highboy dresser at the perfect height for my mouth.

And yes, it's a strange yearning I'm experiencing. It took me a couple of years after surgery, after wearing the artificial limbs, to truly feel comfortable in my own skin again.

I'd met my share of women who had a fetish for amputees and then a few who wanted to smother me with well-intentioned care, but I wasn't interested in playing someone's charge. I wanted a partner and preferably one who didn't try to ride my stump. I shudder at the memory of that night gone wrong.

But there were plenty of women who didn't care. Some just wanted a guy who knew how to use his equipment and who cared if they had an orgasm. Natalie isn't a fetishist and she's not looking to be my mother. But she's not quite in the "I just want to fuck" category either.

To be fair, I suppose some of the women I dated in the last couple of years wanted something more meaningful, but I wasn't interested. Now I am. Real interested.

But if I don't get my act together and pull up my big-boy pants, I could lose her before I even have her.

With that, I set off to find Sabrina. If I'm going to convince Natalie to move in here, I'm going to need to make some changes.

"Hey, sleepyhead," she greets me, but doesn't move from the center island where she's chopping up a pineapple.

"Good morning, Bri." I kiss the top of her head, which isn't that much shorter than mine. Bri's a tall girl. "You got some coffee left over?"

She jerks her head toward an already filled cup, the steam rising indicating it was freshly poured. I take a big gulp before thanking her. "You're an angel."

"Late night, huh?"

"Something like that." Talking about sex with my baby sister has always made me uncomfortable. This time is no different. I can still see her in diapers. I was thirteen when she was born, and my feelings toward her are more paternal than brotherly, which pisses her off. As she regularly reminds me, she already has a father.

But she's twenty-two and knows exactly why I was late coming home last night.

"I hope you practiced safe sex," she smirks, also knowing exactly how uncomfortable it makes me.

I rub a hand over my face and then into my hair that I've forgotten to brush after I showered. It's probably a mess, but I don't care. I'm debating how much to share with Sabrina about Natalie and not just because I want to move Natalie into the townhouse.

"You busy today?" I ask.

"I've got two morning classes and then I'm done. Why?"

"Want to go shopping?"

She squeezes her eyebrows together in confusion. "Are you offering to take me shopping? You hate shopping. You hate spending money."

"I don't hate spending money," I protest. "I object to being wasteful. Spending two hundred bucks on a pillow that I'm not allowed to use because the sequins might rub off is wasteful."

She waves her hand in the air as if my argument has no merit. "I am not buying your new girlfriend anything."

"I asked you to do that one time."

"Three times."

I take a long sip of coffee that's cooling fast. "I didn't want to give a gift that was thoughtless, so I went to my dear sister for advice, and you did a great job. Which is why I'm coming to you again. Competency generates a repeat performance request."

She rolls her eyes. "So what is it going to be? Clothes, jewelry? You know I do not do lingerie. That is still a hard limit."

"Of course not," I say with mock indignation. "If, hypothetically, I were to give you a photograph, could you re-create the room in the picture on the third floor? How doable is that?"

"What? You don't like what we've done to it already? When we were decorating it four years ago, you said nothing too bright and no flowers. This is a totally gorgeous space!" Sabrina exclaims. "People would pay lots of money—lots of frivolous money—for what we did in this house."

I scratch my head and wonder how my intention to bring Natalie here has turned into an indictment of the decorating taste of my mother and sister. I think it's lack of sleep. If I'd stayed at Natalie's place, I would have slept better, longer, and I would have had good-morning sex. Then I wouldn't be making these obvious missteps.

"I have this friend—"

"Is this for the journalist? I thought you broke up with her?"

Gathering the reins of my rapidly shredding patience, I repeat, "I have this friend—"

"If it's not that one chick, then who?" She taps a finger against her lip. "You were out late last night, and Victoria said you didn't talk to anyone at the club when you were out with Ian and her. Was it that lawyer lady from Mom's charity dinner the other night? She didn't seem your type."

While Sabrina runs down her short list of suspects, I refill my coffee. Leaning against the counter, I watch her with some amusement. She is going to be surprised, but in a good way, I think. Natalie and she would get along. Sabrina has a lot of creative energy she seems to try to suppress because she thinks we want her to fit into some business mold. Mom and Dad have told her that she can do whatever she wants, but Sabrina's headstrong. Once she gets an idea in her head, you can't shake it from her. So it doesn't matter that she loves music, she thinks she's got to be a banker or investment fund manager or do something that makes her a "real living," as she calls it.

Kaga is one of those ideas. For some reason she thinks she's in love with him, but like the business thing, once she wakes up, she'll realize the error of her ways. But until then we all watch out for her to make sure she doesn't butt her head against too many brick walls.

At the table, Sabrina gasps and slams a hand down on the pine surface. "Oh my God, I heard that Laura Severson got a divorce recently. Do not tell me you are getting back together with that bitch."

I blink in surprise. "I didn't know she was getting a divorce."

"Not getting, already done. *Finite.* Quickest divorce in New York State. I guess they could not stand each other."

After I broke it off with Laura, she wasted no time in hooking up with a friend of mine. At the time I'd thought he was too good a friend to be comforting my ex with his dick, but after I'd gotten out of the military I realized that I had almost nothing in common with the guys—and girls—I'd hung out with as an arrogant trust fund kid at Columbia.

"Wait, if you didn't know she was getting a divorce, then were you sleeping with her while she was married?"

Sabrina looks as scandalized as if she'd found out I'd been caught having sex in Central Park.

"It's not Laura," I answer, puzzled. I hadn't seen—or talked—to Laura in about two years, unless you counted that time we ran into each other by Rockefeller Plaza. I had popped into the LEGO store to buy Megan's oldest a Harry Potter set, and Laura must have been buying out every store around the rink, because her hands had been full of shopping bags. She'd given me a kiss on the cheek and told me to call her. I promptly forgot her number. At the time I was still seeing the journalist or "Ms. Snoopy," as Sabrina liked to call her.

"So who is she? And why doesn't she like how the third floor is decorated?" Sabrina asks with impatience.

And apparently a thousand questions are what I'm going to have to pay to get this favor done.

"I have a friend," I start again, only to be interrupted.

"Is that what we're calling them now?"

I cut to the chase. "Sabrina, what is it going to cost me to get you to do this for me?"

She sits, knees drawn to her chest, looking like the baby girl I used to push on the swings at the park. "You know what I want."

"Ask for something else." Anything else. The implacability in my tone makes her frown, but wisely she doesn't press.

"Fine," she huffs. "I want you to be there when I tell Mom and Dad about my new job."

I reach over and squeeze her hand. "I would've been there anyway. Ask again."

"Tell me," she implores and grips my fingers. "Tell me exactly what your objections to Kaga and me are. Don't say it's our age—I know that can't be it."

I drag my prosthetic down my face in frustration, wondering if the carbonite fingers would make it more or less painful when I poke my eyes out. "You're right. It has nothing to do with your age difference." It would make me extremely hypocritical, given that Natalie is probably ten years younger than me. "The issue is more complicated than your age. And it's not my story to tell."

"But you won't even let me talk to him, so he can't tell me the story."

"Let it go."

She turns away so I can't see her hurt, but I know it's there. It's painful to see her distressed, and I blame that all on Kaga. It seems that it wasn't so long ago I could coax her out of a pout with a trip to Dylan's Candy Bar or an ice cream in Bryant Park. That ship has sailed. Now she wants to have a relationship with one of my good friends, whose personal life is more fucked up than a Bravo reality-TV show. No, I don't want her involved in that. If that makes me an asshole older brother, then so be it. I've been called way worse for lesser infractions.

But I stay quiet as she gathers her composure and makes up her mind about my favor. "I'll do your little decorating project. I'll reserve my reward to be named later."

"Done," I agree with relief.

"So when does this need to be accomplished? What's my deadline?"

"Today."

"What?" she screeches. "I can't accomplish this today. Are you high?"

"I need it done today. Or at the latest, tomorrow morning." I pull a credit card out of my pocket and slide it across the table. "Whatever it costs."

"Who are you and what have you done with my brother? The last time we decorated this house, you wanted to buy everything used because you could not believe that a sofa could cost more than a couple grand."

"I still don't. I think that the furniture you made me buy was highway robbery. But I'm not asking you to buy furniture. I'm asking you to re-create a couple rooms." I pull up the pictures I've taken on my phone and show them to her.

"Did Barbie decorate this bedroom? I've never seen so much pink outside Victoria's Secret."

I shrug. I kind of liked it. It was different than anything I had and it fit her. It made me feel like . . . I was trespassing into something solely her own and making my own mark.

Sabrina sighs. "I'm going to assume you are redecorating for a woman and not a child. If you'd shown me this earlier, I would have scratched Snoopy off my list right away. She does not look like a woman who sleeps in a Disney princess bedroom."

"What is the kind of woman who sleeps in a Disney princess bedroom?" I ask, curious. Natalie's a grown woman who writes gritty science fiction novels and plays video games in her downtime.

"Someone who didn't get enough time to play with dolls as a kid."

I wonder if that's true. Maybe Oliver forced her to play catch with him. Whatever her reasoning was, it didn't bother me. My dick didn't get any less erect in her sweet-smelling bedroom filled with lace, pink, and ruffles. In fact, if this is what a Victoria's Secret store looked like, I'd have to stay away, because the association would get me instantly hard.

"I want to know more about this chick. You're going to spend thousands of dollars re-creating two rooms for her. I might only be twenty-two, but I'm not dumb. You want to bone this girl. The question is why you have to redecorate rooms that already exist in your own house just to have sex with her."

"Not that it's any of your business, but I don't have to do any of those things just to have sex with her."

"Oh." She nods knowingly. "You've already been in her pants and want to continue to do so. Got it."

"My *friend*"—I emphasize the word—"suffers from severe anxiety. She's living in a place that I don't think is very safe. There are threats against her life. I'd like her to come and live with us for a time. In order to make her comfortable, it makes sense to provide her with familiar surroundings."

Sabrina slaps the table. "Why didn't you just say so? Geez. Men."

I watch her pocket the credit card and stomp off. When she gets to the door, she stops. "I'm happy to spend your money and I'm happy to re-create this Barbie Dreamhouse on the third floor, but I'm not happy with your explanation. And I'm telling Mom," she ends ominously.

That went well.

CHAPTER NINETEEN

NATALIE

I wake up to an empty bed and a text message.

You were sleeping when I left. Text me or call me when you wake.

I reach over to feel the side of the bed that is as empty as it is cold. And there is no indentation, no sign that he spent even a minute in bed after we had sex.

I sit up and look around. There are pillows strewn everywhere and I'm not even under the sheets. Instead, Jake wrapped me up like a burrito.

I have a choice here. I can be hurt because he ran off like I was some one-night stand from a club or I can take it for face value—that we were two people who satisfied a sexual urge with no promises of commitment.

And we're more than two people. We're at least friends. The things we shared last night were too wonderful and too intimate to be the words of a smooth operator who wanted an easy lay.

He didn't leave me exposed, but covered up. Bundled into a cocoon of blankets. And even if I was some conquest, then so what? I opened the door last night. Well, technically Jake opened the door, but I unlocked it, and I didn't freak out when he came inside. That's a huge win.

So I'm not going to be upset that I woke up alone. I'm going to be happy that I was brave enough to have a new friend in my apartment and that I had amazing orgasms with a man, not a vibrator.

Speaking of my vibrator, I kick off the blankets and toddle into the living room. A quick perusal shows that Jake picked up in here a little bit. The pillows from the sofa are stacked, one on top of the other, and the vibe is resting on the coffee table. All of that is going to need to be cleaned. With sanitizer.

But as I stare at it, heat floods me as I remember how he wielded it. Like a pro, if there is such a thing. But if he's not going to be around to use it, then I'm definitely going to need batteries, although I doubt that a fully charged vibe is ever going to make me feel as good as Jake did.

"Hi, Jason. Did a package get delivered to me yesterday?"

"I'll go check, Ms. Graham."

I busy myself with breakfast while I wait.

"Yes, came late. Must be after I left or I would have brought it up for you."

Doubtful, I think, and rude to blame our night doorman. More likely it came during the day and Jason was just too lazy to bring it up, or at least figured that the crazy lady in apartment 3-D wouldn't notice. But who cares? Again, I'm not going to let these little pebbles in the bottom of my shoe ruin my day. There's a pain in my chest and yes, some regret that I woke up alone this morning. I mean, doesn't everyone like morning sex?

I slap the spoon on the counter and shake the granola into my bowl a little too frantically. Granola? This is a morning that calls for sugary cereal. I sweep the granola into the trash and pour a heaping serving of marshmallows and chocolate crunch cereal. Too bad I can't sweep my memories of Jake, damn him and his talented dick, into the trash with the granola.

I slam the cabinet door shut and shove a handful of cereal into my mouth.

A hot chocolate and two pounds of sugar later, I'm ready to tackle my manuscript, so that I can stop avoiding Daphne's increasingly frantic emails. I can see by a quick review of my inbox that she's reaching alarming stress levels. Her subject lines are now all caps and are using more exclamation points than should be allowed in any correspondence that doesn't have to do with the *New York Times* list or a movie option.

Jake's good loving along with my *mild* irritation at his absence spurs some creative organ in my lizard brain, and the words fall out of me. I can barely type fast enough to capture them all. I don't leave to eat, drink, or even pee. It's not until my stomach growls some five hours later that I look up from the screen.

My back and neck and shoulders protest when I push away from the keyboard. Sitting in one position is turning me into a hunchback. I'm going to have to use the treadmill desk for the rest of the day. In the kitchen, I hear the rhythmic bleat of my phone. Picking it up I see I've missed several text messages, but none of them are from Jake. "What the hell" leaps to mind, but I stamp it back down because I don't care. I. Don't. Care.

God, if I cared more, I might crush the phone in my hand, if that were possible. Taking a deep breath, I respond to Daphne's first, because I'm afraid if I don't respond I'm going to give her a coronary.

Me: I was writing. Am writing. You'll be happy.

Her response is immediate.

Her: I'm having a heart attack over here. The managing editor was in asking when I could expect the ms. I can't keep lying to him and telling him it's soon if it is not going to be soon. We can't move the publication date of this book. All the co-op is paid for. The bookstores are expecting it. (1/2)

(2/2) You'll be ruined if you miss the date.

Me: Thanks for the reminder. I know. I'm going to finish. I promise. I've never let you down and I won't start now.

I know she wants to write something further, so I block her, temporarily, so I won't have to see her constant admonishments. After I eat this sandwich I'm going to dive back into the cave and—

And there's a knock on the door. The phone rings at the same time and the face that pops up is Oliver.

"It's me, Oliver," he says from behind the door. "I'm alone," he adds.

I hesitate before walking to the door. Jake is absolutely right, I would feel more comfortable if there were cameras and I could see who is at the door without actually going up to it. As it is, because I can't see, I'm still nervous. Because it's Oliver I only have to give myself a five-minute pep talk to open the door as opposed to the usual ten- to fifteen-minute one that ends up with me walking into my bedroom and putting a pillow over my head.

"Sorry," I apologize as I let him in. "I think I'm still on edge from the clown."

"Don't apologize. I wouldn't want to open the door after that clown showed up in front of mine either." He gives me a one-armed hug and raises a deli bag. "I brought lunch."

"You are the best cousin ever."

"I'm your only cousin, Natalie." He places the bag on the counter while I get the plates. "I was coming home late last night and saw your lights on. I knocked and, well, I could tell you were busy."

My cheeks turn rosy as I guess at how he could tell I was occupied. "Was I really loud?"

He looks away. "I could, ah, tell you were enjoying yourself."

Now we're both blushing. I busy myself with rearranging the plates and forks.

"How much do you know about this guy?"

"A lot."

"Like what?"

How could I share with him the things that Jake had told me? They seemed too intimate and precious to be repeating. I might not know what his favorite food is or what he enjoys doing during his spare time, but I know that he knows what it's like to be afraid, to be different in ways that Oliver will never understand.

"Important stuff," I say to keep things vague. Oliver looks skeptical. "What does it matter?" I ask.

"He could be taking advantage of you. I'm happy that you're not alone, but we don't know this Jake guy." Oliver takes a huge bite of his sandwich.

"He must be decent, or why would you have hired him?"

"Hiring someone to investigate a potential problem isn't the same as knowing him enough to feel comfortable about him dating your cousin." The side of his mouth quirks up and a long crease appears. His fatal dimples don't have the same effect on me that they do on other females, though I'm not immune to the charm.

Reaching over, I squeeze his forearm. I've learned that his biceps have no squeezability. "You're the best and I'd say that if I had a dozen cousins." I take a bite of the ham sandwich he brought me. "But I think Jake is a good guy."

"If he is so decent, where is he now? Shouldn't he be here eating with you instead of me?"

It takes effort not to look toward the bedroom. "I don't ask a lot of questions about your personal life because it's none of my business, but also because you don't have the best relationship track record. And while you aren't as bad as the tabloids make you out to be, you are hardly an angel."

He scowls. "I don't have time for a real relationship right now. You know my focus is on winning. So I look for women who want the same thing. To sleep with a winner."

"God, Oliver, you are more than a football player."

He shrugs me off as if it is unimportant. "Look, I'm not going to be an asshole about it. Just know I'm concerned. Plus, if I need to beat his ass up, I will."

"Noted. Get out of here because I need to write. Daphne is telling me I'm going to put her in the hospital if I don't finish this book on time."

Oliver laughs and ruffles my hair as he leaves.

I check my phone one last time to see if Jake has left me any messages, but the only other ones there are unread texts from Oliver, which I mark as read since he's discharged his brotherly warning in person. After those are discarded, I'm left with an empty screen. Again I remind myself of my victories—allowing someone into my apartment who is not Oliver, Daphne, and Dr. Terrance, and having sex with a real live person for the first time in three years. And that the sex was amazing. Fantastic. Superb. Stuff worth writing about.

If he doesn't call again, then it's fine. I'll be fine. Sure, it will sting. All rejections sting, but the world won't end.

It's not a very convincing argument, but as it's the only one I have, I return to my office. At the very least, I can finish my book.

I close the door, place my headphones on once again, and shut out the rest of the world. The only thing that can exist for me for the rest of the day is this book.

CHAPTER TWENTY

JAKE

When Mike and Rondell, two of my employees who do surveillance work, arrive at three p.m. to start the evening monitoring shift, I give in to the impulse to call Natalie. I'd told myself that if she wanted to see me again, she'd call or text.

That she hadn't all day suggests that she is really pissed off. Generally, pissed-off women are not appeased over the telephone. But whenever I try to grab a moment for myself, work interrupts. We get a call from a West Coast security firm that we often partner with. One of their celebrity clients had decided to make a surprise trip across the country and needed immediate protection services.

Celebrity clients are my least favorite. They require the most work and generally have unreasonable expectations. Primarily because they want to be seen at all times, only they want to control who can see them and where. Whenever I receive a hassled call from LA, it renews my appreciation for my current circumstances. I prefer to make my living off of dull investigative work rather than fending off the paparazzi.

After I convinced one of my new recruits that celebrity work was the best kind of work available and that the hot young actress he'd be guarding would get him a lot of play with the ladies, I was summoned to an investment bank that believed one of their senior employees was embezzling money. Likely he was snorting it up his nose. There is a not-so-shockingly large number of drug-addicted investment bankers and hedge fund managers who have no problem dipping into client funds to support their habits. None of these guys will ever see a day in prison because their firms don't want to reveal anything is wrong in the company. Any dirt that gets stirred up behind the scenes needs to be swept away.

There was one particular hedge fund manager who even threatened to sue his employer for defamation if he wasn't given a good—no, strike that—great recommendation, even after he admitted to losing several hundred thousand dollars' worth of client funds.

I followed the senior partner around that afternoon to see if I could catch him scoring a hit or doing something that would at least give them grounds for termination, but when I hadn't come up with anything other than that he had bad taste in booze, I passed him off to Vic and her partner.

I was able to photograph the soon-to-be ex of one of my clients kissing his secretary outside of David Burke's restaurant on 67th Street. I hope that he enjoyed that kiss, because it was going to cost him about $5 million.

Smart prenuptials have infidelity clauses, and this one gave the wife money for any intimate physical contact including, but not limited to, hand-holding and kissing, as well as emotional infidelity. So naughty texts and pictures were out of the question. She had a good lawyer, but the husband had a lot of money and could afford to be kissing his secretary, I guess.

Sabrina once mentioned she thought that perhaps I have stayed single because I took too many pictures of adulterous couples. That's not accurate. I just figured these people had chosen wrong. If your home life is stale, seeking to spice it up with a third party would only be a temporary fix. At some point that third party would be just as uninteresting, and you would have to move on again. And at that point, you might as well just be single. Which is why I was single. I hadn't met a woman I could envision going home to every night.

Except that's kind of what I want to do right now. Go home to Natalie for a second night. Upstairs is my empty bed and my sister, who is interested in asking me more questions about Natalie or more questions about Kaga. I'm not interested in providing answers on either of those topics.

So it's either go upstairs and let Natalie's resentment, if there is any, fester overnight or call her and make my explanations and hope she accepts them.

"Any activity over in Tribeca?" I ask. If she had a problem, that will give me a legitimate excuse to go over there tonight.

"Nothing," Rondell answers. "It's been quiet all around."

Mike knocks his fist against the wood.

"That's good. That means we're doing our jobs," I say to the two annoyed-looking men. It's a hell of a lot more fun chasing bad guys than sifting through papers, spying on people, and watching security cameras.

"Since we're getting nowhere on the note and the clown, we probably need some eyes on her apartment," suggests Rondell.

"I'll get those set up. I installed the sensors last night, but I think we should do cameras over the doors of the elevator, her apartment, and the balcony. I asked the property management company for permission to install those, but they haven't gotten back to me yet. I think I'll go ahead and install the camera above her door. They can bitch me out later."

"You installed the sensors and you're going to install the camera?" Mike asks. His fist full of nuts stops halfway between the bag and his mouth. He and Rondell exchange looks.

"I can take care of that for you, man. No need for you to be doing stuff like that," he chirps.

From their shit-eating grins, I can tell that they've heard something about Natalie.

"Was it Sabrina?" Someone ratted me out.

Rondell shakes his head. "Nah. Vic put it together. She heard that you were going over to some client's house to do install work. Since when do you do install work? Plus she said that you went out with her man and had no interest in the floor shows. Want us to run a background check on your woman?"

"Rondell, I hope you're not telling your girls that you run background checks on them before you go out with them. That doesn't go over well with people."

"Oh," he says, nodding his head, "so you already ran the background report. Good on you. That's why you're the boss and we're the peons."

"Right, peons I pay a fortune to."

They both laugh at me as I leave. Her phone rings a half a dozen times and I get the voice-mail message each time. Worried that she hasn't answered my phone calls or responded to my text, I call Oliver.

"I'd like to come over and install cameras over her balcony doors and front door," I explain. "Building management hasn't given me the go-ahead to do it, but I figure it's better to have her safe, and we can always pay damages later. I have a tiny camera I can insert on the trim of the front door. It's not my preferred method. As I told Natalie, I prefer the visible cameras. That can provide just as much deterrence as anything. People tend not to do shit if they know they're being watched."

"You're coming back?" he asks, and his surprise irritates me.

It's a good thing we're not face-to-face, I decide. "Yes, I've always been planning on coming back."

"Don't hurt her again," he warns. "I can easily get someone else in here to do your job."

Again? Shit. I swallow my annoyance. "Look, Natalie's not answering her phone, and the sooner I get into her place, the safer she'll be."

"Maybe if you hadn't run off, you could've talked to her this morning about when the best time to install this stuff would have been."

I run my tongue over my bottom lip, tasting resentment and exasperation at this questioning, but he isn't wrong. I did bring this on myself, so I don't jump down his throat. "Last night was a mistake. I won't make it again." It's as much of an apology as he's going to get.

"She's been writing. When she's in the groove like that with a deadline, she doesn't answer phone calls, texts, or anything. Just puts her headphones on. You could probably meet me over here now and make the install. She wouldn't even notice. I'd feel better, and I think she would too, if she had the cameras up. She mentioned it today."

"I'll be over in fifty then."

I gather up the necessary equipment and drive over to Natalie's condo. There's parking right across the street from her place. I text Oliver before entering the building. He sends me a text back letting me know that I should head right up to Natalie's.

Jason, the day doorman, is bent over a magazine. He gives me a nod and doesn't ask for me to sign in. Either he remembers who I am, or he doesn't care. I suppose that he could know who I was based upon Oliver's instruction, but he doesn't give me even a cursory perusal. I'm going to need to move Natalie out of here soon. All a few cameras are going to do is tell me if she's being harassed, not prevent it from happening in the first place.

Graham meets me on the third floor. "How'd you get in here?"

"Your doorman waved me through."

"He what!" Oliver bellows in outrage. It isn't a question. "That fucking prick is done."

I don't know if he's referring to the building manager or the doorman. "You got a key or do you want me to pick the lock?"

The reference to the poor security on the doors garners another glower. He produces a key and pushes the door open. The condo looks empty, but after a moment I hear a faint *clack clack clack* coming from the bedroom that serves as Natalie's office.

"Just do your shit. She won't notice, and she doesn't want to be bothered," Oliver instructs. He stomps over to the living room and takes a seat on the sofa. The remote in hand, he starts flipping through the channels. It's early afternoon and the only thing on is talk shows and ESPN. While I drill holes into the door casing, he watches . . . *Ellen*.

"Didn't take you for an *Ellen* fan," I comment as I fish the wiring through the wall.

"You can only watch so much ESPN before it repeats itself, and I'd rather watch a couple of people be surprised with a free house than hear those asshole reporters who haven't ever played the game talk about how they would do it better." He gets up and strides to the refrigerator. "Want a drink?"

"Too early for me."

"Eh, Natalie doesn't have liquor in here. Only root beer. Pop is my weakness, so I keep it in Natalie's refrigerator. Once I retire, I'm going to be as big as a house. No more watching my weight, working out five hours a day. I'm going to plant my ass on the sofa and never get up."

"And watch *Ellen*?"

"And watch *Ellen*," he confirms.

He sinks deeper into the sofa as I drill into the wall. The audience cheers and music plays in the background while I snake wires through the drywall and screw the base of the camera into the wood frame. I'm hooking the camera wires to the interior power when the office door opens and Natalie shuffles out. She's wearing what looks like flannel pajama bottoms with penguins and a tight tank that stretches across her generous tits. From the way those babies bounce under the form-fitting knit, she's bare under that tank. My fingers itch to push the fabric up until I can press my face between the shadowed valley and lick my way from peak to peak.

It's not until she's at the kitchen counter that she notices she's not alone.

"Oh my God!" she yelps and the cup she had grabbed from the cupboard drops. Diving forward, I managed to catch the glass about an inch from the floor.

Her mouth opens again to scream—in fear or surprise—I'm not entirely certain. I push to my feet and pull her roughly against my chest. I can feel her body shake as I hold her.

Oliver is there too, his frame filling the small kitchen.

"Three's a crowd," I growl when he tries to reach for her. I sweep her into my arms and walk over to the sofa. "Get the door, will you?"

He makes some low, menacing sound as I pass, but I ignore it. I can feel Natalie's little bird heart fluttering wildly against me. I scared the shit out of her, or Oliver did, and I want to make it right. Oliver stands, hands on his hips, observing the whole scene with disgruntlement.

He doesn't like that his place as Natalie's protector has been supplanted. I suppose that's part of how I feel about Sabrina. Maybe I'll share that insight with him someday, but not unless he gets his ass out the door and leaves me alone with Natalie.

When I drop onto the sofa with Natalie curling into me, he finally throws up his hands and strides out. After the door closes, I place a finger under her chin. "You okay, sweetheart?"

"Wh-what are you doing here?" she says.

I can see her fighting for composure, and I pull her closer against my chest. "I was installing a camera above your door."

"How'd you get in?"

"Oliver. When I explained that I wanted to give you eyes in the hallway without you needing to open your door, he said he'd meet me here. Apparently you were writing and he didn't want to disturb you."

"I didn't realize building management would allow that," she says. Her voice is quiet but gaining strength.

I shrug and her body moves too, her lush tits rubbing against my chest. My cock stirs and I try to ignore it, although it isn't easy when her sweet curves are pressing against my lap. I shift her just slightly, so I'm not shoving my inappropriate boner up her ass. "Easier to ask for forgiveness than permission. I don't want you exposed while they dick around approving my request."

"You're serious about this place not being safe, aren't you?"

"As a heart attack. My offer is still open, you know."

"You were serious about that offer too?" She finally looks up and her red lips are slightly parted in astonishment. I really fucked up.

"I'm sorry I left you last night," I say.

"Yeah, it's not a big deal." She shrugs, but her downcast eyes tell me a different story.

"It'd be a big deal if I woke up and found you gone after I'd spent that kind of night with you."

"Then why did you leave?" She sits up and pushes herself away from me. Reluctantly I let her go.

Scrubbing a hand down my face, I rest my wrists against my knees and watch her as unobtrusively as possible as she sits beside me.

In my lap, I've got one hand made of flesh and blood. I can touch her and feel her response, the leap of her pulse, the goose pimpling of her skin, the tightening of her nipple when I palm her breast. My left is a tool that opens and closes. Whatever sensation I have there is pain for a limb that doesn't even exist.

In that moment, I know that before I never cared what other women thought of my new body, one both made by man and whatever higher being is in charge of creation, because I never really cared enough for those women. I enjoyed their company, their bodies. I enjoyed being wanted after those harrowing months of wondering whether I'd even be able to get an erection again.

I enjoyed the simple mechanics of fucking.

And I'd thought, vaguely, of having a family, a wife. But none of those thoughts had any substance, because I didn't care.

But with Natalie, I care. Maybe too much.

I raise my head and look straight into her gorgeous face and her big eyes and realize that I care so fucking much that she could destroy me.

That's really why I ran out last night—not because my leg fucking hurt. But because I was afraid.

And as my heart beats just a little faster and the moisture in my mouth dries up, I get a tiny inkling of what she feels on a regular basis.

Being afraid is a shitty way to live.

CHAPTER TWENTY-ONE

NATALIE

He stares at me with heavy-lidded eyes and I can't read a damn thing in them. I want him to tell me what it meant. No, I want him to tell me it meant something. I can't lie to myself anymore. Last night the earth moved for me. My little world got spun so far off its axis, he's set me on an entirely new rotation.

He's contemplating something, but I don't know what it is. Maybe I was like an ultimate warrior challenge. Find a housebound chick and see if you can make her have an orgasm without her ever seeing you. It's the "sit in" merit badge.

"Whatever you're thinking, stop," he says warningly.

Grumpily I fold my arms across my chest. "What is it that I'm supposedly thinking?"

"I don't know, but it's not good. Your brow"—he waves a finger across his forehead—"is fierce."

Fierce? He doesn't know fierce. I throw up my arms. "You acted like you were so hot to get in here, demanding me to call you and have dinner with you, and then after you *got some* you leave?"

He lifts his hands, spreading his right fingers wide and then his left ones. Today the left hand is black, made of some fucking cool metal. I want to touch it and see what it does.

"After I *got some*, my leg and arm fucking hurt and I was too vain to stay."

"You were too vain?" I echo. It doesn't compute with me.

"I needed to take my leg off."

"Then why didn't you take your leg off here?" I jerk my hand toward the bedroom. "I woke up and I was all alone and that hurt!"

"I know. Shit," he curses, as he shoves himself off the sofa and advances. I back up but the living room is small and there's no place for me to go. "I haven't slept—actually fallen asleep—with a woman since I was injured. I never took off my prosthetic. I've never been around anyone with just my stump."

He makes a sound, a cross between a sigh and a groan. "I never want you to hurt, not because of something I've done. I'm sorry. I didn't place your feelings first, but I promise that if you give me another chance, I'll never make that mistake again."

"Never?" I don't believe it.

"Never." The firmness of his voice leaves no room for uncertainty.

All those *never*s undo me. He cups my face with his right hand, covering my chin, and then drags his thumb across my cheek. His left hand hangs by his side as if he's afraid to touch me with it. It was the same last night. I had to pull his left hand to my breast.

It's hard to reconcile the image of an uncertain Jake with the tall, gorgeous man in front of me. The way his muscles ripple under the cotton of his T-shirt could fool a person into thinking all of him is that hard, but there's a part of him that's vulnerable and he's showing that part to me. I lift his left hand up to my mouth and press a kiss in it. It doesn't feel like his right hand, but it doesn't feel wrong either. It's just part of him, an amazing part.

His fingers curve around my cheek and hold me tenderly. I close my eyes as I lose myself in the embrace. I don't know if some stupid woman rejected him before, but if so, I need to send her a thank-you note, because he's mine now and I'm keeping him. All of him. The flesh parts, the plastic parts, the metal parts. The heart parts. It's all mine.

I raise my face and he bends immediately to fasten his mouth to mine. His tongue invades and his hands, both of them, hold me in place so he can ravish me. I grip his hard biceps and then when that isn't enough, I drag him closer by wrapping one of my legs around his hip. He drops his left hand to help me up and then presses us both against the wall. His thick erection presses against the seam of my thin flannel pajama bottoms and the friction makes me moan into his mouth.

He feels impossibly strong beneath my touch. I grapple with his shirt until it's out of my way and I can stroke my hands over his smooth muscular chest. I map out the ridges and the valleys, enjoying his hiss against my mouth as I scrape my nails over his nipples. I play with them until they, like mine, are hard and erect. Then I drop my hands lower to skate around the waistband of his jeans. He sucks in a breath and then releases it into my mouth.

His kiss becomes hard and fevered and I run my hands along both arms, enjoying the contrast of his warm skin and the cool metal.

His fingers find their way into my pajama bottoms and then into my panties. He strokes me with several fingers, spreading the moisture of my arousal.

"I need you right now." I dig my fingers into his shoulders and try to press closer to him.

"I can't really tell if you're ready." He slips two fingers inside me. The sensation is too good and I lose track of my complaint about the many pieces of clothing that separate us. I allow my head to fall back against the wall and he bends down to lick the pulse point on my neck. I jerk against him and he laughs. The low, throaty rumble vibrates against my frame.

Inside me, his fingers stroke me slowly, as if to tell me that we've got all day to wring out an orgasm. But I'm anxious and needy and want it now.

"I'm ready." I squirm against him to show him how ready I am, but he's working at his own pace, enjoying my immobility. He licks my neck again and then moves up to the sensitive hollow behind my lobe. He sucks the lobe into his mouth, nipping at it and then soothing the tender spot of flesh with his tongue. His mouth moves all over, slowly and leisurely learning all of the sensitive places around my neck and face. His lips never move lower, but I've never been more turned on.

My entire body aches with the need for friction and touch. I clutch him closer and ride his hand while rubbing my breasts against his chest.

Never once do I feel too heavy for him. The thrum of his heartbeat is steady against my chest. He holds me as if he could do this forever, keep me up against him with one hand while he strokes me with his other.

But I won't last forever. I hardly think I can last another minute. With each pass of his fingers and the thrust of the heel of his hand against my sex, I'm growing wetter and hotter. And then I can't hold on to reality one more second. My toes curl and my thighs tighten like a vise around his wrist. I muffle my cry against his shoulder and cling to him as the climax flashes through me from one end of my body to the other and then ricochets back again. Still he works me until I'm a sobbing, weak mess collapsed against him.

"*Shhh,*" he whispers into my ear. He swings me around, still with only one hand under my ass, the other cupping me. Effortlessly he walks me into the bedroom, where he deposits me on the bed.

I whimper in disappointment as we lose contact.

"Don't worry, sweet baby. I'm not done with you yet."

I rise unsteadily to my knees and reach over to unzip his jeans. It's a struggle because he's so hard and so big, but I manage to unfasten the denim without hurting him.

He watches me with glittering eyes—a dark promise there of more to come. I squeeze my legs tight again at the pulse of arousal.

"Are you getting wet again?" he asks.

I don't think I'm ever not wet with him. "I can't help it." I grin. "You're too hot. You should be dumpy and bald with bad habits like picking at your teeth or clipping your toenails while you eat."

"Clipping my what? Is that even a thing?"

"I don't know. It sounded gross when I thought it up."

He's quiet for a moment. "And you still wanted to have dinner with me."

"Yes!" I pluck at the waistband of his underwear, brushing the broad head of his shaft as I do so. "Yes, I wanted to and I want to again. And I want you to get in bed with me and cuddle. I told you I missed that and you said you wanted to do everything that I've missed."

"I did say that." The side of his mouth quirks up.

"Yes, you did."

"The stump isn't an attractive thing."

"It's part of you. You're hot. Ergo, your stumps are hot. Are we done with this conversation?"

He flashes a wicked grin. "Yes, we are done with this conversation. Help me take my shorts off, so I can show you exactly how done we are with talking."

I don't need another order. Or actually I don't mind the orders. And by the glint in his eyes, he knows it. I push down his shorts and then sit back on my knees to await the next instruction.

He takes his heavy erection in his hand and roughly pumps it. A pearl of milky white liquid appears on the tip, and my mouth waters. I lick my lips. I want that in my mouth.

"Get on your knees, sweetheart, and open your mouth. I want to feel your hot tongue around me."

Me too. I slide off the bed until I'm resting on my knees. Obediently I open my mouth and close my eyes. He slides his fingers, the special ones on his left side, tentatively into my hair. I lean into it, this new, wonderful caress. Embolden by my response, he tightens his fingers just slightly, as if he's flexing.

"Okay?" he says in a growl.

"Perfect." I reach up and grip the hand in my hair and squeeze. He's not supposed to feel it, but I think he does because he tenses and then breathes out a sound, half wounded animal, half sigh of relief. And then the tip of his shaft passes over my lips. Once, twice. I lick the salty trail left behind and open my mouth for more.

This time he gives it to me. As with everything today, though, it's slow. He inches inside me and then withdraws. I whimper when he does. I want to be filled up with him. I want to choke on his length and be surrounded by his scent, the thick taste of him on my tongue. "More."

He sweeps the hair out of my face and then holds it in a ponytail behind my head. He jerks my head back and thrusts in, not all the way but deep. Desire pools in me. I close my lips and suck hard, enjoying his gasp.

"Close," he mutters, pulling gently on my hair, but I refuse this order. I want him to come apart above me. I want to swallow him as he spends himself on my tongue. I *love* having him inside me. My resistance proves too much for him and he loses a little of his control.

His hips push forward as he fucks my mouth. I curl my tongue, making a bed for his shaft, and then suck as hard as I can, using my hand as a stop to prevent myself from choking on his thick, long length.

I take him in with unrestrained joy and he responds just as wildly, shoving at my mouth, gripping my hair. The pain and pleasure all blur into one until I feel him jerk in my mouth.

"Fuck," he cries. "So fucking good."

He comes with a low, harsh groan, and I swallow as much of the salty goodness as I can.

"Jesus, Natalie, Jesus," he says as he withdraws. "Your eyes are like stars right now. I'm going to fuck you again soon and I want you to look at me just like that."

He brushes the side of my mouth with his thumb. A little spot of his come rests on the tip. My tongue darts out to lap it up and he shuts his eyes, as if the sight is just too erotic for him to bear to watch.

His thumb tastes salty like his come, but earthier. Like everything else about him, I'm addicted.

He reaches down and lifts me up and then places me tenderly on the bed. And then he takes a seat and proceeds to remove his prosthetics, his actions unhurried and practiced. I don't offer to help, but I do rub the small of his back while I watch.

First his leg and then his arm. He has more limb left than I realized. His forearm ends about four inches from the wrist but most of it is covered in the sleeve that attaches to his device. The same with his leg. I don't find his stumps unattractive, as he warned. They are simply part of him, a part of the whole that I've fallen in love with. I move backward on the bed and raise the covers.

It's probably too early for bedtime, but I want to lie in here, inside the circle of his arms, and fall asleep with my head pressed against his chest. When he stands, I raise the covers and he climbs inside. He tucks his right arm under me and curls me against him.

"You're beautiful," I mumble against his chest.

"That's my line." His palm rubs against my back. I reach across and grip his elbow to draw his arm near me. I'm careful not to touch the lower limb until he gives me the green light, but I want him to know that I love every part of his body.

He resists at first and then allows me to pull his arm close. It rests on his chest and I fall asleep with one hand under his shoulder and the other holding his elbow. As I drift off, I realize that my hand has slipped down, farther down his forearm, but he doesn't move. Not even when I tighten my grip.

Good.

Because I'm not letting go.

CHAPTER TWENTY-TWO

JAKE

I rub her back until her breathing evens out and deepens. One of the skills they teach you in the army is how to fall sleep in a minute no matter what your circumstances. You learn to sleep in a ditch, on top of the crate boxes, or in a hellishly loud helicopter. If you don't rest while you can, you'll be too tired to function, and tired people are dead people. Of course you never get enough sleep, which is why everyone ate the instant coffee and popped Ephedra like it was candy.

So I know I could fall asleep even though it's early. But I don't want to.

Instead, I want to enjoy the feel of her lying next to me. Her head rests on my shoulder and her hand has slid from my elbow down over my forearm. I work it out daily and above the elbow, there's virtually no difference between my right and left side. Below, inside the sleeve, it narrows where the muscle has atrophied.

I've never touched a woman with my prosthetic off, never laid next to one like this, and until now, I didn't realize how much I missed it. The other night Natalie said she missed cuddling. I didn't miss cuddling, but there's an intimacy and closeness that I hadn't allowed myself to experience since being injured.

And because I didn't allow it, I didn't know what I was missing.

Until now.

I had told myself that I preferred sleeping alone, and maybe at the time I did because I never fully trusted any of those other women. It's possible I could have trusted them, that they would have responded like Natalie, but I didn't care enough to want to test that out. To expose myself to them.

Maybe I knew deep down I hadn't cared for them—hadn't felt for them what I feel for Natalie.

I peer down at her pale complexion. Her lips are bruised from our kissing. There's a smattering, a very small faint trail, of freckles right above the apple of each cheek. Her heavy breasts press against my side, and one smooth leg is hitched over mine.

I don't want to sleep with a moment like this to savor. When I close my eyes, I drift off into a somnolent state of peaceful awareness.

When she stirs an hour later, I watch her awaken. She does so slowly, first burrowing her head deeper into my chest. Her small hand opens and then closes on my pectoral. I flex in response.

Her knee slides up and down as if testing the texture of the hair on my leg. I remain still, allowing her to explore to her heart's content. Her touch soothes me in unexpected ways. And arouses me in all the obvious and expected ones.

"I'm glad you stayed," she murmurs with a soft smile. Her lashes flutter softly against her cheek as she blinks. She peers up at me with sleep-filled hazel eyes that are more gold than green tonight.

"I'm not going anywhere." Not anymore. "I should have given you more credit."

Dropping her head as if it's too heavy to hold up, she rubs her cheek against my shoulder. "Was it weird? Sleeping with me?"

"Nope. Was it weird seeing me without my prosthetics? I'm not much of a super soldier without them on."

Her hand on my chest traces a path down the center, bisecting my frame on half. My cock jumps in response but she doesn't touch it. Instead she scrapes a nail along my side and then up under my arm and down to my elbow, finger pausing as if seeking permission. I give a short nod and she continues.

The light touch makes me shiver.

"I love your body. Every inch of it. I look at your arm and leg and hurt for the pain you have suffered, but I'm so happy you're alive. None of the rest of it really seems important." She tilts her head up and smiles mischievously. "Besides, all the important parts are still here."

Her soft hand wraps around my shaft. My breath catches as she gently glides down to the root to cup my balls. I close my eyes to enjoy the sensation of her breath skating across my chest as she stokes my need. Her delicate fingers land on my thighs and hip, tangle into the short groomed nest of curls at the base of my shift. She smooths the liquid that forms at the tip down underneath the sensitive head and then over the heavy blood-infused staff.

"Come up here," I say gruffly, pulling at her hip.

She rises easily and elegantly from the covers and throws one leg over my chest. With my hand and forearm, I urge her up to my mouth. "Place your elbows against the wall and your knees next to my head and sit down."

My mouth waters in anticipation as she repositions herself until her juicy sex is hovering over my mouth. "Down," I order.

She lowers and the smell of her arousal, heat, and musk invades me. I flatten my tongue and sweep it along her folds. She cries out in surprise and then moans in delight. I suck gently at first until she starts pushing down, no orders needed. I circle her clit repeatedly, delivering small bites followed by licks and sucks until I feel her shaking above me.

"Oh Jake, please," she pleads. Her head is thrown back and the long bitable arch of her neck is exposed. I'm going to take her from behind with my hand on that column of flesh.

I reach over with my good hand and press against her clit, opening her with my fingers. She rides me, fucking my tongue. I've never been this turned on; my cock has never been this hard.

Yes, all those *nevers*.

I hold her to me until her thighs quiver and the release floods into my mouth. I stay there, devouring her until her cries of pleasure are just echoes.

"Jesus, Jake," she mumbles, sliding down in a sweaty heap on my chest. "Are you trying to kill me with orgasms?"

"I feel like there is no good answer to that question." Her soft body curled against mine and the taste of her heavy in my mouth does little to abate my erection. My dick is so hard I'm convinced it's poking holes through the sheets. I need her. "You up for a little more?"

She wiggles down until her wet sex hovers over the tip of my cock.

"Doesn't feel little to me," she jokes.

I reach between us and rub the engorged head between her swollen lips.

"Does it feel good, though?"

She sits up and straddles me, pushing the tip inside her hot depths. "So good."

"Condom?" I manage to squeeze out.

She bites her lip and pushes down. Her recent orgasm has made her passage wet but tight. It takes a superhuman effort not to surge into her. The sensation of my bare cock inside her hot pussy is eroding what little control I have around her.

"In a minute," she says. Her eyes are closed as if she, too, can't bear to leave me. She hasn't had sex in three years and I had a test after I broke it off with the journalist.

I plunge upward into the wet suck of her flesh and we both cry out. I hold her still with a hard, implacable grip on her hip. I could come right now. One more thrust and I will spill inside of her. I close my eyes and count to ten. Then to twenty. Finally I'm able to pull out.

"In my jeans," I pant. She bites her lower lip and then nods. Leaning over the bed, she fumbles for my jeans. My cock is red and angry and glistening with her juice. Soon.

Her shaky hands rip open the package and she smooths the latex over my cock. The touch nearly has me coming out of my skin, and then finally she's on top of me again. Her heavy breasts sway above me and her hands dig into my chest as she uses me for leverage.

I hang on because every movement, every tiny sound from her body, ratchets my desire so hot and hard, I could come any moment.

When she finally shakes and cries out her release in a long, tortured moan, I let myself go. With my hand digging into her hip to hold her in place, I slam into her over and over until I'm lost. Maybe I was lost the first time I saw her. I don't care. This is where I want to be. Where I'll always want to be.

◆ ◆ ◆

"I'm serious about having you move." I tell her as we eat a late dinner. I ordered out and Natalie stayed in the bedroom while it was delivered. I didn't bother with my prosthetics, and the most expression Natalie showed was surprise at how agile I was hopping around.

We are both ravenous and I'm glad I ordered more. "You don't have to be at my place." Lie. I wouldn't let her move anywhere else. "But I do think you should think about moving."

Her delicate but strong chin tightens visibly with unease. "I'm not opposed to what you're suggesting; I just don't know how I would get there."

I want to scoop her up and carry her away from all this. Her own time, I remind myself. "Oliver said that you've been sedated at certain times."

She gives a tense nod. "That's right. Dr. Terrance will give me a dosage for special occasions like when Oliver won the Super Bowl and his parents came to celebrate. They wanted me to come up to his apartment and, at the time, I had difficulty making the journey. Once I was in his apartment, it was fine but I don't think Dr. Terrance would support a move."

"I'm wondering if part of your fear has to do with the environment and that maybe if we could make your environment more secure, it would allow you to think about other things." At least she's thinking about it.

"Is it really unsafe here?"

"It really is. I didn't want to say anything before because I figured it would only add to your anxiety. Hell, even my heart races a little faster when I think about you here alone." Her small hand moves to stroke the left side of my chest and I squeeze her hand and then pull her tighter against me. The hard length of my erection responds to the soft press of her hip. When she cuddles closer, I figure I don't have to be concerned about moving it. I rub her back in long, slow motions to ease and distract her as I recite each one of her security problems.

She grows stiff as I run down my complaints, but I keep touching her, keep reminding her with my big body and presence that I'm here and she's safe. I whisper kisses across her cheek and forehead, nuzzling her as animals do in the wild, providing comfort to those in their pack that need it. She leans into my touch, needing it as much I need to give it.

"Would you let me worry about Dr. Terrance? If I can arrange it, would you consider it?"

"I don't know." She worries her lower lip between her teeth. "I'd rather just go into the bedroom and have you distract me with sex."

I cup her face tenderly and press a soft kiss to her temple. "You don't have to ask twice."

She races to the bedroom and is in bed before I make it to the doorway.

CHAPTER TWENTY-THREE

NATALIE

In the end the decision to move in with Jake is easy. I don't want to leave him and he doesn't think this place is safe. I can't think or function when I don't feel safe. Whether he intended it or not, my apartment is no longer the haven it once was.

But Jake offers me a different safe harbor and I want to try. For both of us.

In order to make the trip, I take my medication. Under the layer of drug-induced calmness, I feel my anxiety flutter its wings, like a butterfly trying to escape a net. He doesn't say a word when he arrives to pick me up, dressed in a sweater and the skirt he asked for. He only leads me down to the lobby and out the front door. I'm in the back of a car before I know it. Before the driver starts the car, Jake's mouth is on mine. Surprised and distracted, I lean into him.

He attacks me. His hands and mouth are all over me. The anxiety of being in a moving car is flush against the immediate arousal. Between my legs, I feel the smooth slide of his prosthetic. I widen my eyes and he laughs.

"You okay with this?"

I nod. It's a surprise. He's never touched me like this before. It's strange, erotic, and almost forbidden. It almost distracts me from my anxiety. He doesn't tell me to breathe or relax. He's jacking up my tension, but moving my focus from being afraid to being aroused. The shock of it works.

He doesn't do anything but cup me. His rough mouth and right hand are very busy, though. He places my lax hand against his hard denim-covered shaft. I squeeze it and he springs to life.

I don't even get the chance to undo his jeans as we come to a stop and he bustles me out of the car and up the stairs, faster than I can turn my head. The double doors of the vestibule slam shut behind us and then we're inside the foyer. His left hand is under my ass and his right is pulling down my pants.

Before I can take another breath, he's shoved his way inside me. The broad head of his staff thrusts deep. Each labored breath I take isn't because I'm scared but because I can't get enough. I can't get enough air. Enough feeling. Enough of him.

He slams me against the wall. The force of his thrusts shakes the table beside me. Pleasure grabs me by the throat and throws me down into a kaleidoscope of sensation. Somewhere I hear a cry followed by a low, raspy groan. He moves against me faster and harder until the coil of tension that wound itself inside me, worrying about how I was going to get here, breaks into a thousand tiny pieces and I fall, tumbling hard. I clutch him, gripping him as if he's the only safe port in a very real storm. And he catches me, whispering into my ear that he is there for me. Always.

"I've got you," he repeats over and over as I shudder from pleasure and something more.

He allows me to slide from his palms and drags his heavy, turgid shaft out of me.

"Did you come?" I ask, feeling stupid. I was so caught up in my own pleasure and inside my own head, I didn't pay attention.

He nods and presses a kiss against my sweaty forehead. He busies himself with the condom. I wonder when he put it on. I don't even remember. Before he came to pick me up? In the car? He's very good at distracting me.

"Welcome to my home," he says, and takes me by the hand.

He leads me from the entry hall into the living room. I think this is called the parlor floor, and the tastefully decorated room, consisting of two off-white sofas flanking a black iron and marble fireplace, overlooks the street.

"Here's the oatmeal and brown toast living room." He gestures into the room. I note the deep brown rug and splashes of yellow on the wall in the form of a painting. It's abstract and right now I can't really concentrate enough to figure out what it's supposed to be. Is it a horse? A cow?

Gently he leads me into the room, but I stop him to lean down and take my shoes off. I don't feel right walking on his acres of gleaming oak floors with my shoes. He doesn't stop me, because I know he wants me to be comfortable here. He told me to make it my home too, and I don't wear shoes in my home.

I allow him to lead me down the hall. "Bathroom." He flicks open a door, and I catch a glimpse of a small bathroom with white chest-high wainscoting. I nod to let him know I'm ready to move on. Across from the bathroom are stairs leading up and down.

"The kitchen is on this floor in the back. This place has five floors. The bottom two are my offices. There's a steel door between the offices and the living space. Only I know the code." He tugs on my hand and we walk down one flight. The door takes up almost the entire space, floor to ceiling. There is no knob. On the wall to the right is a square black pad and a visible camera.

"The camera is viewable upstairs. I installed a program on your laptop that allows you to receive the internal house feeds. There are sound and visuals on every entrance and opening in this place. Some clients like the cameras to be hidden, and in a retail setting that makes sense, but from a security standpoint it doesn't. The cameras tell anyone who comes here that we're watching them. Most folks will decide that they'll go two houses down or two houses up to a place that doesn't have such visible security. This door only opens with my biometric handscan." He places my hand on the door and nothing happens. Then he lifts his right palm and spreads his fingers. While I'm watching, he moves his fingers in a pattern, index finger down, pinkie to the right, thumb in the circle, and then the index finger twice more. I hear a buzz and click, and then the door slides open. We're standing behind Jake's desk.

"Shit, this is like a spy movie," I say. The door and opening mechanism is cool enough to shake me out of my post-orgasm, drug-induced stupor. He grins like a big boy with his fun toys and I can't help smiling back at him.

"Yup. You want to see?" He opens his hand in invitation. Do I want to go into his office? I do, but . . . his office is full of people and the door could open at any time. I can feel my heart start to beat a little faster and I step back up the stairs, one step and then two.

"Another time?" I say, but I'm really asking, *Is it okay if I just stay in this pretty house and never leave?*

"No problem." He swipes his fingers down and the door thuds shut. "Up the stairs and I'll show you the rest of this joint."

"The rest" consists of a big kitchen on the other side of the living room. We walk up a flight of stairs and when we stop on the landing, he directs me to the right. Although the shape of the room isn't the same—mine is basically a square, and the room here has a curved nook because the townhouse front has a sort of turret built into the side—I stare in amazement. The queen-sized bed—the same size as mine—is topped with pink and white pillows and a rose quilt, just like mine. There are several windows, but all are covered with shades that keep the light and street noise out. It's only bright in here due to the lamps and the crystal chandelier. I can't speak. I'm so overwhelmed.

Jake turns me away and then leads me down the hall into the other room, which has a fireplace and is set up to mimic my living room and office. It has a similar sectional and there's a corner desk. "I figured we could put your treadmill over in the other corner. I couldn't make it exactly the same without knocking stuff out, but I figured you'd like the wet bar here. I added a hot plate, a convection oven, and a microwave, and if you stay longer, we can have a full kitchen installed here. You don't have to go downstairs to the kitchen if you don't want to. Above you are two more bedrooms. One is my sister's. I'm going to introduce you to her later if you're okay with that. The top floor is my bedroom with an exercise space."

His hands are tucked into his pockets and he rocks slightly on one foot. It's as uncertain as I've ever seen him. He's nervous, nervous about making this perfect for me.

Even with the dullness of the diazepam, I'm overcome with emotion. My knees feel weak and I barely make it to the sofa before collapsing.

"It's so much, Jake." But I can tell he wanted to do this, so I don't make the mistake of telling him that he shouldn't have gone to such effort. I raise my arms to him. "Hold me," I ask. He drops down next to me and gathers me up. Into his neck, I whisper my paltry thanks: "You're never getting rid of me."

His hold tightens. "That's the idea."

I lick the salty skin on his neck and revel in the shudder it produces. "Take me into the bedroom and let's see how well your performance holds up."

He powers up to his feet with me in his arms and strides down the hall. "You're on my turf now. Let's see how *your* performance holds up."

The sad fact is I can't keep up with Jake, and after the second orgasm, I beg for him to get inside me and when he does, I nearly pass out with the pleasure.

He leaves me snuggled under the covers while he goes to use the bathroom. I'm getting used to having sex with him while he wears his pants. It's actually kind of deliciously sexy to be completely undressed while he's half clothed. It's as if we're doing something naughty and getting away with it.

"Okay if I go downstairs to work?"

I nod. "Okay if I lie like a slug in my bed and fantasize about you?"

He grins and bends down to stroke my face. "Write down a list of your fantasies and we'll check them off."

"How do you know that you'll want to do them? Maybe one of them is you wearing a French maid's costume."

"I look damned good in a skirt. It might be too much for you. Besides, we both know how that fantasy ends."

"How?" I raise a haughty eyebrow.

"With the feather duster up your ass and my cock in your pussy."

I squirm under his hot gaze. "I've never done that before. Maybe I won't like it."

His hand pulls down the covers to stroke between my legs. "Hmm," he muses. "You're getting turned on just by the mention of it." He slips a finger inside me. "Let's feel how wet you are." I leak all over his hand. With a low satisfied chuckle, he withdraws and then sticks his finger into his mouth and sucks as if he's trying to absorb every drop.

God!

I reach for him, but he shakes his head with regret. "Sorry, I really do have to go." He bends down to kiss me. I can taste a faint hint of myself on his tongue. "Later," he murmurs.

With that, he picks up his knit shirt and tugs it over his head and is gone.

Not removing his clothes does make it easier to fuck and go. I lie for a few more minutes in bed, making a mental checklist of fantasies before I force myself to get up. I spend more time exploring.

There's a completely empty walk-in closet and a bathroom with a shower/tub combo, a sink, and a toilet. The single window is again covered.

Out in the hall, I find two other doors. One is the entrance to the elevator and the other is a storage closet. I don't open either door.

Inside the office/living room, there's another set of shades covering doors that Jake had explained earlier led to a small balcony. I take a seat at the desk and click on the video feed program. Each feed is labeled and my computer screen is big enough that I can watch eight cameras at once. Jake's place has a lot of doors. The back cameras show the small courtyard where nothing is happening. The courtyard must be on the same level as Jake's office. The front door has two views, one of the stairs and one of the street.

I watch the street view for a long time. Cars pass by. A cab stops and drops off a passenger, and I tense but relax when I see the person go to the opposite side of the street. A black SUV pulls up and parks illegally. The driver, a big man with a shaved head, steps out and trots down the stairs. Hurriedly, I switch over to the camera marked "TSE," which I presume stands for Tanner Security Entrance. The man walks in without knocking. I don't hear a thing.

Jake was right that I wouldn't even know that there were people below unless I wanted to. Part of me wonders what it's like down there, but as more people arrive and leave, with me tensing each time, I'm glad I don't hear them. Eventually I have to turn away from the cameras.

I open my emails, which consist of a few fan queries that have been screened by Daphne's assistant and then two emails from Daphne. I don't read Daphne's emails. I know what they are going to say. I answer the sweet fan emails and then open my manuscript because Daphne's right. I won't have fan emails if I don't put out another book. And my amazing fans deserve more work than I have done.

I force myself to write and then, unlike before when I've taken diazepam, I find myself pouring out words, fun words, fun dialogue, an action scene. I barely notice when Jake checks on me later, inviting me down to dinner. I'm too engrossed to break away. When I finally look up from my screen, hours have passed and I'm both hungry and exhausted.

CHAPTER TWENTY-FOUR
NATALIE

The smell of coffee and fried batter lures me off the third floor, down the stairs to the bright kitchen with its huge marble counters. Off-white rustic cabinets run the entire length of one side of the long room, with a long counter space breaking up the storage on top and the bottom. In the middle is a center island large enough to hold five barstools. Across are more cabinets and all the fancy chrome appliances that a person would need and then some. At the back of the long slim room, a small nook overlooks the postage-stamp-sized backyard—which, by Manhattan standards, is actually sizable. Jake is ensconced in one of the chairs with the *Times* spread out in front of him and a plate empty of anything but a few traces of syrup.

A girl is standing in front of a large six-burner stovetop pouring batter into an ancient-looking cast iron pan, which is a perfect snapshot of the townhouse—a blend of new and old but all sturdy, workable items. She must be Sabrina. The similarity in their features is unmistakable.

There are no delicate vases or strange pieces of art that you often see in these more expensive townhouses. I've lived in New York for going on six years so I'm well aware of the price tag attached to a place like this. It is in the millions, could even be eight-figure millions.

Oliver and I came from a solid Midwestern background, and while we have both achieved some form of financial success, there is an air of almost disregarded wealth here, as if Jake and his family have been surrounded by this environment for generations.

Jake lifts his head from his paper. His super-soldier hearing, as I put it, must have alerted him to my arrival. He tilts his head in invitation and I trot over to his side without another thought.

"There you are," he says, stroking the back of my legging-clad thigh under the overlong T-shirt that I'm wearing. It's his. I found it folded on the top of the tufted dark brown leather chair situated in the corner of the room. It's mine now, but I haven't told him that yet. "Like your shirt."

I lift the collar to my nose and inhale Jake's scent—a mix of sandalwood aftershave, fresh soap, and clean sweat. My favorite new cologne. "It smells good too."

His full lips spread into a wide smile. He fists the shirt and drags me down for a long, wet kiss. It's almost too long and too wet to be having in front of his sister, but I've found I'm pretty much unable to resist anything Jake wants. Who am I fooling? I want this too. In fact, I'd like the hand that is now gripping the back of my thigh to be down my leggings. I break away from the kiss before I climb onto his lap and start grinding like a shameless wanton.

At least he's breathing a little heavily too. "Get some dinner," he says and squeezes me hard on the ass.

I wander over to Sabrina. She's taller than I had guessed from her picture, with a willowy body that probably makes everything she buys look amazing. She's the type who can literally wear a potato sack and still look elegant. Today she's chosen a pair of skinny jeans and a slouchy knit shirt. Her caramel brown hair is caught up in a high ponytail, and when she turns to greet me good morning, I almost stumble back at the beauty of her unusual blue-gray eyes.

She raises a perfectly shaped eyebrow and I give myself an internal slap on the face. Of course she's beautiful, because Jake is beautiful. Their beauty is different but still the same. They have the same high cheekbones, but where Jake's jaw is more chiseled, hers is softer. His eyes are a deeper blue and hers are light. But the slope of the cheeks and the full lips mark them clearly as related.

"Hi, I'm Sabrina." She holds out the hand that's not gripped around her spatula. "We're having breakfast for dinner. Is that okay?"

I wipe my sweaty hands on my pants, grateful that I've taken diazepam, otherwise I probably wouldn't be able to do this. Maybe I should be giving the drugs a little more credit.

"It smells amazing and who doesn't like breakfast?" A familiar uneasiness washes over me and this time my anxiety has nothing to do with my surroundings and everything to do with wanting Jake's little sister to like me.

"Exactly."

"Sorry I didn't come down earlier." I search for an adequate excuse. *I was busy having sex with your brother, and then I got caught up in writing, so in addition to my phobias, I'll never act like a normal person.*

She waves her spatula to indicate she didn't mind. "Jake told me you were going to be out of it. It's no big deal. Want a pancake?"

I nod enthusiastically and try not to panic about what Jake might have told his sister. *Oh by the way, I'm bringing a fruitcake to stay here. She might break down and start crying if the doorbell rings. Pay no attention to her.*

"Jake tells me you're at Columbia. What's your major?"

"Business." She sounds unenthused. "My mom was a lawyer and my dad was a banker. Megan, our sister, took the lawyer position and Jake was supposed to be the banker, except he joined the army. But he owns his own business, so it's all good now. So I guess I'm going into investment banking."

She sounds unenthused *and* resentful.

I glance over my shoulder at the table, where Jake's head is buried in the newspaper. His left hand is curled around a hot cup of coffee and I watch distractedly as the left arm moves up slowly to his mouth and then down again. I notice then that the markings of this prosthetic are different than he ordinarily wears. The fairings are a dark gray, and the area near the elbow bulges out.

"That's his DARPA arm," Sabrina informs me quietly when she notices where my attention is pinned. A quick twist of her wrist and three more perfectly shaped silver-dollar pancakes are poured into the cast iron pan. "It's more advanced, but it has a lot of bugs, so he wears it only at home where he can shut it down and change it out."

DARPA is the Defense Advanced Research Projects Agency. I remember doing research on robotics during my first series and coming across a lot of DARPA-related papers. They were mostly focused on creating super soldiers, but one step toward a super soldier was having amputees test out various devices. Jake would be the perfect subject. He's very fit and active. Plus if super soldiers looked like him, all they'd have to do to win would be send in a few advance scouts to ladies' night at the local bar. The women would fall in love and then fight to keep their new lovers in their beds—

"You're drooling."

Sabrina's whisper catches me off guard. Turning away from Jake, I wipe a hand across my mouth. Dry. I give her a mock scowl and she winks back at me.

"I never thought I'd say this, but it's nice to see you perving over my brother. Some girls are turned off."

"By what?" I can't imagine that there's anything about Jake that's objectionable. Although Sabrina has known him longer, so maybe she's privy to some terrible personality flaws. Lowering my voice, I say conspiratorially, "Does he squeeze the toothpaste from the middle of the tube? I would hate that."

She rolls her eyes. "Oh no, Jake is precise. He squeezes from the bottom and he'll go into your bathroom and straighten out your tube from time to time."

"Oh, so he is constantly invading your privacy?" I nod. "That would really be bothersome for me."

"No." She shakes her head. "He doesn't do that either. And he doesn't send people to follow me all over town or watch me, like his friend Ian does with his wife, Tiny." The side of her mouth quirks up as she flips the pancakes.

"Ian? Oh, Ian Kerr?" I'd read about him in the *Observer*. Everyone in the city knew who he was, and supposedly we were all supposed to mourn that he'd been taken off the market by some down-market girl who rode a bike for a living. I was more intrigued by his bike-messenger girlfriend, or wife, I guess, than I was by some Wall Street billionaire who bought and sold half the city. I didn't realize that Jake ran with that crowd. I wrinkle my nose.

"Don't worry. Ian's not like that. He's down to earth." She jerks her head at Jake. "He has a low tolerance for bullshit." Then she sighs. "All his friends are amazing."

The wistful tone makes me wonder which one of Jake's friends she has a crush on. I'll ask him later. For now, there's just something amazing in being able to sit down in a new place with a new person and not be totally freaked out.

I'm a little anxious. My heart rate is definitely up, and one loud noise may have me scurrying upstairs, but overall? I'm pretty damn jubilant.

◆ ◆ ◆

Life at Jake's is so much easier than I thought it would be. The house is bigger and while I don't go outside, ever, the different floors give me a sense of openness and freedom that I hadn't experienced before. I feel like I accomplish something by going from my set of rooms down to the kitchen and back up again.

Sabrina flits in and out, going to classes and coming home to study. The only downside is that they have a lot of people ring the doorbell. Most of the activity is downstairs, but Sabrina gets deliveries to the house regularly. I hide upstairs and watch the delivery trucks on the computer monitor Jake has set up, and I don't come out until they leave.

Other than that, the transition is a lot smoother than I imagined.

Four days after I've moved in, a blonde woman, slim and lovely, appears at the door. I take a break from writing and am sitting on the sofa contemplating my next scene when I hear the doorbell. From my vantage point, I watch as Sabrina goes to answer it. My office door is closed, but my heart picks up, just a bit.

Sabrina opens the door and allows the woman in. The woman gives her a warm embrace that Sabrina returns half-heartedly. They talk and Sabrina disappears. The woman removes her jacket and looks around. She smooths her hand over the iron-and-marble console table in the entryway and then moves toward the living room, out of view.

My breathing starts to escalate and I reach for my breathing bag, but my action is arrested when Jake shows up. I hear footsteps racing up the stairs and then a knock at my door.

"It's Sabrina, can I come in?" she asks.

"Yes, it's open," I answer, but I can't take my eyes off the camera. The woman, back in view, has her hand on Jake's right arm and she's standing really close to him. Too close for my comfort. She says something and strokes his arm. *That's my arm, bitch!*

"Who is it?" I ask sharply when Sabrina settles into my desk chair. She double clicks on the video feed and it fills the big monitor screen. I'm not sure I'm happy about this new, improved vision because I see now she's beautiful, and even in the grainy footage, her skin looks impeccable.

She has that very wealthy, very polished look of a woman who's successful and well off. Her jeans are skintight and her tight top is short enough that a flash of skin shows between the tops of her jeans and the bottom of her shirt. She takes another step closer to Jake.

"It's Laura," she answers, as if I know what that name means.

"Who's Laura?" I ask Sabrina.

"His ex. He was going to marry her before he joined the army and then broke it off. She got married, while he was deployed, to an old friend of his. Then like a few months ago, I heard she got divorced and was wondering if Jake was single. That's what Megan told me, at least."

"His ex?" The word tastes sour and bitter. "What do you think they're talking about?"

"She's probably wanting to know when she can get back into his pants and he's telling her to go away—I hope."

Me too, Sabrina.

The fear that's spiking in my blood isn't anxiety based.

It's that I just found Jake and I'm not prepared to lose him.

CHAPTER TWENTY-FIVE

JAKE

"Laura, this is a surprise." When Sabrina came downstairs to tell me I had a visitor, the name Laura didn't immediately ring any bells.

"Really? You told me that we needed to get together again sometime, and I was just in the neighborhood and thought I would stop by." She holds out her coat and I take it. In the neighborhood, I think dubiously. Laura lives on the East Side and I can't think of a thing that would bring her over here. It's not like she's taking the bus. I don't think Laura has ever put her ass on a public transport vehicle ever.

"Do you need some help?" I ask. "My offices are downstairs."

She laughs and presses a hand against my right arm. When she leans in, she looks like she wants a hug, or worse, a kiss. I step back slightly and turn to disguise the rebuff by draping her coat over the console table. She frowns and looks at the closet door.

Oh no, I'm not hanging her coat up. That would imply I wanted her to stay. Today's been a frustrating day—I'm not getting any closer to finding Natalie's tormenter. Whoever ordered the clown hasn't reused the email address, and the note is a dead end. Anyone could have written it, including myself or even, hell, Oliver. We've followed her ex-boyfriend around—the most boring asshole on the planet. He's not agoraphobic as far as we can tell; he just never leaves the house. He's glued to his gaming console. Two of her former coworkers are living overseas, another couple are in San Francisco. The others are living normal lives. No one appears to be a threat there. We've even investigated Oliver to see if there were any credible threats against him. Right now any connection to him is tenuous. The notes, the clown, are all personal to Natalie.

The bright side is that she and Sabrina are bonding and that she's happy here.

She's even been up to my bedroom. I used sex in the elevator to lure her upstairs and now she associates the small box with good things like pressing her face against the glass walls and both of us coming like freight trains.

I want to broach the idea of her meeting with Isaiah instead of Dr. Terrance, but I don't want to spring a hundred new things on her at once, or make her think that I feel she's defective and I'm trying to fix her.

The last thing I want to deal with is Laura, a woman I've seen once in about six years and thought of even less. Unfortunately for me, I'm going to have to deal with this myself instead of hiding behind Natalie.

"I'm here to see you, Jake," Laura trills. "Your place is lovely. Who decorated for you?"

While it'd be great to feign ignorance, her flirtatious smile and the touching are signals that are hard to miss. "My mom and sisters," I answer as repressively as possible and shift so her hand falls away.

Belatedly I realize that my answer implied I had no woman in my life. Her eyes light up and she advances into the living room. I have no choice but to follow. "Well, I might have used a little less of a lemon yellow accent, but it's still nice. Was it renovated when you bought it?"

I nod curtly, refusing to sit even as she settles into one of the brown leather chairs. "I'm working, Laura. If you need help with something, why don't we go down to my office?"

She shakes her head. "Surely you can take a coffee break. Or donuts? Cops like donuts, right?"

I sigh and scrub a hand down my face. Where's Sabrina? At least she could come and help me. "I'm not a cop. I run an investigative and personal protection service firm."

"That sounds naughty." She raises an eyebrow and licks the corner of her lip. Laura is attractive and I've had sex with her many times before, but none of her antics move me. But I cared for her once; hell, I might have even married her had my life not made such a dramatic turn, and I don't feel right about placing my boot in her ass and kicking her out.

On the other hand, it doesn't feel right having her in the same house as Natalie. I glance at the entry, where just a few days ago, I'd taken Natalie. I still feel the soreness in my abs from the long bout of predawn sex we'd had this morning.

I curl my fingers into my palm. No, it wasn't right that Laura was sitting here without Natalie knowing.

"I'm seeing someone," I say baldly. "My donut breaks are saved for her."

"Oh." Laura looks down at her hands and then at the fireplace. Anywhere but me. "When did this happen? Because when I saw you in Rockefeller Plaza, you implied you were single."

I didn't remember saying anything like that, yet it's possible I might have told her that I wasn't too busy to have a drink with her. I see now Laura took that to mean I was open to getting back together. "A few weeks ago."

"Then it can't be serious." She rises from the chair and sways over to me. I step aside, adroitly but obviously. A frown creases her forehead.

"It's serious."

"It can't be *that* serious. You said you just started seeing her a few weeks ago. Don't you remember what we had together?"

"It was a long time ago." *And I never asked you to marry me. It was just something that both our families thought would happen. I never needed you, not like I need Natalie*, I think.

"We have a long history and had some really good times, Jake. During my divorce I couldn't stop thinking about you. When I saw you at Rockefeller Plaza, I knew that we'd made a mistake all those years ago." She places her hand on my chest. Her eyes dart to my left side. "Even that doesn't bother me."

I raise my left hand and make a fist. "This? My stump or my prosthetic?"

She grimaces at the word. "I can get used to it."

I walk over to the entry and pick up her coat. "You're a nice woman, Laura, but so long as Natalie wants me, she's going to have me. Hell, even if she doesn't want me anymore, I'll probably spend the rest of my days trying to convince her to give me a second chance. There's nothing for you here."

Hurt mars her pretty face and I can see the spiteful words form before she opens her mouth. But then her good manners take over and she manages to sniff haughtily. "Your loss."

Silently I hand her the coat, which she practically rips out of my hands. She spins and jerks open the door and then runs out. Behind me I hear a shuffle on the stairs.

"You should go upstairs," Sabrina says.

I nod. "Thanks."

As I pass she says, "You made the right choice."

"There's no choice to be made," I tell her. "It's Natalie or no one for me."

"Same."

The one word strikes me hard. Does she really feel that way about Kaga? I push that worry aside and hurry up the stairs to reassure Natalie.

"Can I come in?"

Natalie turns away from her desk. The computer monitor that shows all the exterior feeds is asleep and her manuscript is up on the main screen. "How am I supposed to finish with all these interruptions," she teases while gesturing me forward.

"It's a conspiracy," I quip. "Did you see we had a visitor?"

"We?" she says with a raised eyebrow. "That lady looked like she was here to see one person only."

I pluck her from her chair and then sit down, settling her on my lap. Talking about exes necessitates a closeness. I want Natalie to know she's it for me, and I can't fully express that with her across the room. "That was Laura. I dated her when I was in college and then for a couple years after. I hadn't seen her once in eight years, and then about six months ago I ran into her at Rockefeller Plaza. She said we should get together and catch up and I told her to call me because it seemed like the social, polite thing to do. I put it out of my mind and didn't give it another thought."

"But because you took a long time she showed up at your doorstep."

"The hazards of working out of one's home, I suppose." She buries her nose in my neck. "We okay?"

"Yeah."

"Do I need to worry about your exes showing up?"

"No, Adam and I didn't have that kind of relationship, and in the end, he was mad that the game was taking so much flak and I was mad he didn't defend me more. I think we were glad to see the back of each other."

"Speaking of exes, did you have a chance to look through your emails?"

She stills in my embrace and then shudders. "I can't. Oliver told me I should go through my old emails, make a list of potential perps, but I can't, Jake. I just can't go through all the horrible stuff again. I'm afraid they'll eradicate every tiny little bit of progress I've made."

"All right. We'll work without it."

"Thank you." She snuggles in closer.

I tip her head up for a long kiss before I head back downstairs. We might not be married, but it feels like it. And it's not a bad feeling. Not at all.

I end up working late and Natalie is still in her office. Sabrina is gone, but there's pasta in the refrigerator. I reheat it and then head upstairs.

"You hungry?" I knock on the door.

She opens the door. "Sabrina fed me a few hours ago."

"Do you mind then?" I gesture toward the food. She shakes her head. "Mind coming upstairs?"

"No, I can do that. Can we ride the elevator?" Natalie believes the elevator inside the house is tremendous. After our sex ride, I'm beginning to agree with her.

"Yes, but I need to eat before I can service you."

She sticks out her tongue. I whip out my left arm and drag her to me, burying my nose in her neck as she squeals. It's a tremendous relief not to worry about which arm I'm using to touch her.

"Come on." I drag her into the waiting box and press the button. I shovel the pasta into my mouth as the elevator rises from the third floor to the fifth. She stays snuggled up to my side. "How's the writing going?"

"Good, I'm nearing the end. I can feel it. I think a couple more days and I will finally be able to answer Daphne's emails."

We walk out and my knee locks up. Stumbling, I drop the bowl and it crashes to the ground. "Fuck!"

Natalie grabs my arm to steady me, but my heavy weight nearly takes her to the ground. I shove her roughly away—too roughly. Cursing, I apologize. "Jesus, I'm sorry."

There's glass everywhere. The sauce has splashed the walls, the carpet, and me. The burn of humiliation crawls over my skin. Natalie tries to pick up the glass.

"Stop. Just stop," I snap.

She does immediately and scuttles back, looking hurt and concerned. *Fuck.*

It's the first time I haven't felt completely competent around her and it's pissing me off. I close my eyes and gather myself. "Sorry." It comes out grumbly so I try again. "I didn't want you to hurt yourself on the glass."

She swallows. "I just wanted to help."

"I know, sweetheart. I'm a fucking beast."

"You're not, but I know what it's like to not always be showing your best side."

I take a deep breath and then another. "I want you to think of me as a man."

"I do."

"A normal one."

"You are."

I wipe my hand across my mouth and start picking up glass.

She watches me for a few moments, and then says, "You know, Jake Tanner, you talk a good game."

"How's that?" After she gets to her feet and disappears inside the bathroom, I limp over to the dresser and pull out some T-shirts. I dump them on the floor to cover the mess. I'll get someone up here tomorrow to clean it up. The best I can do now is make sure Natalie's feet don't get cut.

"You tell me I'm fine when we both know I'm not, yet you have to be perfect at all times? Even if you had your two original limbs, you would trip and fall because you're human. I trip and fall. I drop things. It doesn't make me less of a woman. And, if you do think that flaws make you less than normal and not worth loving, then what am I?"

She dumps the towels at my feet and drops to her hands and knees to clean up the mess I made. Poleaxed by her comments, I don't try to stop her. I'd thought I'd made the big sacrifice by taking my prosthetics off in front of her, but I hadn't fully let my guard down. She wore her flaws on the outside, like me, but she'd accepted them and allowed herself to be loved.

So I owed her the same or I didn't deserve her. She's allowed me to see her at her most vulnerable and to help her. I can't turn her away now. I limp over to the bed and unfasten my jeans, pushing them down until the top of the compression sleeve shows.

"Will you help me?" I gesture toward my leg.

Her eyes widen and she nods. Halfway across the room, she turns back to look at the spill. "What about the mess?"

"Leave it for tomorrow. Someone will clean it up. Right now, I need you." I needed to hold her in my arms and reassure myself I haven't fucked it up too badly.

She kneels between my legs, looking like both a supplicant and aggressor. "What do I do?"

"There's a valve behind my knee. Turn it to the left. You'll hear the air displace and then the compression sleeve will loosen. Pull the sleeve down."

She does as I instruct, her hands all over my prosthetic. But she doesn't look revolted or, worse, turned on. The fetishists, the ones who get aroused by the amputations, the stumps, the devices, are worse than the ones who pity me. But there's none of that in Natalie's face. She's full of intense concentration as she twists and then sits back to wait for the vacuum seal to evaporate.

"This is really cool. I'm going to incorporate some of this in my next story."

She might be turned on a little, I guess, but just by the technology and the marvel of it all. Truth be told, it is cool and I'm glad that fascination is her response rather than revulsion. She pulls on the sleeve, her warm fingers a welcome touch. The sleeve goes nowhere.

"More force," I say wryly.

"I don't want to hurt you."

"You won't.

She reapplies herself to the task and as she pulls, her little tongue appears between her teeth. My body responds in predictable fashion.

"Does this feel good?" she asks in surprise. My newly formed hard-on is hard to miss.

"Nope, this is just the result of being near you."

This generates a smirk. She gives a hard jerk and the compression stocking gives way. When her hands pull down the inner lining and her knuckles brush against the tender skin, I shiver.

"Did *that* hurt?" She tosses the liner behind her and pulls my jeans all the way off and out of the way.

"No." It's my turn to laugh slightly. "It's sensitive."

"In a bad way or a good one?"

"Don't know."

She runs her hands down what's left of my calf and I flinch at the sensitivity.

"Too much?"

"A little," I admit. "I haven't had anyone but a medical professional touch me. It's not a very erotically charged situation."

She rubs her hand on my knee. "Maybe another time."

I don't say no. The sensation was strong and maybe if I had time to steel myself to it, it might end up being very arousing.

I hold out my arm and she stands between my legs and helps me off with the arm. She picks up both devices and takes them over to the chair. I watch her with bemused affection.

I could get used to this. It was a lot easier with her help than doing it by myself.

"You up for a shower?" I ask.

"Tonight?" she says, turning around and climbing on top of me. I steady her with my forearm and squeeze her plump ass with my right hand.

"The hot water can make it harder to get into the prosthetic in the morning."

She nods eagerly and we go into the bathroom. The shower has a wide marble bench for when I want to lie down during a steam. I place a couple of heavy towels on it and turn on the steam to warm up the enclosure.

Sitting down, I pat my lap.

She crawls on top of me. The rain head sprinkles hot water down on us and we make the sweetest, most tender love of my life.

I didn't know it could feel like this. I've come hard for her and wanted her more than anything, but this?

There's no describing it. There's her slick flesh rubbing against mine. Her bouncy tits squish against my chest as she rides me. I grip an ass cheek and hold her hip steady with my forearm.

The water sluices over us, a stream that we drink in as we kiss each other in deep open-mouthed caresses. She rocks against me and I swell inside her, getting harder and bigger with every thrust. We make love for an endless amount of time, until our skin is wrinkled and we are dizzy with pleasure.

With love.

"I love you," I whisper into her mouth.

Her breath catches and then releases on a half sigh, half sob. "I love you too, Jake. So much."

And then the words as much as anything drive us over the cliff.

CHAPTER TWENTY-SIX
NATALIE

Dr. Isaiah Crist is one of the most imposing men I've ever met. I fight not to cower under his dark stare. He doesn't intend to be intimidating, but he's got a command, a presence. Jake has something similar, but he wears it more casually—only occasionally trotting it out in the bedroom, to my eternal dirty-girl delight.

Crist's demeanor is familiar in the way he holds himself, slightly erect, slightly alert. It doesn't remind me of Dr. Terrance, though. I agreed to meet him at Jake's request. After all, Jake met with him, and frankly, I'm at the point where I'm willing to do most anything to be *better*. I do believe that Jake accepts me as is. The other night when he allowed me to help him off with the prosthetic, I felt like the tectonic plates had shifted and I was right where I needed to be.

But it isn't *enough*. I want to be able to go out with Jake, meet his friends, make new friends. I want to eat at a new restaurant and see a Broadway show.

So I said yes to Dr. Crist. I'd say yes to anything at this point.

As he greets me, I try hard to concentrate on the fact that I'm safe, that no one is going to hurt me, that no one would even be allowed into this house without Jake's say-so. I can't hide from the good doctor, and when he hands me a white paper bag, I take it gratefully.

Shoving it up to my mouth, I take one gulp and then two.

"Easy now," he says and I concentrate on slowing down and taking more measured breaths. He settles into the sofa across from me and sets his overcoat to the side. "I thought it might rain today," he says, tilting his head toward the coat. "I'm not a fan of umbrellas."

When I'm in control enough to set the bag aside, I share, "I saw this invention for a hover umbrella. It displaces water through air, so it's like holding a big hair dryer over your head, pointing to the sky."

He stares. "I think I'd rather get wet."

"You probably would if you used it on a windy day." When I go to fold the bag I notice it bears the words Dr. Isaiah Crist's Breathing Bags. "You have personalized barf bags?" I gawk.

He smiles, a big giant smile. His perfect teeth set against the dark skin are almost blindingly beautiful. I blink at the full force of his charm. "One of my men gave me that."

"Oh?" Then I realize that the familiarity stems from Jake. There's something vaguely soldierish about their bearing, I think. It's in the way they walk with precision and the watchfulness in their eyes. "Did you serve with Jake?"

"No, I predate him by a decade, but bless you for thinking I'm so young." He leans back and undoes another button on his vest. "Jake's a very special man. Have you talked about his service?"

I shake my head. "No, he's never seemed particularly interested in talking about it. I didn't want to press if there were bad memories."

"That sounds like Jake. He was a Ranger."

"A forest ranger?" I ask dumbly.

"No, an Army Ranger. An elite soldier. Only the very best are Rangers. He is one of those people who is deadly by just existing. You could not ask for a better protector. He is fierce with the ones he cares about."

The implication that I am one of those he cares about is not lost on me, and I feel a tingle of happiness that Jake's letting people know I'm important to him.

"He's pretty terrific," I answer with a bright smile, but my lips kind of sag when Dr. Isaiah doesn't return it.

"His business is very successful," Dr. Isaiah continues. "In fact, he's turning away business. He says he doesn't want to grow so big that he can't spend time with his family."

I can see that by saying that Jake is terrific, I've somehow misled Dr. Isaiah into believing that my feelings toward Jake are tepid, changeable things.

"I love Jake," I tell Dr. Isaiah. "I love him and I want to get better for him."

Dr. Isaiah shakes his head slowly. "Oh no, you cannot get better for him. You can only get better for yourself."

I rush to cover my mistake. "Obviously for me too."

"Jake will never make you happy if you're not already in that mental space. I've spoken with Dr. Terrance and he's explained many things to me, things I should have considered before agreeing to see you as a patient. Jake brought you from one cage to another. Dr. Terrance and I think you should return to your apartment. Restart your aversion therapy and then come back here. When you're ready to be a partner to Jake."

He cuts to the core of my fear with ease. Distressed, I drop my gaze to my lap. "Is this marriage therapy?"

"It can be. Do you know what your greatest fear is, Natalie?"

I swallow hard. I hate answering these questions. At least with Dr. Terrance I don't have to repeat these weaknesses. He already knows what a mess I am. Having to repeat that to a new person, even a therapist, makes me feel small and unworthy. "That I won't be better. That I will always be afraid of everything."

"But you aren't afraid of everything. You are afraid of *some* things. New people, new experiences, new places. All things you can't control, including love of another person, require the largest measure of trust, because you can never fully control another person, particularly not what they love or who."

His words are like stabbing knives and my breath catches and I can't swallow. I remember Laura coming to the door. I wonder about all the times Jake will be out on the town alone, or all the nights he will be forced to stay inside with me. I begin to choke on air. Dr. Isaiah grabs the barf bag and presses it against my mouth, commanding me to breathe. He counts as I gasp into the bag. His large hand slaps against his leg with each beat. My breaths come in short pants and I feel lightheaded.

"Stay with me, Natalie. In one, out two. In one, out two," he chants. "Listen to me."

I concentrate on the rhythm of his voice, the thud of his palm striking his thigh until my breathing regulates and I no longer feel like I'm either going to throw up or pass out or both. Even as he is counting, he reaches into his jacket pocket and hands me a large white handkerchief. I wipe my face, not even realizing I was crying. The tears come with big giant gulps. Dr. Isaiah moves next to me and places a comforting hand on my back as I sob out the grief over the loss of my parents, over the loss of my friends, over the loss of my career. I mourn it all and for a while, for a long while I fear I will never stop crying and that the ache of those losses will tear me apart.

I don't hear him come in and I don't feel the displacement of Dr. Isaiah's body, but when Jake's arms close around mine, I begin to feel that hollow place inside me knit together.

"Shhh, Natalie, I've got you, sweetheart. I'm here for you," he whispers into my hair. I feel the reassuring touch of his prosthetic, sturdy and capable against my cheek and then my head. I turn my face into it, so I can feel how Jake has made his losses into triumphs.

The door closes with a quiet click and then it is just Jake and me and my endless tears. He rocks me tenderly, his mouth finds mine, and the sweetness of his kiss fills me up.

Dr. Crist is right. My fear isn't of falling apart in public or being attacked. My fear is loss. And when my world spiraled out of control last year, I felt that all I'd achieved—my status, my friends, my freedom—had been taken from me and it was one loss too many.

And I know, oh God I know, that I can't depend on Jake to make me better, but I don't turn away from his caress. I drink it in. I allow him to press me against the cushions of the sofa or maybe I drag him down. I can't remember later. I only know that our clothes fall away and soon he's inside me, thick and long and full.

"Sweet darling, my sweetest darling," he whispers, smoothing my hair away from the sticky residue of tears on my face. He kisses my stained cheeks with exquisite care, all the while moving inside me in a slow and measured taking. He cherishes me with every touch and caress.

"Jake, oh Jake. I love you." I strain for him, rising to meet his downward thrusts, matching his rhythm with an ease that I've never felt before and I fear I'll never feel again. He digs his knee into the cushion and twists into me, striking me hard and making me gasp in need.

"Love you too." He shudders against me. He wraps me in his arms and this cone of protectiveness drops around me. In his arms, there's safety. I lace my fingers through his hair as he makes love to my mouth with his firm lips and his strong tongue. There's not a part of my body he's not touched with those lips or licked with that tongue.

These memories I've made with him will keep me warm for months to come. I'll get better, for myself and for Jake—if he'll still have me. But while I'm gone, I'll at least have this.

I curl into him. Wrapping my arms and legs around him, I ride the wave with him until we're both coming, a long, languorous orgasm that sweeps over us in wave after wave of pleasure. We hold fast while it buffets us and we're still together when breathless, it throws us ashore.

I love you, I whisper silently. *Love you. Love you. Always.*

I pretend to fall asleep and Jake quietly gets up. He goes to the bathroom and cleans himself and then readies a cloth for me. He's always taking care of me, Sabrina, his family. He loves us all so much. He gives of himself selflessly. And he deserves someone who can help him each day instead of add to his burden.

He slides the warm washcloth between my legs and wipes away his come. I want to cup his seed to my opening so that the sperm takes root in an egg. Then I wouldn't have to leave him. He wouldn't let me, and we'd be bound together forever. But that's so wrong that I only allow it to torment me for a moment before banishing the thought.

He leans over and kisses my temple and whispers something that I can't quite make out. I try to memorize every sensation so that later I can replay it, later when I'm back in my apartment retracing my steps from the door, to the elevator, to the lobby, to the subway. Until I can get on that train, I know I can't be with Jake. I won't be good enough for him and he'll realize that and it'll be one loss too many for me again.

◆ ◆ ◆

After I break down with Dr. Crist, Jake doesn't bring up any more visits with therapists, and I hide myself in my office, pouring out all the emotion inside me onto the page. I'm nearly done, only a chapter or maybe two to go.

There's a small knock on the open door. My heart rate spikes, but I remind myself that there is no harm here. The security cameras are up on the monitor and I notice one that says "office door." I click on it and it shows Sabrina.

The length that Jake has gone to ease the anxiety of moving into a new place is so enormous it is hard for me to wrap my head around it. And it just reminds me of how many sacrifices he's already made and how many he's going to have to continue to make and it makes me both angry and sad.

"Come in," I call. I rise out of my chair to greet her.

Her head pokes around the corner. "I hope you don't mind my

bothering you. It's almost lunchtime. I was going to make some soup. Would you be interested?"

At the mention of food my stomach conveniently growls.

I point to my stomach. "My stomach says, 'Yes please.'"

"I can bring it up here if you'd like."

"You definitely are not waiting on me. I'm coming downstairs."

We walk down the hall and I stop. Sabrina is halfway down the stairs before she realizes I'm not right behind her. She turns around with one hand on the balustrade. "Everything okay?"

"There's not anyone downstairs, right?"

"It's just you and me today. I think Jake had a meeting."

I concentrate on my breathing and count the steps. When I get to the second landing, I pause before turning toward the kitchen. Sabrina says nothing, but I know she's wondering what I'm doing. "Just having a moment," I laugh weakly.

"It really isn't a problem to bring you food," she assures me.

I give her a grateful smile. "A lot of my anxiety has to do with fear of the unknown. It's not rational, of course, but no phobias are, right? But I'm going to be fine. Let's go."

"I get you on the phobia thing. It's not like snakes and spiders are going to kill me, but I can't stand the idea of them around." She shrugs as if my anxiety keeping me housebound for over three years is no big deal. Either enlightenment runs in her family or I've been making too big a deal out of my own issues. Maybe it's both.

"Tell me what to do." I rub my hands against the cool marble counter. "I want to help."

"We're making potato soup, so if you want to cut up the carrots and potatoes, I'll get the rest of the stuff ready."

As I chop, she busies herself with broth and herbs and onions and ham. I nod my head toward the soup she's creating. "Have you thought about opening your own restaurant? You love to cook, and everything you make is delicious."

She hesitates. "No. I mean, I do love cooking, but this is a hobby. I want to DJ."

At first her words don't register. Is that even an actual job? Fortunately I don't say the words out loud. "Interesting. Have you done that?"

"I've been doing some clubs, mostly small ones and underground ones for raves that don't have licenses and stuff like that. I've done frat parties and other kinds of small house parties at college, but I've never done anything on the big stage."

"And you think that your parents won't be supportive?"

"I'm the youngest, so I don't know that they expect much out of me. But the last thing I want to do is disappoint anyone."

"Your family loves you, though, and they would want to see you happy."

"I guess."

Her solemn and unhappy response makes me wonder if there's more to the story. But I don't know her *that* well and I don't feel comfortable prying.

"Do you have a brother?" she asks.

"No, I have a cousin. Oliver. My parents died when I was five and his mother took me in and I was raised with him. He's two years older than me."

"Jake wasn't really around when I started dating and Megan says that he wasn't a jerk to her boyfriends. But ever since he's been out of the army, it's like because he doesn't have citizens to protect, he has to stand guard over me."

"He just loves you," I try to console her.

"Maybe, but I wish he would love me from farther away. Maybe I should move. You know the most popular DJ is from the Netherlands."

I shake my head; I did not know that. I don't know anything about DJs other than they play music and people dance to it.

"One of Jake's friends is Tadashubu Kaga. His family owns a big beverage company in Japan, but Kaga opens nightclubs all over the world.

He owns the Aquarium and 69. When the Aquarium opened, there were so many people you couldn't even see your own hand."

"Sounds interesting." Sounds horrible. I would never want to do that—go out to a club with a bunch of people where it's so crowded you can't even see your own hand. Sounds like my very worst nightmare. I have to clench my hands to keep from shuddering. "Tell me about DJing. I don't know much about it."

"It's not just about mixing music or even mixing beats. A good DJ understands her crowd and keeps the energy up until the last song is played. The DJ Kaga brought from Germany was amazing. This guy held the crowd in the palm of his hand. When he said jump, they all jumped. When he said get down, the whole crowd writhed on the floor. Celebrities, models, actresses, they all listened to him. A good DJ makes the crowd move their bodies, but also moves the heart. With every song he played, every beat he ground out, it was like a spell. They were his. For like five hours."

She sighs in memory of this amazing artist. Whatever she had seen had made a big impact on her. I didn't point out that she sounded a little Napoleonesque in her desire to rule everybody in her vicinity.

Before I can ask her any more questions, the doorbell rings. At the discordant sound, my hand jerks and I knock over a box of broth. Fortunately it wasn't open yet. I look at Sabrina with panicked eyes. Could I tell her not to answer the door?

"Why don't you go upstairs," she suggests.

I don't exactly run up the stairs, but I don't walk either. When I'm in the office I collapse on the sofa. Dr. Crist's magic bag is on the table and I grab it and start puffing into it.

There's a knock. "Hey, it's just me, Sabrina."

She waits for a response, but I can't give her one. I'm frozen in my chair staring at the door. My hands are clenched together between my thighs in an effort to stop the shaking.

"The package is for you."

"Sabrina, I'm sorry," I say. "I'm sorry I am so fucked up."

"Don't apologize," she says, her soft voice soothing through the door. "Do you want me to leave the box out here?"

I nod even though she can't see me, and I keep nodding and start counting. By the time I get to one hundred my heart rate has slowed. I'm able to open my eyes.

"Sabrina, are you still there?" It's been a while since I had a panic attack. I was settling in and my sudden outburst surprises me.

"Yes," she says brightly, apparently not at all concerned that I made her wait for a response for five minutes. I open the door to find her sitting on the floor with the box, a medium-sized one, beside her. I wonder if my old doorman forwarded this to me. She rises, easily and elegantly, to her feet and hands me the box. I carry it into the office and lay it on the coffee table in front of the sofa. The exterior of the box has my name on it and Jake's address.

"I wonder what it is?"

"You didn't order anything?"

"No. It's probably some gag gift from my cousin Oliver."

She makes a face. "What's he like?"

"Overprotective." We both laugh. "He's very sweet. But he's pretty focused on his career right now and that takes priority in his life."

I take a pair of scissors from my desk and cut open the top. It's taped tightly shut. Inside is a Styrofoam container almost like a cooler.

"Ohhh, this looks like dessert from Milk Bar," Sabrina coos. She bounces a little in her chair and I admit that I am excited. What a sweet, thoughtful gift.

When I pull off the top, a terrible stench rises. We both peer into the box and then scream. I shove the box away. Sabrina lunges for it.

"What is that?" she cries.

I don't know what it is, but I know what it means. It means that there is no safe place for me. I can feel myself shutting down into a huddle at the corner of the sofa. Wave after wave of panic hits me. I gasp for air, but my lungs have tightened and seized and every breath I take is painful. I stare at the box, not seeing the cardboard or the white foam lining but the red mass that lays inside. The acid bile in my stomach gurgles and burns a scorching path up my throat. I clench my teeth and try to swallow it back. The tears come, but I can't stop everything.

Distantly I can hear Sabrina talking, but I don't know if she's addressing me or someone else. It's too much. The sound of her voice, the scream, the stench of rotted flesh, and my own putrid fear.

I draw down into myself trying to make myself small and unseen. I tuck my head to my chest and roll my knees up and let the panic drown me.

CHAPTER TWENTY-SEVEN

JAKE

"Tell me what happened," I demand. Sabrina is shaking in anger and fear while Natalie is rocking in a near catatonic state in a corner of the couch. I raced up here, having heard the screams even downstairs in my office.

"A package was delivered," Sabrina repeats for the third time. She points to a cardboard box no bigger than a foot square. "Some guy in a white truck delivered this. She thought it might be a gift from Oliver. Who would do this?"

I pick up a pair of scissors discarded in the table and drag the flaps of the box downward. Inside is the body of a very small animal. Because it is so damaged it's difficult for me to discern exactly what kind. Dog, cat, a rabbit? It is vivisected, and some of the internal organs are pushed out. Sabrina is weeping and Kaga, who was in my office at the time discussing the background checks of his new employees, leads her away. I let them go. I don't have time now to be worried about the Kaga situation, because someone sent a dead animal to Natalie.

I approach her slowly. She doesn't move. She's somewhere lost in her own headspace. Bending down, I pick her up. Her limbs are clenched together and she doesn't loosen them even as I carry her to the bedroom. Holding her with my right hand so that I don't drop her, I grapple with the blankets, shoving them down awkwardly. I lower her gently and pull the covers over her. She doesn't move or speak. I only know that she's alive by the small rise and fall of her chest. Her skin feels cold and clammy to the touch.

I wonder about taking her upstairs to my room, but decide against it. When she wakes up she will want to be somewhere familiar. I'm not leaving her, so I text Kaga. He appears at the doorway about five minutes later. I can tell by the look on his face that he's annoyed at being dragged away from Sabrina.

"I left the office door open. Can you shut that for me? I don't want to leave her." I motion toward the bed.

"No problem."

"And send Mike up here. He's the tall blond. Looks like a Viking."

Kaga leaves and a few minutes later I hear Mike thundering up the stairs. Ordinarily I wouldn't have anyone in Natalie's space, but we need to be on this right away.

"This way," I tell him, intercepting him at the top of the stairs. In the office, I show him the box. "Someone delivered this today. I want you to find out who the deliverer was, where the carcass came from, who paid for it. I want this information within the hour. I don't care how many people you have to pull off existing jobs. This needs to be done now."

"Want me to call the police?"

"No, not until we know what we're going to find. Sometimes it's best if we take care of it ourselves."

He nods. The police knowing about this could be a hassle if I need to teach someone a lesson about messing with me and mine.

I dismiss him and return to the bedroom. The huddled shape underneath the covers has not changed. In the back of my head, I hear Oliver barking at me to call Natalie's therapist. I'm not doing it. She doesn't need sedation or therapy at this moment. She needs answers. I'm going to provide those to her. While we wait, though, I'm going to address her physical needs. Her body is going to be cramped and sore if she doesn't loosen her muscles. I start by pulling gently on her legs drawn tight to her chest. After a few tugs, they give way.

I start rubbing them to get the circulation going. Everything is tight; even her feet are curled. I press my thumbs into the soles of her feet until her toes straighten, and then move up to her calves and the muscular thighs. Beneath my hands, I can feel her relaxing, inch by slow inch. It's no hardship to touch her, but it breaks my heart that she's nearly comatose because her safe place—my safe place for her— has been desecrated.

Whoever did this is going to pay for a very long time.

I roll her onto her stomach and stroke my hands down her lovely skin. She sighs, a hiccupy, sad sound.

"*Shh*, I'm here. No one can hurt you now."

She seems to understand and better, even believe, as her body sinks into the mattress under my massage.

Mike comes up a half hour later, coughing slightly at the door. I cover her and walk out, shutting the door behind me.

"The delivery truck is from a private delivery service based out of Newark. Our security cameras picked up the license plate and had the background information already available. I talked to the driver, one Kelly Pierce. He is forty-two and has a drunk-and-disorderly charge from three years ago. Zachs is pulling the police report on that along with all his financials."

"What's the name of the delivery service?"

"The delivery service is Here Today, Gone Tomorrow. It delivers packages locally. This one was a fax order with a Western Union payment. They were directed to pick up a box from a pizzeria in the Financial District and then deliver it here."

"What does Western Union want from us in order to get their videotapes?" Western Union, like most cash exchange places, records every transaction.

"The manager said nothing without a warrant."

I rub my forehead. I do not want to get the police involved yet. "Is there anything that you have on the manager that you could use to leverage the information out of him?" Mike shakes his head. "We got nothing yet. Maybe in a day or two?"

I think quickly. Oliver would help even if it meant leaking the secret of his connection with Natalie. "Is he a Cobras fan?"

"Who isn't?" Mike says quizzically.

"Go to the pizzeria and see why they are in the business of dealing with dead pets. In the meantime, I'll go to Western Union. Which one?"

Mike gives me the address of one in Midtown on the East Side before he leaves. I find Kaga and Sabrina in the kitchen, looking slightly mussed and guilty, but I can't summon a give-a-damn.

I dump some milk in a pan. My mom made warm milk for me when I was a kid, and it always made me feel better. I'm at a loss as to what to do for Natalie. Sabrina comes over with a small bottle in her hand.

"Put a little almond extract in it."

I give her a tight smile, and she shakes two small drops into the pan.

"Is she going to be okay?"

"Yes. I don't know when or how, but I do know that she is strong. She's gone through a lot and made tremendous progress. Coming here, away from her home, was a lot to ask of her." My fist tightens around the handle of the pan, but there's no pain there. I turn to Kaga. He sees what I need immediately. I turn off the burner and pour the mixture into a mug, which I hand to Sabrina.

"Sabrina, why don't you go upstairs and sit with Natalie," he says.

"What are you two going to do?" she asks skeptically.

"I have some information that might be helpful to your brother."

We don't exchange a word as we walk into the cellar.

"Do you want to change?"

I look down at my jeans and T-shirt and shake my head.

"Very well, let's go."

In the cellar we enter a padded room the staff and I use to train. Kaga shrugs off his thousand-dollar suit coat and his expensive shirt. He slips off his shoes and crouches. It's not a fair fight. It wouldn't have been even if I had two regular legs and arms, because Kaga has been fighting since he could stand. I'm faster with a gun and probably better with a knife, but in hand-to-hand combat, there are few people who could ever beat him. Because of that, he is the perfect person for me to spar with. And I need pain and punishment before I can go back up and face Natalie. These are blows she should be landing; this is pain that she should inflict. Kaga does it for her. For forty-five minutes, he spins, strikes, and jabs.

And I take it because it's only a fraction of the suffering I deserve. Kaga calls a halt.

"We're not done yet," I snarl and spring forward.

He glides away. "Yes, we are. I have no intention of receiving another blow."

I notice with some grim satisfaction that I managed to land a punch on his upper cheek, which is bruising.

"Your sister will think that we've had yet another disagreement about her."

I pull my shirt off and wipe my sweaty face with it. "You know, Kaga, you're so hell-bent on having her. I'm not gonna stand in your way. But if you think for one minute she's going to accept the life that you can give her, then you're not as smart as I think you are." I shrug the shirt back on. "And if you hurt her, we're done. I will always choose my sister over you."

He nods his head, almost a bow, to acknowledge the rightness of my statement. Family honor means everything to Kaga, which is why he's in the bind he's in now.

"I vacillate back and forth," he admits, "between wanting everything and wanting just one thing."

"Make up your mind before you go ruining people's lives."

He takes the hit, absorbs it like none of the physical blows I was able to land. And I'm almost regretful, but this is my sister. And I fear that whatever future she might have with Kaga will be too painful for her big heart to endure.

Back in my office I exchange my sweaty clothes for clean ones and ask for another report, ready to go to Western Union.

"I offered a signed Cobras jersey and the owner coughed the information up immediately. One of the frequent customers of the pizzeria is Daphne Marshall. She's an editor at Brook Myles. There was a dog that ran out into the street and got hit by a car. It lay in the street for some time, so finally someone from the restaurant went and picked it up. They were going to throw it away, but Daphne objected. She said that the dog should have a funeral and that she would pay for it. She asked them to box it up in some dry ice and said that she would send a driver for it."

"Daphne Marshall?" I repeat dumbly.

"That's what they said. I ran some preliminary information. No criminal record, but she's in debt up to her earlobes. Credit cards maxed out and one month behind in her rent. She lives in a complex downtown."

"Shit, I thought for sure it was a dude," Zachs says.

"Thanks. I'll take it from here." I'm not sure how I'm going to break it to Natalie that the person who has been tormenting her for the last few weeks, who has been instrumental in destroying the progress that she's made in conquering her anxiety, is her closest friend and editor. I can't even fathom why.

Natalie has the answers, and she deserves to know what I've discovered. I don't even think she's ready to hear it. Knowing who the perpetrator is, though, makes it easy enough to shadow her to make sure no other harm comes to Natalie. "I want a tail on her twenty-four/seven. She doesn't take a shit without us knowing."

Mike nods and Zachs trails behind. "Are you sure it's not a guy?" he asks in disbelief. He had been so convinced it was a man. His notion of females as the weaker, milder gender is taking a blow.

I'd laugh if the situation weren't so fucking tragic.

With a heavy heart, I climb the stairs. In the bedroom, I find Natalie packing. Sabrina is gone and the almond milk lies untouched on the end table.

"What's going on?"

She draws in a shaky breath and then turns to me. "I should go home," she says. "I don't belong here. I've embarrassed myself enough. I called Dr. Terrance. He said to take two diazepam and go home."

"This is your home." I fold my arms across my chest and stand in the doorway, blocking her way.

"Then I called Dr. Crist and he told me the same thing. To go home."

"Your home is here," I repeat.

Her eyes fill with tears, but she swallows hard, fighting them back. "It's not."

I push away from the door so I can gather her into my arms. "Natalie, I love you. You love me. This is *your* home. I want you here with me."

Her lips tremble and her face scrunches up as she tries to keep the tears in her eyes from falling. "I'm embarrassed and ashamed and maybe I shouldn't feel that way, but I do. I want to be able to lick my wounds in peace."

"I'll leave then, just for tonight, but don't go." She's shaking and feels slight and frail. I don't want to let her go. Not now. Not ever. "Listen, sweetheart. I know who is doing this to you and I can make it stop."

"You can? You can magically make all my anxiety go away?" She twists out of my grip and zips her suitcase closed. "With your penis or what? You are so well adjusted. You've conquered all your demons and now go around saving others. Well, you can't save me. I'm a mess. I know this. But I just want to be a mess by myself."

The shame and anguish in her voice is killing me. "You don't have to go this alone."

"You know agoraphobia isn't fear of the outdoors or crowds. It's the fear of having a panic attack in public and not being able to do a damn thing about it. It's literally fear of fear itself. That's why even in my own home sometimes I have a hard time with change. When I first moved in, I stayed in the bedroom. Sometimes I slept in the bathroom because it was the smallest room in my house and I figured if I passed out, pissed myself, or vomited, I'd just have to reach up and turn the shower on. I can't do that here. There's too much space. It's just all too much. I can't stay here." She shuts her eyes and the water leaks out. I wipe her tears away with my thumbs and when I place my lips against hers and she opens in response, I feel like the crisis is momentarily averted. I taste salty tears and infuse as much love and tenderness into the kiss as possible.

I brush her hair back. "You're stronger than you know. This too shall pass."

It is the wrong thing to say. She gasps and breaks away. Bending down, she grabs her suitcase. It swings around and hits me in the knee joint and I fold, like a stupid house of cards.

"Fuck," I cry, sounding like a goddamned broken record.

"Oh my God," she cries and claps a hand over her mouth. "I'm so sorry. I—I have to go. I'm sorry."

She runs out and because of my stupid fucking prosthetic, I can't get up and chase after her. I crawl to the bed and pull myself up, and then limp downstairs only to see her run out the door. Adrenaline must be overcoming her fear. A car service is waiting. She dives into the backseat. I see her bending over, blowing into a paper bag as the car speeds away.

CHAPTER TWENTY-EIGHT
JAKE

"You bastard," I say, ripping the door open.

Isaiah is on his phone and he looks at me coolly as I charge in. "I have to go now," he speaks into the receiver, "an emergency has arisen. Here's Sarah. Make an appointment, first available free date."

"You're goddamned right this is an emergency," I snarl. "What the fuck did you say to Natalie today?"

I want to leap across the desk and strangle him.

"Have a seat, Jake." He gestures toward the chairs.

I plant my palms on his desk and lean over. "No, I won't fucking sit down. Now tell me what you said to make Natalie leave. I know you said something and I want to know what the fuck it was and how you're going to fix it." He stares at me. "Now," I roar and pound on the desk.

Isaiah jerks back and then rises. He waves to the person behind me. "No, Sarah, we are just fine. No need to call the cops."

"You don't know that," I fume. "I'm two seconds away from taking you down, no matter what our history."

He pinches the bridge of his nose in exasperation. "Now, son—"

I cut him off with a slash of my hand. "No, you don't get to 'son' me. I am not your patient. I am not in your platoon. You don't get to tell me what to do. You are going to sit down and you are going to listen good. You took something from me that was vital. You broke her, and you need to call her right now and fix it."

Hands spread, he shrugs helplessly. "That's just it, Jake, she is broken, but I can't fix her and neither can you. She has to get better on her own. I spoke with Dr. Terrance—"

"You did what?" I ask incredulously. "I came to you because I fucking trusted you, Isaiah. You knew I didn't like this guy and that I thought he did more harm than good."

"So are you."

I rear back as if he struck me. "What?"

"You aren't good for her either."

"What the hell are you talking about?"

Isaiah comes around his desk and stops a little too close to me for his own safety. My right hand curls into an involuntary fist and the left follows seconds after.

"You were enabling her. In your house, she didn't need to go anywhere. You saw to her every need."

"So what? She was having therapy. You yourself said she'd get better in her own time."

"She wanted to get better for you, not for herself."

"That's bullshit. She wanted to be better before I ever met her. She was outside her apartment and walking down the street, going to local cafés. Her progress and subsequent reversal had fuck-all to do with me."

He takes a step back and then another as I advance on him. "You're not a therapist, Jake. You were her lover."

"Am," I say stonily. "I *am* her lover. Will be. There will be no one else for her."

He shakes his head. "You'll never be happy if she's not sufficiently well."

"Fuck you, Isaiah. You don't know what makes me happy or what I need. As long as she was happy, that's what fucking mattered. When she was ready, she would have left the house. When she was fucking ready. You think taking her away from people who love her was really the best decision?"

"I do, yes," Isaiah says, with the pompous reassurance of a man who's fucked with one too many minds.

"If you weren't twenty years older than me, my fist would be in your face. Don't ever call me again, Isaiah. I don't want to have anything to do with you."

"Jake, wait," he calls.

I don't turn around or answer any of his pleas. That man is dead to me. I want to break something or someone, and if I stay another minute in his presence, I will lay him out. He messed with me; worse, he shit on Natalie. He'd said something to her, made her think she was weak and less-than.

Instead of building her up, he tore her down. Did no one recognize how strong she was? In her own time, my ass. Everyone was imposing a time line on Natalie that fit their idea of when she should be at what mental health marker.

Did I care that she didn't leave the townhouse? Fuck no. Did I care that she preferred to spend her time locked up in her two rooms on the third floor? Double fucking no. I care that she looks at me like I could lift the world on my shoulders. I care that when she smiles, my whole day gets better. I care that she's clever and talented and can think rings around me. I care about the sweet way she and Sabrina have bonded. I care that she loves me and that I love her. That she, in the noncorniest way, is my other half. Probably my better half.

At home, I find Sabrina in the kitchen. There are already two full boxes of cookies and from the looks of it, she's well on her way to a third one. She gives me a sad, trembly smile. "I thought I'd bake some cookies for her."

Folding Sabrina in my arms, I try to comfort one woman in my life. "I'm going after her. She'll be back here sooner rather than later. I have her treadmill desk. She loves that damn thing."

"Do you think she's all right?"

"She will be."

And I'll be there to hold her hand and celebrate every success, even if it's just answering the door.

CHAPTER TWENTY-NINE
NATALIE

Jake calls, but I can't bring myself to answer the phone. I huddle nude in the shower. I couldn't make it from the car into the building without vomiting. I had to lean over the planter and spew my guts into the soil in front of a bunch of strangers. Chris, the night doorman, held my hair and my suitcase and then helped me upstairs to my apartment.

I managed to get to the bathroom before losing whatever was left in my stomach. Shaking like a leaf, I stripped down and sat in the shower waiting for the hot water to warm me up. I'm sweating like I ran a marathon and I can't catch a full breath. When I break down into full-on ugly sobs in my apartment, there is no one to hear me but my walls.

I hear the phone ring, and I can see Jake's face smiling back at me. He let me take it one morning after he'd gone down on me. He had this intensely satisfied look, and I thought it was wonderfully perverse to take a picture of him right after he'd wiped his mouth with the back of his hand.

His smile was full of wicked intent and it thrilled me to look at it. Even as wretched as I feel now, I still can't prevent my body from reacting to that look and the memory behind it.

I close my eyes to shut him out. I can't bear to look at all that I've lost, at all that I could have if only I didn't let my fear rule my life. In such a short time, he'd come to mean so much, but God, I require so much work, so much sacrifice.

He turned his world upside down for me, re-creating my office and bedroom down to the last pink pillow. He set up eyes to the outside world to alleviate my anxiety. He showed never-ending patience. And what do I give him in return?

A freak show.

I can't allow him to make more sacrifices for me. I remember when Adam, my ex, broke it off, telling me how he was done explaining how I'd hidden away under the guise of someone else's name. He wanted me to go out and defend myself. I tried, but the deluge of abuse was too much for me.

I understood why Adam didn't want me anymore. I was too much trouble. Eventually Jake would feel that way and I can't bear for that to happen—to see the love in his eyes replaced with resentment. It's better this way, I think.

Eventually the hot water runs out and I am forced to leave the shower or turn into a Popsicle. The phone dings and a message from Oliver pops up.

Read your email. It's important.

With a trembling hand, I pick up the phone and open my emails. There's one from Oliver that I swipe on and I see immediately it's a forward from Jake. The contents send me reeling.

I don't want to believe a word of it. It's all so circumstantial. Roadkill, a restaurant, a delivery service. It doesn't compute. She's my friend, my only friend, and the betrayal strikes deep. I hate Terrance, but I love Daphne.

If it was Terrance, I'd believe it, but not Daphne. Never Daphne.

I delete the email and stumble toward the bed. I haven't changed the sheets and they smell like Jake, which makes me cry harder. The diazepam must not be working. The pain of emptiness and loss wracks me, and I feel worse, a hundred times worse, than when the only thing that surrounded me was fear.

I huddle under the blankets, wanting to rewind the clock, only I don't know when I'd stop. Do I go back to four weeks ago when I first met Jake? Or six weeks to the time I got the note? How about three years ago when the subway attack happened, or maybe all the way back to when my parents died?

Why did I come here? I can't remember. I don't feel safer. I don't feel better. I don't feel less shame or embarrassment. Instead I feel alone. So alone.

It's the unbearable emptiness that makes me take the phone call. It's the twelfth one.

"Why?" is the only thing I can think of to say when I answer the phone.

"Let me see you. Let me explain in person," she begs. Her voice is thick with emotion. Is she crying because she betrayed me or because she got caught? How does she even know? My guess is that Oliver or Jake called her to tell her to leave me alone.

"Why?" I repeat. I can't see her. I shouldn't want to talk to her, but she's someone I love and I have this need to hear her out.

"We needed another hit. You were way behind. These notes, the clown, spurred you like nothing else. I would have stopped them once the book was done."

"For the book? That's it? Because it's done. It was done this morning. I was going to email it to you." The manuscript that I finished after working all night and into the morning rests abandoned on the floor of the office at Jake's house. I wonder if it will ever see the light of day.

"What do you mean, that's it?" she cries. "That's everything! I did this for you! I would never have sent the dog if I'd had the manuscript. You were too busy with Jake." She says his name like he's the devil.

"No!" I sob. "No, you did this for yourself. You fucked with my head, Daphne. I trusted you and you—you did this horrible thing for your own gain. I don't want to talk to you ever again."

I move to hang up, but she yells out, "Stop."

"What is it?"

"The book? You said it's done? Can you send it to me?"

I shake my head in disbelief. "No." And then I end the call.

I drag the comforter and pillows into the bathroom, turn my phone off, and try to sleep, but my mind is racing. I want to call Daphne again and yell at her until she says she's sorry. I want to hurt her so she knows what it feels like. I close my eyes and envision kidnapping her and locking her in a box until she screams for release. But then somehow, it's not her in the box, but me. I'm the one screaming and afraid and no one is there to hear me.

I see Jake, but he can't hear me. I yell for him and slam my palms against the box, but the barrier is too thick and he walks by. I gag on my own saliva. Crawling to the sink I fumble in the drawer until I find my bottle of Restoril. It takes thirty minutes, but eventually I find peace in a drug-induced sleep.

I wake up with my face glued to the bathroom tile. The Jake-scented sheets cocoon me, and for a moment, in the dawn space between sleep and awareness, I feel him next to me. He's curved around me with his right arm under my cheek and his left arm resting on my waist. I have my legs tangled with his and my toes are pressed against his calf.

But then the smoke of sleep dissipates and I'm left with the cold tile and the sheets that are quickly losing his special scent. My body protests as I rise. In the mirror, a puffy-faced monster stares back at me. My hair is both knotted and limp, a spectacularly ugly nest. I had told Jake I wanted to fall apart alone, and here I am, more unraveled than a ball of used yarn.

My eyes are red and tired. Below my puffy eyelids, my cheeks look extra pale—nearly ghostlike. An insistent pounding sets in around my forehead. I swallow two aspirin before I leave the bathroom in search of clothes. Three antianxiety drugs yesterday, a sleeping pill and two aspirin before breakfast. I've become a regular pill popper.

I dig my laptop out of the suitcase that yesterday I tossed just inside the door on my way to the bathroom. I bypass the kitchen because the thought of food makes me ill. In my office, I take a seat and then power up the laptop. The room looks enormous and bare without my treadmill desk.

I ignore the new emails—all of them from Daphne—and dig out the deleted email. In plain and unmistakable detail, Jake spells out what he knows. That Daphne sent me a dog that was already dead to scare me into finishing my book. He believes she was responsible for the note and clown too. He ends the email saying that he loves me and that the third floor is waiting for my return. I get misty-eyed when I read that part.

I open the manuscript. The dedication reads:

To Daphne, a tough but necessary taskmaster. Without your encouragement, I would never have finished this book.

My finger hovers over the delete button. Is she right? That without the notes, the clown, I would never have finished? When I was achieving my biggest milestones—leaving the apartment, walking into a café, traveling all the way to the subway stop—I'd forgotten about the book. Or not forgotten about it, but it wasn't my priority. I'd done the three books in the trilogy. This was the start of something new, and I felt that I had time to pay attention to fixing myself rather than the words on the page, and so the book was pushed aside.

I'd been selfish, because Daphne had made me a commitment and needed me to fulfill my end of the bargain. But I'd ignored her pleas, too wrapped up in seeing how far I could push my phobias.

But then I remember the cold sweat and nausea that hounded me for days after the note came. I remember the sense of utter defeat when I couldn't bring myself to open the door. Her methods worked but at a great cost because once again, I'm a prisoner of my own making.

That's not entirely her fault, though she played a part in it. I press down and watch the letters disappear. The cursor blinks at me. I can't write what's in my heart, so I shove away from the computer and pace. The walls of the apartment feel confining rather than protective. I pull open the curtains of the French doors and look outside. There's a blue sports car and then a red one. And then a town car and then a taxi and then a black Audi and then a white delivery truck—my eyes swing back to the black Audi. It's hard to see inside the tinted windows, but I believe I see the shape of Jake's perfect head.

A knock at my door has me swinging around. My breath catches and then accelerates. Is it Jake? Daphne? Do I feel fear or anticipation? I rub my sweaty palms together and call out, "Who is it?"

"Dr. Terrance."

I drop my head into my heads and press the bridge of my nose between my two index fingers. The pain in my head doesn't go away. Neither does Dr. Terrance, judging by the repeated knocking on the door.

"Oliver is worried about you," he calls. "I promised I wouldn't leave until you opened the door."

"I can't open the door. I'm too sick," I lie. I probably could open the door, because I can see by Jake's security setup on my laptop that it is indeed Dr. Terrance alone and outside my door. But I don't want to. I want him to go away and let me wallow in my misery.

"I heard about Daphne. That's a difficult situation. I'm sure you feel betrayed."

I squeeze my entire head between my spread fingers, but Dr. Terrance's incessant knocking continues.

"Use the key," I finally call out. I know Oliver has given it to him.

The lock disengages and the knob turns. I slam the top of my laptop down and fold my arms, waiting for him to step inside and close the door.

"Your curtains are open. Are you feeling well enough for that?"

I glare at him in mulishness. I don't want him here. There's nothing he can do for me today.

"I see you're in a mood." He sets a small white bag on the table. If it was Jake bringing me this bag, I'd guess there was something flaky and delicious inside. Because it's Dr. Terrance, I'm certain it's drugs. He wanders into my office, where I'm sure he's counting the prescription bottles and the number of pills I have left. Predictably, he returns a short while later.

"I see you haven't been following my medication regimen."

"I believe at our last meeting you said that the drugs were 'as needed.'"

"And you believe you haven't needed them?" Skepticism abounds in his tone.

"I believe I took them when I needed them."

"*Hmmm*," he murmurs. He crosses one elegantly shod knee over the other. Dr. Terrance is a handsome older man and dresses well. I wondered at times in the past whether his success was largely reliant on his looks. He'd once lamented to me how he'd do well on television and thought we could work together in shining a new light on anxiety-based disorders. I said no. "It's unfortunate about Daphne. Were you able to finish your book?"

"Yes." I wonder how long it will take until he leaves, or rather how many questions I'll have to answer before he leaves.

"Really?" His eyebrows arch, just slightly. "When was it? After the dog was delivered or before?"

"Before," I say stonily.

He leans forward. "How fascinating. So the note and the clown were all you needed to push you forward? Tell me, how did it feel when you received the dog? I'll need to document this all for your charts."

"It didn't feel good."

He continues as if I hadn't said anything, or as if he can't hear me. "Daphne's methods, although unorthodox, worked. Interesting."

"Interesting? How is it interesting that my best friend royally screwed me over." Disgusted, I rise and pour myself a glass of water.

Dr. Terrance waves his hand as if to say "never mind." "It's an interesting data point to help me treat you better. The more information you provide to me, the better I am able to help you cope. Now why do you have a camera installed above your door?"

I hesitate because Jake told me to keep the details of my security in the apartment a secret. But since the danger is gone, what's the point?

"It's so I have eyes on the areas that I feel present the most danger to me. Jake thought if I could see what's going on outside my door, I'd feel better."

"Was he right?"

"Yes."

"Interesting," he muses. "Are there any other security precautions that Jake installed for you?"

I open my mouth to say yes, but then close it. He doesn't need to know. I need to keep some things private, and the night that Jake installed the sensors, the night I opened the door and let him in, is a memory I don't want to share.

Dr. Terrance senses that I've shut down and gets to his feet. He taps the white bag with his finger. "This is a prescription for a higher dose of your sleeping aid. Take it tonight and for the rest of the week. When you're better rested, we'll start therapy again. I'm confident that now you are no longer being targeted by an unscrupulous person, you'll be able to make great strides. But it all begins with rest. So take the prescription and help your body recover. Your mind will soon follow."

He leaves me with this sage advice.

There's a kernel of truth in his statements. The more tired I am, the more emotional I get. I stare at the white bag. If rest can help me get better faster, then that's what I should do. I should sleep, get rid of these headaches, and start therapy again.

Maybe if I can get better soon, Jake will still be available. I'd take a taxi to his apartment and stride up the stairs and knock confidently on his front door. When he opened the door in surprise, I'd invite him out on a date. We'd go to the local Chinese place with its wonderful, cheap food. We'd hold hands and walk along the Hudson as the joggers and tourists pass by.

I reach for the white bag and open it. Inside I find one pill bottle. "Take two," it states. I swallow them and go into the bedroom to start my recovery.

CHAPTER THIRTY

JAKE

The four days that have passed since Natalie left have not been good. I wake up every morning with an ache I can't massage away. It's not unlike a phantom pain—one that you feel but can't alleviate because the limb is just gone.

Today, I arrange things so that Mike will take all the reports and assignments and report to me on an hourly basis. I won't be in the office.

I make an appointment to see Daphne Marshall. I tell her assistant that I'm John Vinton, a former Army Ranger with two prosthetics. I'm interested in writing a memoir about my time during the war. I hear those are popular now.

The assistant couldn't book me an appointment fast enough.

Other than the glassed-in bookcases filled with the latest bestsellers and large pasteboards on the wall of book covers, I am hard-pressed to distinguish this sterile set of beige office walls from any other type of office. A slender, young woman about Sabrina's age arrives in the lobby. She's wearing a skinny skirt and a sweater with a big chunky necklace.

Her eyes discreetly take me in, pausing only seconds on my hand

and lingering on the jeans leg that hangs perfectly straight to the floor. There's no visible sign of my lower leg prosthetic with pants on.

"John Vinton?" she asks.

I hold out my right hand, which she takes without hesitation. "Yes, and you must be Katie Robinson." I smile and she blushes. Her hand clutches mine for a heartbeat too long and her appraising gaze returns to my chest and then my face. She likes what she sees and isn't shy about letting me know it.

"This way. Daphne and I talked about your project this morning. She's very interested in working with you. How old did you say you were?"

"Thirty-five." I hold the door open that she unlocks with her card access. "My girlfriend says I'm getting old."

"You don't look old. Maybe you need a younger girlfriend."

So much for my attempt to deter this young lady's flirtations. I give up and silently follow her down a long hallway until we get to a corner office. She knocks on the door. "Daphne, Mr. Vinton is here."

"Come in!" she calls.

Katie opens the door and positions herself so I have to brush by her in order to get into the office. Kids these days. Daphne rounds her desk and comes forward, holding both hands out in front of her to take mine. "Mr. Vinton, how nice of you to approach me. Come in and sit down. Can Katie get you anything to drink? Coffee, tea, water?"

"I'm fine, thank you." I move into the office, but I don't sit. Daphne has quite the view of Midtown from her corner office. Windows cover two of the four walls.

"Of course. You may go, Katie," she orders. Katie pauses and then reluctantly closes the door.

"Please sit." Daphne gestures. She, like Katie, is tall and slender. She's dressed in a black dress and thin stiletto heels that look like they could kill someone. I much prefer my penguin-pajama-wearing Natalie to this sleek machine.

"I think I'll stand."

"Oh?" She takes her seat behind the desk. "Because of your leg? Tell me more about your story. Will you write it or will you want a ghost-writer?" Her pen is poised to take notes.

"None of the above. I'm Jake Tanner of Tanner Securities. Oliver Graham hired me four weeks ago to discover who'd been stalking and harassing his cousin, Natalie."

The blood drains from Daphne's face as she makes the connection. I walk around her office, noting that Natalie's books are placed in a prominent position, but that those aren't the only books Daphne edits. "Do you terrorize all your authors or is Natalie a special case?"

"I terrorize them all. It's how I get the work out of them I do. If authors were left to their own devices, they would dawdle over one sentence a day. They need constant encouragement and motivation. I provide both." There's not an ounce of repentance or regret in her voice. It makes my job easier.

"The dog thing was inspired, but you couldn't secure the silence of the restaurant. Did you really think you were going to get away with it?"

"It was a minor miscalculation." The fingers around the pencil tighten. "There was every indication our transaction would be kept private."

"You should have slept with the owner instead of threatening him with exposure to the health department. Love makes you do things that fear won't or can't. Take Natalie, for example; she cared for you and worked tirelessly to finish her book because of that love. But you shit on that love and now you're not going to see a single word."

She snorts. "You've known her for how long? Please. Natalie will deliver that book to me. If not today then next week. She'll forgive me in the end because she knows I did this for her. Out of love."

"No, you're going to announce your retirement today, and your project will be passed on to another editor, one of Natalie's choosing. After you announce your retirement, you will go home and pack, and then you will get on a plane and fly to Columbia, Missouri, where your parents still live. If you make any attempt to contact Natalie, you will be brought up on embezzlement charges."

"What? What are you talking about? I'm not an embezzler! I don't even have access to financial accounts here!" she cries.

I look bemusedly at her. "Really? Because I'm fairly certain your bank account has at least four suspicious deposits from your employer. You should go and try to straighten that out before the information is turned over to the police."

"Did you plant this on me? Did you?" She screeches. She jumps to her feet and starts shoving things in a bag.

"Let's just say that building security in New York leaves a lot to be desired. If you were staying, I'd recommend that you look into a security firm to assess the safety and security of your building. And if you'd hired someone like me, I'd tell you that a person would be able to pass by the front-desk security under the guise of delivering flowers and that the two locks on your doors can be bypassed with a bump key and opened in under twenty seconds. Both locks. I'd also tell you that leaving your passwords taped to your desk under your keyboard is practically an invitation for hacking. I'd think it would be hard to get another job in this town with that kind of black mark on your record."

"Get out," she snarls as she runs by me.

"Don't forget," I call after her. "No contact, or the next person that walks through your door will be wearing a blue uniform."

She wrenches the door open and runs out. I follow at a sedate pace. Katie is standing beside her office cubicle with a confused look on her face.

"She forgot she left her iron on at home." I shrug. "Another time."

"Oh, okay. Do you want me to reschedule?"

"No, I've changed my mind. I don't think a memoir is in the cards for me."

I call Mike to let him know that Daphne has twenty-four hours to quit her job and get out of New York before we leak the information planted in her bank account. I climb into my car and drive to Tribeca.

I flash my lights at the car parked across the street from Natalie's building and Rondell pulls out, leaving me the empty parking space. I park, push back the seat, and pull out my laptop. For as long as it takes, this car will be my office.

Around four, Oliver exits the building and walks across the street toward the car. I get out, needing to stretch anyway.

"You planning on sitting here all day?" he asks.

"Yes."

"She got an email that Daphne quit her job. You have something to do with that?"

"Yes."

He nods with approval. "I'd been thinking of contacting her publisher and saying that I'd write a memoir for them if they'd fire her. What was your take?"

"Her bank records reveal several large financial transfers from her publisher into her private account. If she steps out of line, that information will be provided to the police."

He whistles. "That's better than my idea."

"It appears to be working. Although I don't mind if she sticks around, because her ass belongs in prison. I tried to make it easy on her for Natalie's sake." I tilt my head up to look at her third-story balcony.

"She's doing okay," Oliver says, answering my unspoken question. "She's hurting, but I think if you give her time . . ." He trails off.

"I'll wait for her as long as it takes."

He looks surprised, but pleased. "I don't know what that feels like."

"What?"

"To care about a person outside my family that strongly. Is it a good feeling?"

I rub a hand across my chest where the ache set in and hasn't left. Then I remember the short time we were together. The pleasure we had in bed and the time we spent out of it, just talking. "It's worth the pain," I finally say.

"Kind of like the game."

I nod in agreement and we stand in silence for a few minutes watching the balcony. He breaks the silence. "This is some kind of Romeo and Juliet shit, isn't it?"

"I hope not, since they ended up dead."

"Yeah, but Natalie's safe now. She'll come around." He doesn't say it with confidence, though. I don't care. I have enough confidence for the two of us. I have enough belief for everyone.

"I know."

"You going to sleep in the car tonight? You can come upstairs and stay at my place."

"She won't be able to see me then."

"You think she's watching?"

He stares up at the balcony again, where there's been no movement. "I know she is."

Oliver shakes his head. Whether in dismay or disbelief, I'm not sure. He slaps me on the back and jogs back inside.

At six that night, I text her.

Going home for the night. The car out here has two women—
Chloe and Elaine. They'll watch over you until the morning. I love you.

There's no response. Not an immediate one and not one when I get home.

There's not a response two hours later.

I break out the whiskey at the three-hour mark. Maybe I should have used a winky face.

Ian and Kaga arrive at ten. Sabrina must have called them. They step into the pink bedroom, where I've been sleeping since Natalie left.

"It's late," I note sourly.

"Heard you broke out the reserve. You can't drink that alone," Kaga protests. He settles into one of the two pink velvet chairs flanking the front window.

"Jesus. Did Barbie throw up in here?" Ian takes a seat in the other chair. "Why do these chairs have no arms? Where are you supposed to rest your elbows while you're drinking?"

I glare at both of them. "I haven't drunk enough to tolerate you two jackasses."

Ian shifts, uncomfortable in the armless chairs. "I can't get comfortable. Can we go to the den?"

"You can, but it's now Natalie's office."

"Fuck." He takes a glass of Kaga's special reserve and downs half of it. I tip my now-empty glass toward Kaga, who provides me a refill.

We sit silently staring at the liquor as if it holds the answers to the world's questions.

"Don't bite my head off," Ian says, "but Natalie sounds like a lot of work. She worth it?"

"Yes." I don't have to think twice about it.

"Okay." He accepts it without more interrogation. "What can I do to help?"

The chill that set in when Natalie left eases a bit. I've got good friends who'll help me drink my sorrows away and who'll open their wallets, if necessary. To show them how much I appreciate them both, I kick my legs out and lean back. "Armless chairs are good for fucking."

Ian leaps out of the chair, as if I told him there was a snake underneath. Kaga just smirks.

CHAPTER THIRTY-ONE

NATALIE

On the seventh day, my prescription runs out and I can't sleep. I toss and turn all night long. Worse, whenever I close my eyes, I see Jake. I see him standing above me, one hand gripped around his shaft and the other in my hair as he holds my head steady while he feeds me his big, swollen cock one delicious inch at a time. I see him underneath me and feel his muscles bunch and flex as I ride him. My body aches with the memory of him next to me, under me, over me, inside of me.

I pull out my phone and read his text messages and emails. My favorite is the winky face. No, my favorite is the one where he tells me that someday my fear will be the thing that keeps me sharp instead of making me bleed. I'm bleeding now because I don't have him next to me, holding me in his arms while we fall asleep. I don't have his sunny smiles to greet me every morning. I don't hear his deep laugh or the loving concern in his voice when he speaks of his sister.

Every day and every night that I look out of my balcony, the black Audi is there. I know that it's not him all the time. He texts me when he comes and goes. He has things to do, but he's always back. I wonder that he hasn't gotten a ticket yet, or a cop hasn't stopped to warn him that he can't sit outside the same apartment building for seven days straight. I guess he's right. The security in this neighborhood really does suck.

The nights with the sleeping pills are dreamless and I feel calmer than I have in a while. It's making me think more clearly. When I ran out of Jake's home, my mind was a whirlwind of competing emotions—fear, anger, sadness. I was already feeling the loss before I'd even walked out the door. Since then I've had time to think about being alone in this place that I've called home for the last three years.

It's no longer the haven that I once thought it was. I keep looking outside, but not because I'm wistfully longing to join the masses. Instead I look toward Jake, and all my reasons for leaving him seem hollow now.

Both Dr. Crist and Dr. Terrance are right. I can't get better for Jake. That's a fruitless goal. I have to get better for myself, but truly, that's always been my desire. I've wanted to get better so that I could live a fuller, richer life. But that full, rich life of going to museums and restaurants and movies and riding the subway isn't appealing if there's no Jake there.

In my office, I open my laptop. The large blank space under the centered all-caps word DEDICATION stares back at me. I deleted the dedication to Daphne. She doesn't deserve it. At this point, I don't know what she deserves. She never did me any physical harm. For anyone else, the pranks would be laughed off. I wish I could laugh it off, but it's more my problem than hers. I should have answered her emails instead of ignoring them. I should have been more open about how I was creatively depleted while I was trying to get better. But Daphne shouldn't have jumped off the deep end either.

We were both at fault, but that didn't mean I could forgive her, not yet.

But I need to forgive myself and accept myself for who and what I am. I'm full of anxiety and I will always be a little fearful. Right now, I prefer to stay inside my home. But this apartment isn't my home anymore.

After some time, I allow myself to write what's in my heart.

When I was lost, you found me.

When I needed safety, you protected me.

When I fell, you caught me.

When I needed time, you stopped the clocks.

Wait for me. I'm coming.

I take two of my diazepam. It's what I took when I left Jake's town-house, and I figure any larger a dose I may just pass out on the street. According to Jake's text, he had to go see a client, and Mike and Rondell are watching the condo. I wait until the car service pulls up, and then I start to count. It's ten steps to the entry and five more to the door. It's twenty steps from the door to the elevator. There are forty-seven steps from the elevator to the exterior doors. I don't look up. I keep counting.

My heart is racing and my palms are so sweaty I can barely keep a hold of my breathing bag. Once outside, I put it up to my mouth and start panting into it. The crinkle of the bag reassures me in the same way the counting does.

"You sick, lady?" the driver asks. I don't look up at his face. Sweat pours down my back and covers my forehead. Despite that I'm cold as ice. "I ain't an ambulance."

"No." I shake my head. "Allergies."

I don't give him time to refuse me. I climb into the back of the car and buckle my seatbelt. I throw two hundred-dollar bills over the seat. That's enough for the driver. I make it four blocks before I have him stop the car. I stumble out and retch on the sidewalk.

"Gross."

"That's disgusting."

"God, I thought these homeless people were supposed to be in shelters."

Behind me I hear the car squealing away. I crawl toward the side of the building and pull out my phone. My shaky hands prevent me from dialing so I use the voice command.

Thankfully it works and the phone starts ringing.

"Natalie, where are you?" he answers immediately, and I almost start sobbing in relief. "Mike and Rondell saw you leave, but lost you in traffic."

"I'm at . . ." I struggle to sit up and look around. "I'm at Leonard and Hudson, I think. On the east side of the street."

"Are you alone?"

A gurgly sob breaks loose. "I wish."

"I'm coming, sweetheart. I'm at Rector and Greenwich. I'm fifteen minutes, at the most. Stay strong."

I nod even though he can't see me and then bring the breathing bag up to my face again. Those fifteen minutes stretch like a canyon. I labor into the bag and count the seconds, literally.

A nudge against my foot causes me to look up. The silhouette of a beat cop is outlined by the sun. "You need to get up. There's no loitering."

I should say something and explain my predicament, but I'm afraid if I stop breathing into my bag, I'll barf all over this cop's shoes. That would probably get me arrested. My folded legs begin bouncing rapidly. He leans over me and grabs my arm. "I said move."

Dizzy and shivering violently, I allow him to push me down the sidewalk. I stumble and catch myself against another building. My legs are too weak to hold me up and I start to crumple again. The cop shouts something, and then I hear a screech of brakes and a slamming of a car door. Heavy footsteps pound toward me, but his uneven tread is something I recognize instinctively.

"Jake?" I mewl.

He reaches down and picks me up as if I'm a child weighing no more than an ounce or two. "I have her, officer, thank you."

"I'm going to have to take her in for questioning. She looks like she's on drugs."

I burrow into Jake and clutch him to me. I can't leave him.

"She's agoraphobic and is having a panic attack." I feel him shift under me. "Here's my card. You can follow me home and question her there."

"Oh, hey, sorry, man. Did you lose your arm in service?"

"Yeah, army. Ranger out of Fort Benning."

"Okay. Just take her away and make sure she's not wandering around by herself anymore."

"No problem, and thank you, officer."

Jake slides me into the back of the car and taps on the window. It takes off. He doesn't stop holding me. The whole way up Hudson, he strokes my back and whispers into my ear. The sixty blocks up Hudson to Jake's townhouse seems endless. I puke another time into the breathing bag. The sour smell of vomit fills the car, and a moment later, wind whips through the enclosed space as Jake and the driver lower the windows.

I sob into his chest, humiliated but weirdly happy. I couldn't make it back to Jake on my own, but I didn't have to. He met me more than halfway. His embrace feels strong and reassuring.

He carries me into the house, up the stairs to the third floor, and into my new bedroom. The shades are drawn and it's blessedly cool and dark. Jake lays me on the bed, and then hustles away. I hear the faucet in the bathroom turn on and off. When he returns he has a tall glass of water. I take it with shaking hands.

"What were you doing? Why didn't you call me?"

I look like shit. My nose is full of snot and my eyes are red from my crying. I can barely hold the glass in my hands. "I don't want to lose you," I say.

"You aren't going to lose me. I'm not going anywhere." He bends down to try to kiss me, but I avert my face.

"Don't kiss me. I puked a couple of times. I have vomit mouth."

He chuckles. "All right, but even your vomit mouth isn't going to turn me off."

He settles for kissing my forehead. He helps me off with my clothes and then takes off his own, including his prosthetics, and then climbs in bed with me. His body is so deliciously warm. I curl into it, seeking to draw as much heat from him as I can and absorb it into my own body.

When I inhale, I no longer smell the sour of my sickness but his warm, earthy male scent. The one that covered my sheets for too short a period. Behind me I can feel his arm moving up and down in long languid strokes. His hair-roughened limbs rub against mine. All the sources of friction are heating me from the inside. Instinctively, I shift toward him. He runs a hand along my thigh and then lifts it to drape over his hip. I'm open to him and he takes wonderful advantage. He licks his fingers and then spreads the moisture between my legs. One finger slides inside me.

"You're wet inside," he whispers into my ear.

I squirm, trying to get his finger deeper inside me. He obliges and thrusts another finger in, and the fullness of those two long digits makes me sigh with anticipation.

"Did you think about me while I was gone?" he asks.

"Every day." It is more of a question of when didn't I think of him.

"Did you use your vibe?"

I shake my head.

"Why not?"

"Because it wasn't you. It wasn't good without you."

"Poor baby. Seven days and no relief. You must be so hungry. Your sweet pussy is squeezing my fingers. I can't wait until my cock is inside you. My hand doesn't do it anymore either."

His filthy words have me writhing against his fingers. He drives me out of my mind with just a few more thrusts. Then he withdraws and I hear a crinkle of foil. Before I register what it is, he's back between my legs, spearing me with his big cock. I come immediately again. He's right. It's been so long and I'm so, so hungry for him. His hand comes between us to pinch my nipple and then he rolls me on my back so he can suck my nipple into his mouth as he works me with his shaft.

The double sensations have me arching off the covers.

"You taste so good," he says. "But I need more."

He withdraws completely and dives between my legs. The firm feel of his mouth curls my toes. I dig into the covers and push up to meet his mouth. He attacks me, devours me until the lightning strikes behind my eyelids. I feel like I come endlessly, like it's one big orgasmic wave after the other. He works his jaw against the tender skin of my thighs and his hard tongue stabs me repeatedly until I'm begging him to stop or for more. I don't know what I want.

He does, though. He rears up on his knees and roughly drags me down until my sex is kissing the tip of his cock.

"Watch," he says darkly. And I do.

I'm arrested by the sight of his thick ridged cock disappearing inside my body. He takes it so slow, moving tiny centimeter by tiny centimeter until he's fully seated inside me and his balls are pressing against my ass. He does this slow, torturous action three more times before he loses control and falls to his elbows. His body cages mine, and below me, he uses his knees to leverage inside, making sure he strokes every tissue and nerve inside my pussy. My legs bracket his hips and I dig my nails into his shoulders. We move as one, in perfect synchronicity, and the fire he'd started from the moment he climbed into bed roars to life again and consumes me. It burns up all the hurt, the acid, the loss until I'm a bright white light of pleasure and joy.

"I love you." It's a scream and a promise.

He thrusts inside of me and punctuates each stab with his return vow. "I love you. Always. Forever. Natalie. You're all that matters to me."

The raw and honest words dig into my heart and take root. Clenching him tight, I let go and allow him to catch me.

CHAPTER THIRTY-TWO

JAKE

If anyone asks, I will swear I saw a holy being as Natalie sucked me to the back of her throat. Later, after she brushes her teeth three times, she lets me kiss her, and after a week of deprivation, I can barely stand upright after our kiss. And that's not even because I'm without my fake leg.

The next morning we sleep in and then order breakfast to be delivered from a local deli.

"I'm going to restart therapy with Dr. Terrance," she tells me. I try to hide my frown behind a bite of my breakfast sandwich, but I'm not successful. "He was right last week, maybe not about leaving, but he gave me a one-week supply of sleeping pills, telling me my mind and body needed to rest. I wasn't thinking straight with the stress of finishing the book and living in a new place."

"And having someone intentionally fuck with your mind," I finish for her.

She shoots me a wry look. "That too. But after a week of sleep, I was able to think more clearly, and it brought me back to you."

I capture her hand and press a kiss against it. "I'm here to support you, not tell you what to do."

"I know. I love that." She rubs her head against my shoulder, the long strands tickling my skin.

Abruptly I shove aside breakfast and push her against the covers. "Breakfast is over."

She laughs and spreads her arms wide. "I'm down with that."

Later she tests my ability to sit back and allow her to do her own thing. A frown settles in as she sorts through her manuscript.

"Have you chosen a new editor?" I ask.

She shrugs. "Not yet. When you have an editor that you . . . love, it's more than a business relationship. It's a true meeting of the minds. I guess that's how Daphne was so effective." She gives me a wincing smile. "She knew me like no one else."

"Have you answered any of her emails or texts?" Daphne has been trying to open a line of communication but so far, Natalie has resisted. I wish she'd block Daphne.

"No. I'm not ready. I may never be ready."

I have no sympathy for Daphne. "You don't get extra life points for forgiving someone who dicked you over."

This time when she smiles, it's without as much pain. "I know. It's hard, and I really, really appreciate you allowing me to deal with this in my own way."

"I'm a prince." I wink. "Since I'm not hassling you about Daphne, will you let me go over and get your stuff?"

She wants her laptop and suitcase full of things she took with her when she left, including, she says in a ploy to get me to agree, my favorite pair of underwear. It's pink with white lace and bows and it's tremendously naughty, and I don't really want to explore what about that schoolgirl look turns me on.

"No, I want to come."

I nearly bite my tongue off to avoid reminding her of what a mess she was yesterday. "Fine, but we're going to have a driver and you're going to sit on me while we're in the car."

"Ooh, let me think about that very hard decision. Um, okay, yes."

In the end, I just finger her while she gives me a hand job. Unfortunately I don't come and I have an erection that makes it difficult to walk when the car stops outside her Tribeca condo. She's in a better state than I am in. We kiss fiercely on the way up to the third floor, which does nothing to abate my hard-on. Only the phone call I get does that.

"Go ahead and answer that while I pack," she says as my phone rings.

It's Mike.

"I was closing up the file on Natalie when I noticed that there was a message left by the Western Union owner. I called him up and he said that all he was willing to tell me was that the person who paid was not a woman, but an older, well-dressed man. He thought he was in his late fifties, but that the man colored his hair because his eyebrows were graying."

"So, a second person?"

"Sounds like it."

"Do you think this guy would be willing to look at pictures?"

"You know who it is?"

"I have an idea."

"It's worth a shot."

I hang up and find Natalie in the bedroom. She's changing into my favorite panties. I lick my lips.

"What's up?"

Me, I think. But business before pleasure, especially when that business is Natalie's safety. "Mike was closing your case and found a weird anomaly. Apparently the Western Union clerk said the person who paid for the delivery truck was not a woman. I want to go down there and talk to them. Maybe Daphne had someone working with her. Will you be okay here? I'll be an hour, two if traffic is bad."

"I'll be fine. I have my laptop and can do some work."

"Good." I kiss her on the forehead. "Call me if you need something, anything."

"I will." She makes a shooing gesture with her hands.

I don't wait for the elevator and am grateful for the car service. I won't waste time finding a parking space. I bark out the address and the driver pulls away. In the car, I pull up Dr. Terrance's website and find a picture of him. Late fifties, colored hair, and gray eyebrows all fit.

After a meeting with the Western Union manager, I confirm that the person who placed the order was Dr. Terrance. Son of a bitch.

I look at my watch. I've only been gone for forty-five minutes. Dr. Terrance's office is on Madison Avenue and in the midday traffic, it shouldn't take more than twenty minutes to get there. I make a snap judgment to go confront him. This time, I'm not allowing him to leave the city. This man is going down. I'm going to ruin him.

When I arrive at the address, I let myself into the building. His office is on the second floor. I make a show of limping and place my left prosthetic on the lobby table. "I'm here to see Dr. Terrance."

"Sure. Just a minute." The guard makes a phone call. "No one is answering the phone, sir."

"He's there," I protest, acting as if not seeing my therapist is an affront. "I just called."

I grimace and rub the substitute arm as if I'm in a great deal of pain. The security man waffles and then says, "Okay, sign in, though."

I do and then I slowly make my way to the elevator, pretending to drag my leg behind me. I step out on the second floor and continue the charade until I get to Terrance's office. It does look like it's locked up and closed. No matter. His locks are better than those on Natalie's door or Daphne's door, but all locks are vulnerable. I shove the door open and a security alarm blinks. I wave at the camera in front of the door.

I could care two shits about him knowing I broke in here. I want him to feel vulnerable and afraid. I bypass his secretary's desk and open his office door. It's a standard psychiatrist's office. He has a modern leather sofa and two pricey chairs in front of a massive cherry desk. Along the back wall is a row of matching cherry file cabinets.

I have limited time until the security people show up, so I go to the desk first. If my guesses are right, then he keeps this information close to him. When I discover Natalie's file in the upper right-hand drawer, all of my guesses are confirmed. On the top, taped to the left side, is a letter from Daphne inviting Terrance to write a book, *The Girl Imprisoned*, for a million-dollar advance. Below the letter are audiotapes and on the other side, affixed by a metal clamp, is a stack of notes. I peruse them quickly.

Subject responding well to extra-high dose of Restoril. Increase dosage next time by half to see if hallucinations set in.

Subject obeyed directive to return to old condo. Minutes spent counseling: 5.

Subject left condo. Responding to outside stimulus that is not within control. Must disrupt.

That fucker is dead.

CHAPTER THIRTY-THREE

NATALIE

My phone rings and it's the downstairs lobby. "Hi, Chris. If that's Jake, just let him up."

"No, it's Dr. Terrance."

"Oh, okay, he can come up too."

I have everything packed and ready to go. I read an email from Daphne's boss, who informs me that Daphne is taking a leave of absence, and she wonders if I had any preference for a new editor out of a short list she attaches. That's depressing in so many ways.

I shoot back a reply.

I don't know any of these folks.

She must be refreshing her emails constantly, because my inbox receives a reply almost immediately.

We can set up appointments for you to meet with them. Brook
Myles has a whole stable of really wonderful editors and they
would all love to work with you.

I'm not sure what I want to do with my manuscript. I guess it's time to get an agent. I hadn't had one before because Daphne bought all the rights for the three books. I had Oliver's agent look at the contract, who shrugged and said it looked standard. After the option sold, I got a film agent, but I don't have a publishing agent. Maybe if I'd had one, this debacle with Daphne would never have happened.

Without Daphne around, though, there are hundreds of emails to answer. She's not filtering them so I start the task of responding to each of them. As I make my way through the first ten, I wonder why I had her doing this in the first place. The emails are so wonderful and encouraging. I could have used these when I was struggling with writing or just struggling in general.

I frown, wondering how much Daphne has hidden from me over the years and why I let her do it.

A knock on the door jolts me and for a moment I freeze. Then I force myself to relax—it's Dr. Terrance. The video feed that is still working confirms that. I manage to go to the door, ten steps and then five more. I open it and allow him in. The door closes behind him and I lock it for good measure.

"Look at you." He beams. "Opening the door. The Restoril did its job, didn't it?"

"It helped," I admit, but eye the white bag in his hand.

He spots my suitcase immediately. "What's this?"

"I'm moving back to Jake's. What are you doing here?"

He shrugs out of his coat and drapes it over my kitchen chair. "Natalie, I told you I would return in a week, and here I am, a week later. We're restarting your therapy. After learning about Daphne, I've decided to change your prescriptions and try a couple of new coping techniques. Her betrayal must be cutting you deeply. I imagine that you are going to be suffering a setback shortly and I want to minimize its effects."

He picks up the suitcase and carries it into the bedroom. "Let's start by unpacking. You aren't going back to that townhouse."

I stare at him, refusing to follow. "I'm not unpacking. Why would I? I can see you at Jake's place as easily as I can here."

He heaves a huge sigh. "Natalie, you are unwell. You aren't in any position to make decisions."

"I'm not unwell. I'm improving. I—"

His mocking laugh interrupts me. I stand in shock because I've never, ever heard him denigrate me like this.

"You're so foolish. You think one week of good sleep and you can conquer your crippling anxiety. Look at you." He waves a hand over my figure. "You can't even open the door to your own condo most of the time. Listen to me. You count opening a door, something normal people do countless times a day, as a victory."

I flush hot with anger and humiliation. "I don't think I'm cured or recovered. I just want to live with Jake. I'll get better every day. I'll take my medication and I'll do therapy. Heck, I'll even do group therapy. Whatever it takes, I'm going to do it."

"You'll never make it," he taunts. "You step outside that door and you'll be puking and passing out in less than five minutes. In fact, let's time it." He unlatches his watch and waves it in the air.

"Dr. Terrance, I think you should leave." I put on a brave face, but he's not wrong. He's describing everything that happened to me the other day when I tried to go to Jake's. I didn't make it more than four blocks before vomiting on the sidewalk. The cop thought I was a drug-addled homeless person.

My palms feel slick as I rub them together. A chill settles into my bones and starts to make me shake. I lock my knees together, but the shaking is too violent for Dr. Terrance not to notice. He laughs with a low, menacing sound. He reaches inside the pocket of his coat and pulls out a big black metal handgun. "Out there, the world is a scary place." He advances on me, and I back up until my calves hit the sofa cushion and I fall. I scramble backward without taking my eyes off the weapon. "There are madmen with guns who'll hurt you. There are people who will attack you in the subway for fun. There are people who will pretend to be your friend and stalk and harass you. There's no one for you to trust. There is no safe place."

He shoots and I scream, covering my face. Frantically I pat myself but I feel no injury. Then I see the hole in the wall that separates the living room from my bedroom.

"You are pathetic. Look at you, huddled in the corner. I am nearly forty years older than you, but you, a girl in your prime, are too afraid to defend yourself." He marches to the door of my apartment and wrenches it open. He tosses the gun on the threshold. "See. You could get the gun and get me to leave, but you're too paralyzed by your own fear." He sits down in his chair and takes out a recorder. "Subject is cowering in the corner. She is crying, not silently, though. I hear small snivels. She has showered today, likely after coitus with her lover. He is not present. Make inquiry into whether he has abandoned her." He continues to dictate, and I stare at the gun.

The door. Get to the door, I tell myself.

I unlock my cramped legs and stand. I shut everything out and start counting. It's fourteen steps into the kitchen. I pause. My breathing sounds unnaturally loud in my ears. Every sense is heightened. Ten steps to the entryway.

"Fifteen minutes have passed. Subject has moved from sofa to kitchen. Still shaking. Still crying."

I swipe my hand across my face and it comes away wet. I didn't realize I was still crying.

The gun. The door. The gun. The door.
Ten steps.

I take one step and then another until I am standing in the open doorway. Sweat is drenching me, and the bile in my stomach swirls like a tornado.

"Subject is at the door. Has stood there for four minutes and counting."
Bend down, I order myself. *Bend down*!

I lunge forward and grab the gun. The metal feels solid in my hand. Behind me I hear Dr. Terrance yelp. He runs toward me and I'm knocked to the ground. It's the subway all over again. Fight or flight. *You're pathetic.*

I'm not. I'm not. I'm not.

I reach out and punch him, my fist hitting flesh. The sound encourages me and I draw back and hit him again. He pushes through my fists and then straddles me. "Stop it, Natalie." He's red-faced or maybe that's the blood from my fists.

I refuse to listen to him. I want to live and this motherfucker isn't taking me down. Surging forward, I head-butt him. He jerks backward. The gun clatters backward into the apartment. I crawl toward it and he drags me back.

Kicking and screaming, I reach for the gun. He slams on top of me. His reach is longer, but as he pointed out, I'm younger and stronger. I throw him off and grab the gun while rolling over on my back. He lands on top of me and I feel the recoil in my hands.

He looks at me in surprise and then falls off. "You've shot me," he whispers in hoarse surprise.

With my hand to my mouth, I cover a gasp of horror. "Oh my God." The red stain is spreading. "I didn't mean to."

"If you hadn't I would have," I hear a grim Jake say behind me. He holds his phone to his ear. "I need an ambulance and police car. My girlfriend shot an intruder."

It's then that I pass out. *I deserve it,* I think, as I lose consciousness. It's not every day I gain a boyfriend and shoot my therapist.

◆ ◆ ◆

"It's a beautiful day out here," I say to the man standing at the end of the sidewalk. His feet are planted shoulder width apart and his arms are folded across his chest. The one hand looks like it is covered in a dark leather glove, but upon closer inspection, one would see it's a fully articulated hand made out of special carbon fiber polymer. It's attached to a special forearm that has wires connecting to electrodes implanted in the man's arm and attached to the ulnar and median nerves. Those wires and electrodes provide sensation, like temperature and, I blush, vibration.

"It is. A little windy but the breeze feels good."

The wind ruffles his hair and then mine. I don't bother to turn away from the wind. Instead I face it, enjoying the flick of my hair as the breeze blows the strands across my face. "Feels real good."

We stand there, silently, as I take deep breaths. I tilt my head up to catch the sun's rays and the man's breath stops.

"God, you're beautiful," he says.

I smile with my eyes still closed. I know what will happen next. He steps closer and then that special hand wraps around my waist while the other hand tangles in my hair. He presses his lips against the hollow of my neck and then the underside of my chin and finally my mouth. *Feels real, real good.*

My eyes flutter open to see him watching me, his gaze full of love and joy. A discreet cough behind me reminds me we are not alone. I disentangle myself from the man's embrace, but keep his special hand tucked in mine.

"Do you want to walk another block?" Lindsay, my new occupational therapist, asks. Her job is to walk with me on Mondays. This is my fifth week since I shot Dr. Terrance, and I'm now standing three blocks from my home. It's a really good day.

"Yes, just one more, though. I don't want to stretch my good luck," I say, squeezing my man's hand. He lifts our joined hands to his mouth, where he presses a kiss to the back of mine.

"It's not luck, sweetheart. It's all you."

"That's right," Lindsay interjects. "This is the result of your hard work, not any luck."

I look at Jake Tanner and the fact that his hand is entwined with mine. Did I win him as the result of hard work? No, it's luck. Or good fortune. Or some sort of destiny. I didn't deserve him, but he's mine anyway.

"Don't look at me like that," he murmurs. "Or I will be the one who can't walk an entire block."

My gaze drops to his pants and I see the faint outline of a hardening arousal. I swallow a giggle. "Don't tempt me," I say.

Lindsay is used to our flirting and walks ahead of us, mumbling something about how we're like newlyweds. Not yet we aren't, but soon. A beam of sunlight bounces off the new shiny ring on my left hand and forms a circle of tiny slivers of rainbow on the ground, granting us a thousand new opportunities to hope.

"I'm proud of you," Jake says, as we walk along, and I concentrate on the feel of his hand in mine and try to shut out the number of people around and the knowledge that I'm so, so far away from the safety of our home.

"I'm proud of me too." I count the lines cut into the cement and the number of trash bags littering the sidewalk, waiting to be picked up. I may never be able to walk the streets of this city with ease. I may never get farther than five blocks from our house, but I'm outside. I'm no longer a prisoner, not in my home or in my own mind.

And most of all, I'm with Jake.

And in the end that's all that matters.

ACKNOWLEDGMENTS

First I need to thank my dear husband and daughter for their endless patience and nonstop encouragement.

Thank you to the wonderful Montlake team that made this book happen. To Helen, who invited me to be part of the family; to Maria, who has shepherded this project from birth to publication; to Krista, who pushed me hard to make this the best book I had in me; and to Jennifer, who helped me polish out the errors.

I also want to thank Daphne, who is a marvelous person in real life, for letting me borrow her name. Your emails and texts and phone calls are a constant source of pleasure.

Thanks also to Robin and Sunita, Jess and Meljean, Melissa and Lea, Elyssa and Kristen, Michelle and Lisa, for their support and friendship.

Finally, thank you to all the bloggers and readers who take the time to read my books. I know you have thousands of choices and it is a privilege that you allow me to entertain you in this fashion.

ABOUT THE AUTHOR

Jen Frederick is the *USA Today* bestselling author of *Unspoken*, part of the Woodlands series. She is also the author of *The Charlotte Chronicles* and has had several books on the Kindle Top 100 list. She lives in the Midwest with a husband who keeps track of life's details while she's writing, a daughter who understands when Mom disappears into her office for hours at a time, and a rambunctious dog who does neither.